I0594307

THE
PILGRIM ROAD
TO DEATH

THE
PILGRIM ROAD
TO DEATH

A GWEN ARMSTRONG MYSTERY

CAROL BRUCE

First published by Level Best Books/Historia 2025

Copyright © 2025 by Carol Bruce

All rights reserved. No part of this publication may be reproduced, stored or transmitted in any form or by any means, electronic, mechanical, photocopying, recording, scanning, or otherwise without written permission from the publisher. It is illegal to copy this book, post it to a website, or distribute it by any other means without permission.

This novel is entirely a work of fiction. The names, characters and incidents portrayed in it are the work of the author's imagination. Any resemblance to actual persons, living or dead, events or localities is entirely coincidental.

Carol Bruce asserts the moral right to be identified as the author of this work.

Author Photo Credit: Ariel Thomas

First edition

ISBN: 978-1-68512-884-5

Cover art by Level Best Designs

This book was professionally typeset on Reedsy.
Find out more at reedsy.com

For Mary and Margot

Praise for The Pilgrim Road to Death

"A suspicious death, a centuries-old talisman that may be stolen, and a sense that every character has something to hide makes *The Pilgrim Road to Death* an archaeological thriller to delight fans of Agatha Christie and Elizabeth Peters. Set in England and northwest Spain between the two world wars, this fine mystery effortlessly blends mystery, danger, and a touch of romance with its meticulously researched historical backdrop. Kudos to author Carol Bruce for the debut of a sparkling new series."—Mally Becker, Agatha Award-nominated author of the Revolutionary War mysteries

"*The Pilgrim Road to Death* is a treat for those who are fascinated by the Camino and Santiago de Compostela. Well-researched and with a murder at its core, Carol Bruce has created a masterpiece in historical story-telling. And throw in some smuggled antiquities for good measure!"—Laraine Stephens. Author of The Reggie da Costa Mysteries

Prologue

Santiago de Compostela, April 1928

The scrape of footsteps on stone made Emily freeze at the top of the cathedral steps and look behind her. A thin, cold mist swirled around the empty stone-paved stairs.

Not a soul could be seen across the murky expanse of the Plaza Obrador, except distant figures moving across the colonnaded ground floor terrace of the Hostel de los Reyes Catolicos.

She shivered and clutched tighter at the letter in her pocket, then stepped toward the massive doors, only to stop again. Did something just move in the shadows?

Events of recent days had her seeing things. Angry at her own timidity, Emily hurried forward and pushed open the carved oak door.

Inside, twin archways led into the nave, past the original façade, a masterpiece of sculpted stone depicting the Last Judgment, now protected from the eroding rains of Galicia. Throngs of medieval pilgrims once gathered here, at the end of the Way of Saint James, exhausted and footsore, yearning for the final blessing.

On impulse, Emily slipped her fingers into five deep indentations at the base of the pillar, pressed into the cool, smooth stone by the hands of countless supplicants through the centuries. She took some kind of comfort from the ancient ritual.

Even in this time of fading faith, pilgrims still came. Since the horrors and losses of the Great War, she suspected there had been more of them, looking for salvation.

The cavernous nave of the church was almost deserted. Massive, fluted columns rose upward into the gloom. Candles glimmered in every niche and side chapel like swarms of fireflies. In the distance, the main altar glowed with burnished gold. Few figures moved in that vast space. Dipping her knees, she crossed herself, then walked quietly down the centre aisle.

The night prayers of Compline had already been said and there would be no more services until Lauds at daybreak.

Reaching the altar rail, she knelt, bent her head to her clasped hands, and closed her eyes. Her fingers slid down the cold metal railing and held tight.

Sanctuary, if only for the moment. Breathing in the heady scent of myrrh and frankincense that permeated the atmosphere. The huge incense burner called the botafumeiro hung low above the altar, almost five feet tall and gleaming silver, suspended by ropes and pulleys from a crossbar in the octagonal dome far overhead.

Earlier she had come to the special pilgrim mass to see the unique ritual when the botafumeiro 'flew.' They filled the censer with pounds of incense and burning coals. Eight *tirebolieros* in red robes took hold of the ropes, then began to swing the heavy vessel so that it soared higher and higher over the heads of the congregation. The pilgrims ducked and flinched, with the burner roaring and smoking like an express train. She liked to think the sacred smoke would carry her anguished prayers to...someone.

A priest crossed her path, head bowed, soutane flapping like black wings behind him. The air hung heavy, like a blanket stifling a low murmur from the rows of curtained booths lining the wall. Was that the sound of the flock confessing their sins? If only she could seek solace there. She shivered and pulled her tweed coat tightly around her. It felt so cold in here tonight. She stood up and pulled the terse note from her pocket.

Be there at 11:40. Sit near the altar.

She found a chair and sank down beside a soaring stone pillar. This man had her trapped, but what did he expect her to do? She refused to do what he demanded, but how could she face the inevitable disgrace and humiliation?

No one would ever believe the truth. Or at least, the truth from her perspective. She had been so stupidly naïve. In a woman of her age, it was inexcusable.

What about Gwen? When she got the parcel, would she understand? It was wrong to involve her, but in some ways, the girl was her only hope. Emily knew that if she went down in disgrace, it would put an end to Gwen's advancement at the college. The Dean would lose no time putting Gwen back in her place.

As for her, the thought of prosecution, even prison, paled in comparison to the crushing thought of her colleagues' contempt. Everything she had worked for would be forever tainted. Any thought of telling Gwen the whole story of her past would be impossible.

No, there must be a way out.

Above all, she must master this physical fear. In her fifty-seven years, she had faced everything from desert sandstorms to warring tribesmen. Perhaps age was catching up with her at last, and a couple of near accidents in a civilized country were enough to make her feel unexpectedly frail.

Whatever this man wanted, he wouldn't hurt her. He needed her too much. She had to use her brains and nerve to find a way out.

She sat up straighter in the chair. A dark figure swept past, then whirled towards her. Something silver and glittering came hurtling out of the darkness. Remorseless as the old pagan gods, seeking sacrifice. In that instant, she knew this was the end.

Chapter One

If going to places where rock tombs abound, excellent quarters can be had in them; no dwelling is so warm at night or so cool in the day.

"I wonder if they still do that?" Gwen murmured.

The thick porridge bubbled like a volcanic pool on the old cast-iron stove. She dragged the wooden spoon through the glutinous oatmeal with one hand, as she flicked the pages of the leather-bound book on the kitchen table with the other.

"Do what?

She turned to see her brother Reg coming into the kitchen, tying his kerchief and tucking it into his collarless shirt.

"Sleep in rock tombs." She gave the pot a final stir, then started spooning porridge into three earthenware bowls.

She gestured toward the book. *"Ten Years Digging in Egypt.* Flinders Petrie says that travelers can sleep very comfortably in rock tombs. Of course, that was thirty years ago."

Reg chuckled. "He might be right about those tombs. Got to be a deal warmer than this place." He jerked a thumb upward. "There's a draft up there'll freeze your... feet off." Tall and rangy, his dark eyes and sharp cheekbones made him the very image of their father as a young man. But the warm humour in Reg's expression had long since fled from his dad's.

He grinned and turned the book so he could read it, then chuckled. "So, you'll be away to Egypt then? Just let us know so we can see you off, eh."

"It could happen." She banged the bowl down in front of him. Cheeky lad! Who was he to scoff at her dreams, however unlikely they might be.

A series of thuds and a slamming door announced that Billy was up. He came clattering down the stairs in his hobnailed boots and flung his lanky body into the kitchen chair. One day, those cheap deal frames would collapse under the onslaught. She ladled up another bowl of oatmeal. Her brothers spooned it into their mouths with the single-minded intensity of young animals.

She watched them with a mixture of tender-hearted love and deep irritation. They took everything for granted—the plain food she laboured to put on the table, the small stone cottage kept neat and clean only by virtue of her working late into the night and rising early the next morning. But with their mother gone, who else was going to keep house?

While both boys were tall, and gangling, at twenty Reg's handsome face bore a serious expression that hid an impish sense of humour, while sixteen-year-old Billy had the smooth, pale cheeks of an angel and shared with Gwen their mother's copper hair and big blue eyes. Gwen didn't like to think how much havoc they created in the hearts of the factory girls in Durham. And one day, they would both marry and make homes of their own, and then where would she be?

While the boys ate, she hurried into the sitting room to make up the fire. The ticking clock on the mantel gave an urgent reminder of what needed to be done before she left for work. These days, she couldn't wait to get there.

Until last year, her prospects had seemed very limited. Continue as a low-paid secretary, if not at the college, then at some office in town. Look after her father for the rest of his life. Read books about world travelers while stuck in this village, decaying into impoverished spinsterhood. She shuddered. That had all changed when she took the job at Seathorne College and met Emily Temple.

Gwen ripped off a page of the Yorkshire Post, folded and twisted it into a compact knot, and added it to the small pile of paper spills on the iron grate. Dad would be home first, and he'd need a fire.

Pale light filtered into the room as she raced through her mental list. There had been just enough meat left from Sunday's joint to leave Dad a cold plate in the pantry and give the boys something substantial in their bait boxes, along with slices of bread slathered with dripping. Bread and jam would do for her.

Kneeling on the hearth, she grabbed another sheet of newspaper and scanned it quickly, habitually incapable of not reading any text that presented itself to her eye.

A scholarship of not less than 50 pounds...

Scholarship? She snapped the sheet open again. In a paragraph entitled, *A Pioneer Business Woman*, Gwen discovered that one Lady Boot had married well, developed philanthropic tendencies, and had enough spare cash to encourage other educated women. She reread the paragraph avidly.

With the Scholarship the holder takes a course of advanced study or research work in relation to Domestic Science. She crushed the paper into a ball and threw it onto the grate. "Domestic Science! What a travesty!"

Tossing some slivers of kindling on top of the paper, she quickly added chunks of coal from the brass scuttle, building a neat pyramid of the dull black rocks. With all the wide, wonderful, exotic world open to you, why on earth study Domestic Science?

"Domestic Science. What does that mean anyway?" she murmured to herself, "Determining the chemical formula for Spotted Dick?" With a snort, she threw the last chunk of coal on top of the pile, dusted off her hands, and sprang to her feet.

Stepping out into the passage, she saw the thin, stooped figure of her father hesitating at the head of the stairs. She fought back the jolt of guilt as he began his painfully slow descent. He hated her running up to help him.

"Morning, Dad. How are you?" She put on a bright smile.

"Quite well, my dear." His laboured breathing, and gaunt, grey face gave the lie to the cheerful reply. The boys burst out of the kitchen, and her father winced at the racket as they jostled each other in the rush to pull on their coats in the narrow hallway.

"Do you have to behave like ignorant louts?" His strained, high-pitched voice emerged on a choking cough. They looked up at him, shamefaced.

"You were educated to be better than this," he went on. "Better than a couple of navvies on the railway. You've mixed with the lower classes for so long that you've forgotten how to behave properly, you've forgotten every refinement I tried to instill."

Reg flushed and spoke up, with an obvious effort to stifle his resentment, "You're not being fair, Dad. For a start, we're not navvies, and you know it. There's not much use for Latin and Greek in mechanical engineering, but it's a respectable profession. We'll both make good money one day."

Their father gripped the banister, as if he might lose his balance, his face drawn and bleached of all emotion. "Money! No matter how much money, you'll still sound like an oaf."

"An oaf with a decent job and friends…" Reg went on. "An oaf who fits in. You gave Gwennie those elocution lessons, so she'd fit in when she went to that posh school, right? Well, it works the same for us."

He started buttoning up his jacket, looking suddenly regretful. He wasn't her willful little brother anymore. He'd asserted himself as a man. But at what cost?

Billy had been standing silently behind Reg, his fair cheeks stained bright pink. Suddenly, he ducked past his brother and shot out the door, with only a hurried goodbye.

Reg followed him more slowly, giving his father and Gwen a brief nod. "Bye." She couldn't bear to see the pain in her father's eyes.

Back in the kitchen, Gwen finally ate her own porridge as she watched her father pick distractedly at his breakfast.

"Treacle, Dad?" She pushed the tin towards him encouragingly, but he only gave her a thin smile and shook his head. You'd almost think he wanted to fade away.

A surge of anger and frustration took her by surprise. She jumped to her feet. "Better get going, or I'll be late. Are you in at the school today, Dad?"

"This afternoon." He gave a weary sigh. "I'm trying to get some local Northern history into the curriculum. The poor little mites should learn something about their heritage, though God knows, the way the world is going, it won't do them the least bit of good."

Gwen looked at him helplessly. After a moment, she said, "Remember to light the fire in the sitting room when you get home." Halfway out the front door, she turned and raced back to the kitchen, snatching the Petrie book off the table.

She shoved it into her bag, feeling the weight of it bump against her side as she hurried down the narrow high street of the small village. Taking a breath of the cool, damp spring air, she felt a lot calmer. Dr. Temple was due back today, and she might need the book. Not that Emily would say anything if the return was delayed. A surge of excitement quickened her steps on the bumpy cobbles. She couldn't wait to tell Dr. Temple that during her absence, she had got through the entire reading list and was ready for more. By the summer she might even have learned enough to go on an official dig as an archaeological assistant. Emily implied that she would use her influence to get Gwen a place. Her soaring hopes fell abruptly. Dad would never stand for it. Who would look after him and the boys?

Her steps quickened as the pony and trap rattled into view around the corner of The Ginger Man Pub. Old Fred flicked the reins as the horse trotted past the tiny village school where her father would teach later that day.

She could remember when he'd been passionate about teaching the children of farm labourers and miners about the ancient heritage of these northern lands going back to before the Roman conquest. She thought of the volumes on her father's shelves that had first awakened her sense of wonder and fascination with history and learning.

Was it wrong to want more from life than this circumscribed little world? Was it wrong to want to see for oneself the shimmering marble heights of the Acropolis, the fabulous sculptures in Hadrian's villa at Tivoli, the towering pillars of Karnak, and the pyramids of Giza? Dad used to understand her dreams.

The war changed everything. She had been ten when he went away. He returned four years later, a mere ghost of himself, with a perpetual cough and a graveyard pallor. More than that, his very soul seemed to have gone out of him.

"Mornin' Gwennie." Fred tipped his disreputable old hat in her direction and gave her a toothless grin as he brought the pony to a halt. The head gardener of Seathorne College, Fred kindly offered a ride in the trap to any of the staff who lived in the village, to save them the long walk past the gatehouse and up the drive.

"Good morning." She smiled back and swung herself up onto the wooden seat behind him. This was her favourite part of the day. As they left the straggling stone cottages of the village behind and trotted along the narrow road up to the headland, a milky sun broke through the clouds and shimmered on the broad expanse of ink-blue sea. The mild air carried the sharp scent of gorse and the salty tang of brine. Scoured by constant breezes, no trees grew up here, and the grey mass of the College dominated the skyline.

By local standards it was quite new, built in early Victorian times by a coal baron with a taste for medieval crenellations. His aspirations to the nobility depended on his only child, Letitia, who had been expected to make a brilliant marriage. Alas, her bluestocking tendencies were widely blamed for repelling all comers. Her disappointed father had no sooner shuffled off this mortal coil than the spinster heiress put her Fabian beliefs into action and turned the place into the Seathorne College for Women. Grudgingly, the old universities now admitted small numbers of young women but had been very slow in granting degrees. In fact, Cambridge still denied women that recognition.

Before the War, when her father took a position as the village schoolmaster, the family had moved from Newcastle to the tiny north-east village. There had been a tacit understanding back then, that one day, if she studied hard enough and did well on her exams, money would be found, and she would be one of those privileged young women admitted to the college. But then the world changed.

Her father came back from France, barely able to teach a few classes a week for a tiny stipend, and the following year, the influenza epidemic had swept her mother away. Now here she was, going to the college all right, but entering through the servants and tradesmen's door.

The breeze carried distant shouts and laughter from a group of students playing hockey on the recreation ground as the pony trap jingled up to the back entrance and pulled to a halt. Gwen jumped out, shouldered her bag, and ran into the building, hurrying along the echoing, drab-brown service corridor.

Emerging through the green baize door, she entered a world of academic hush. A portrait of Letitia Henderson dominated the oak-panelled entrance hall. Sargent had painted the founder in her youth, looking imperious and gravely beautiful in classical drapery.

The college modelled itself on Cambridge's Girton and St Hilda's at Oxford. Most of the two hundred-odd students were undergraduates, with a small number of graduates pursuing doctoral studies. The lecture halls and accommodation were at the far back, and the students rarely intruded on this part of the building unless attending a professor's study for a tutorial, so early morning calm prevailed.

The morning post sat in a basket on the hall table. Gwen leafed through the pile of letters and parcels, extracting all those addressed to the professors. As the academic secretary, she looked after the small group of resident lecturers by typing their letters, managing their correspondence, and helping to keep them organized. She was good at her job, and she liked it well enough, except...now there was the tantalizing promise of so much more.

She noticed the return address on one of the letters to Dr. Temple. *The British School at Athens.* Probably an invitation to go out there again. Gwen didn't even want to let herself hope that she might one day accompany the professor.

She sighed. What she wouldn't give to have that woman's life!

With the stack of letters in hand, she turned and ascended the broad staircase that led to the offices on the first floor.

"Miss Armstrong." A low, authoritative woman's voice stopped her halfway up. She turned to see the spare figure of the Dean, Dr. Bridgeman, in her usual grey tweeds and tightly marcelled hair, standing at the open door of her study. "May I have a word, please? I have some rather dreadful news."

Chapter Two

Gwen sat in stunned silence. A letter with an official crest lay on the desk between them.

She couldn't quite take it in. Emily? Gone?

"The Consulate have made sure that everything was done properly. Dr. Temple was buried in the English Cemetery in Santiago, apparently some friends of hers took care of the details." Dean Bridgman's iron composure wavered a little. "The College will send a wreath, of course."

"This accident...I don't understand what happened." Gwen's voice emerged in a whisper.

The Dean, frowned down at the letter. "I sense there is some uncertainty about the precise nature of the event, but it seems she may have been struck down by the thurible at Santiago de Compostela..." she paused at Gwen's perplexed look, "A thurible is an ecclesiastical incense burner, and this one is quite famous. It's very large and ornate. During the service, they fill it with burning incense and swing it in an arc above the worshippers." Her lips compressed into a thin line of disdain. "So flamboyant. So very Catholic."

"But how?"

"The Consul does not elaborate, except to say that the thurible was not actually in use at the time." The Dean bore onward. "One can only speculate that the vessel was not secured properly." She sighed. "Accidents like this are by their nature inexplicable. Perhaps a rope breaks, a heavy object obeys the laws of gravity, and swings free. An unfortunate person happens to be in the way...." She shrugged and shook her head.

Gwen felt a sudden surge of anger. "Speculation just isn't good enough.

It's all so vague. Didn't they investigate?

With an air of irritation, the older woman took off her pince-nez and rubbed the bridge of her nose. "I know you are upset, but don't be naïve. You must understand the delicacy of this sort of situation. The Consulate are experts at dealing with the Church and Civil authorities. You can be assured they have done their job."

"But…"

Dean Bridgman raised a restraining palm that told Gwen discussion was at an end. "This is difficult for all of us, but we must carry on as calmly and professionally as possible." Her voice softened a fraction. "I know that Dr. Temple considered you an extremely bright young person and gave you duties that might more properly have been assigned to a post-graduate. I also understand that she had taken a particular interest in you, that she invited you to tea at her cottage several times."

How did the Dean know about those Saturday afternoons, and why did it make her feel as if it were some kind of guilty secret?

Dr. Bridgeman replaced the spectacles and looked at Gwen over the top of the gold-rimmed lenses. "Normally, I would not condone friendship between one of our most accomplished academics and a mere secretary. Nor did I approve of her intention of making you a research assistant and blurring the distinction between scholars and administrative staff. I'm not sure it sets the correct tone or a good example for our young ladies. They must revere and respect the faculty."

"I have…" Gwen stumbled over the word, "I had nothing but respect for Dr. Temple. She was so very kind to take an interest in me. I certainly didn't push myself forward if that's what you're thinking." A lump had risen in her throat, and Gwen fought to keep her voice even.

"No, no," the Dean said hurriedly. "I didn't mean to imply any such thing. In fact, I am telling you of this terrible news right now as a courtesy, before I address the morning assembly. I thought it better you hear it directly than through some gossip in the servants' hall."

"Thank you," Gwen said quietly, stung by that oblique relegation to the same status as the cleaners, or the maids.

The Dean drew herself up and tucked the letter into a folder on her desk with a brisk finality that gave a clear signal the conversation was over. "There will be a memorial service at some appropriate time. All the staff will be notified."

Gwen rose to her feet. "Thank you," she said again and turned to go, her vision blurred by tears. To her shame, the wave of sorrow for Dr. Temple was nearly swamped by the dismal knowledge that her own hopes for the future had also died.

At the door, she paused and took a deep breath, forcing herself to assume a professional demeanor. "What shall I do with her correspondence? She got several letters only this morning."

The Dean considered a moment. "We will need to notify her colleagues. Please make a memorandum listing all outstanding correspondence and the names of any colleagues with whom she was in regular contact. I will draft a letter from the College delivering the news. And, of course, we must send a notice to the most important scholarly journals regarding this sad loss."

Back at her desk, Gwen looked over the twenty letters that had accumulated in the two weeks Dr. Temple had been away. She wrote out the list of correspondents, which included some of the most prominent archaeologists and historians of the day. Had it been only that morning she'd coveted Emily Temple's life? And now, Emily Temple was dead.

* * *

The letter arrived a week later.

Hurrying home from work, Gwen stepped through the gate to see Mrs. Simkins in the front garden next door.

"Your Dad left school early again." Her voice held a distinct note of triumph that went with the derision on her slab-like face. "He comes rushing past me, gasping fit to burst and so agitated. My Willy told me there'd been some kind of set-to between your Dad and Mr. O'Brien."

Gwen felt an ache of weary dismay. Not again. "Oh, I'm sure it was nothing. The headmaster has different ideas about education, and sometimes they disagree."

"He'd better watch it, your Dad." She crossed her arms under her hefty bosom and raised her chin. "We all know he had a bad war, but so did lots of the men round here, and there comes a point when people don't have no patience no more."

Considering how Arthur Simkins had spent his war at a nice, safe supply depot in Newcastle, that was a bit rich.

"Thank you very much for your opinion, Mrs. Simkins," Gwen said curtly. "You've always been such a kind, compassionate soul," and swept past her toward the front door.

"Don't say as how I didn't warn you, pet." The tart comment followed her into the house.

All through the evening meal, as Reg and Billy bantered and talked, she watched her father push the food around the plate and barely eat a morsel. He looked particularly haggard and was wheezing badly.

After supper, he muttered that something had come for her in the post. He fumbled among the clutter on the hall table until he found a pale blue envelope and handed it to her with a shaking hand, his eyes averted.

"Are you all right, Dad?" she asked gently. "How was your day?"

"O'Brien's an idiot. He thinks you can beat knowledge into children." He gestured toward the letter. "It's from Spain."

She recognized the writing, that clear and upright hand she knew so well. A jolt of grief went through her.

"Dr. Temple."

"Ah." He still didn't look at her, but at his hands, which he kept tightly clasped as if to still their restless movements.

"It's a shame you didn't meet her. You would have had so much in common."

"In common? Hardly!" His harsh tone shocked her.

"She was a good woman. Intelligent, sympathetic." Gwen was aware that it sounded like pleading. "I just don't understand what you had against her, Dad. After all, she was helping me—"

"Helping you!" He turned on her with a fierce glare. "What help is it to give a young girl false ideas and make her think she can rise above her station?"

Gwen stared in disbelief. "My station? Dad, people don't think like that any longer. Things have changed since the war. Women can go into the professions…"

"Nothing's changed for the likes of us. Man or woman, you need money in this world, money and influence. It was cruel and misleading to make you think you could ever get a job in archaeology. Those Oxford types would make mincemeat of you. Laugh at your accent and ridicule where you came from."

His bitter anger stunned her.

"Perhaps I'm tougher than you think," she said.

He turned away, shoulders sagging. "It doesn't matter now anyway. The woman's dead."

With a sense of utter desolation, Gwen watched him shuffle slowly into the front room and close the door.

She'd tried for the past year to have them meet. Somehow, it never happened, and she had slowly realized that her father was actively avoiding the encounter. His resistance had confused and disappointed her. And then, when Emily died, his impassive reaction to her sorrow had hurt deeply. Like so many other things, she put it down to that inner misery he suffered, that went deeper than any physical wound. But now, a wave of anger swamped her compassion.

Her throat tightened, and tears sprang to her eyes. Could she not even count on him for a father's sympathy and affection when his child needed it? For him to support her ambitions the way he once had in her childhood.

She took the letter into the kitchen and hesitated for a moment before tearing open the envelope, her hand shaking.

Santiago de Compostela, April 27th, 1928

Dear Gwen,

By the time you receive this letter, I hope to be back at Seathorne, but certain things have occurred that prompted me to put pen to paper.

In my travels across Northern Spain, I've been visiting with friends and preparing for my role as 'historical impresario' for the upcoming tour. On this trip, I intend to go beyond the Pilgrim route and the cathedral and introduce aspects of the Celt-Iberian culture and the Roman occupation. To that end I've been to see Professor Hunt at Finisterre and yesterday I was in Corunna.

My purpose in writing is to ask a favour of you. I am sending a package to the cottage, which may arrive before I do. For reasons I cannot go into now, I ask that you go to the post office and take it into your care. It is vitally important that it be concealed and protected. Should the postmistress prove awkward, I have included a signed directive.

I am sorry, my dear, that I cannot explain what this is all about. There have been a series of untoward episodes that have left me uneasy. It is possible these are meant as a warning. I am afraid there is a long and shaming story behind all this, which I cannot discuss in a letter.

You may wonder at me confiding in you in this manner, but I have come to think of you as a sort of protégé. In you, I see myself, in youth, thirsting for knowledge and constrained by the absurd social attitudes that keep young women from achieving their potential. On my return, we must have a serious talk about your future.

Kindest Regards,

Emily Temple

Bewildered, Gwen read the letter through several times, then stared unseeing into the flickering hearth.

A series of untoward episodes...a warning... What did that mean? A cold shiver went through her, despite the heat of the fire. It meant that tomorrow, somehow, she had to get to the Post Office.

* * *

"Miss Armstrong!"

Gwen looked up guiltily from her seat behind the large desk where she

13

had been organizing Emily's papers and realized that her name had been called at least twice before she registered it.

The Dean stood in the doorway of Dr. Temple's study, accompanied by a striking younger woman.

Dragging her attention back to the present, Gwen stood abruptly. "Dr. Bridgeman. Good morning."

She wrenched her thoughts away from Emily's letter. Unable to sleep, she'd read it over and over again, trying to decide what it might mean in the context of Emily's death.

"Dr. Spenser," The Dean turned to the tall, slim woman at her side, as sleek as a mannequin in a photo magazine, with a cloud of blonde bobbed curls and a silky jersey two-piece. "This is Miss Armstrong, our academic secretary." She turned to Gwen, "Dr. Amanda Spenser is taking over Dr. Temple's position on the faculty.

The elegant woman looked critically around the office and raised her eyebrows. "Yes, well.…. Perhaps over the summer, we can have the place spruced up a bit."

Gwen felt her cheeks burning. She loved this room.

Amanda Spenser walked over to the desk, pushed aside the stack of papers Gwen had just organized, and set down her glossy leather case. "When will Dr. Temple's effects be removed?"

She glanced over the shelves of artifacts, Emily's mementos of a lifetime of archaeological digs, then casually picked up a clay lamp. "Common little thing," she murmured. "First century, I should think."

Gwen tried to resist the rush of resentment at the woman's casual disdain. After all, it was a typical object, found by the score in Roman digs.

"It's from Corstopitum," Gwen volunteered. "Near Hadrian's Wall."

Dr. Spenser shot her a sardonic look. "I know where that is."

"I was born there," Gwen said, "In Corbridge, I mean. That's the town nearby." A rush of heat rose in her cheeks. Why had she said that? She sounded like a gormless idiot.

"Really. How fascinating." The Professor sounded anything but.

"Dr. Spenser has published extensively on Romano-British settlements, as well as Celtic sites," Dean Bridgeman said. "Her area of expertise is very similar to that of Dr. Temple, which is why she will also be taking Emily's place on the upcoming tour."

For several years, the college had provided lecturers for educational tours of Europe aimed at well-heeled travellers, very often the friends of Letitia Henderson, the college founder. The tour for which Emily had been preparing was the 'historical impresario.' No one ever said it out loud, but Gwen suspected the tour primed the pump for donations.

Dr. Bridgeman had told her that a replacement had been found for the tour, but this woman couldn't be more different than her expectation.

"We have Dr. Temple's notes to help you prepare," Gwen said.

"Thank you, Miss Armstrong, but I do not require any...help," Dr. Spenser said, with a faint curl of her perfect lips.

The Dean swept her out of the office to continue their tour of the college. Gwen watched them go with dismay. It was wrong to go by first impressions, but she had a sinking feeling that Dr. Amanda Spenser was going to make her life miserable.

Chapter Three

In the lunch hour, Fred kindly took her to the Post Office in the pony cart, where she discovered that a parcel had arrived addressed to Miss Temple, but it had already been delivered to her home.

That afternoon, with a heavy heart, Gwen started clearing out Emily's office, carefully wrapping the little clay pots and fragments of Roman glass bottles that had littered the shelves and packing everything into boxes. Who would be getting all these things, she wondered.

Opening the top desk drawer, she noticed the red tassel peeking out from a sheaf of papers. Gwen pulled out the old iron key, weighed it in her hand, then slipped it into her pocket. She needed to find that parcel.

The next day was Saturday. In the morning, after breakfast, Gwen prepared a cold luncheon and left it in the larder, then told her father where she was going, and that she expected to be there all day.

"I don't see why you have to go there." He sat hunched over the kitchen fire, and she knew that was where he would probably stay. "Whoever gets the place can clear it out. What do they think you are, some kind of skivvie?"

Gwen struggled to be patient. "It's nothing like that, Dad. Emily was my friend. I got permission from the Dean to make sure the cottage is locked up and that any valuables are taken into care."

They hadn't spoken about Emily since the day the letter came, which was alright by her. Gwen still felt stiff and resentful. She even wondered if Emily's death left her father relieved in a way and if he felt guilty about it. It wasn't unusual for widowers to expect unmarried daughters to look after them for the rest of their lives, but he knew this daughter wanted so much more.

Her father had been sleeping badly, which made him even more fretful than usual. "What about the lads?" he asked querulously, "Who's going to feed them?"

"The boys are quite capable of making themselves a sandwich when they get back from football." She reined in her annoyance and said more compassionately, "I've left you all a big pot of stew and some fresh-baked scones in the pantry."

"Be sure you're home before supper." He gave her a long look, then turned away in silent disapproval that both hurt and infuriated her.

Gwen had calmed down a little by the time she hurried along the narrow, rutted lane toward Emily's cottage, half a mile from the farthest edge of the village.

Clearly, Dad's pride was battered. Emily had been helping his daughter in a way he could not and offering her a way out of this narrow life. When a man couldn't provide for his own family, he sometimes resented help, illogical as that might be. Even in their small village, she had seen too many examples of men who survived the war, only to return home bereft of resilience and humour.

Turning a corner in the lane, she saw the small cottage, looking as lovely as the illustration on a box of chocolates. Birds sang in the nearby woods, where a carpet of bluebells and a haze of green buds foretold an early spring. Sunlight warmed the old grey stone, and masses of saffron daffodils overflowed the flowerbeds and filled the air with their heady scent.

With a pang of sorrow, it hit her that Emily would never see this again. Her old bicycle sat propped against the garden shed, and Gwen smiled at the sudden image of that slim, upright figure sailing in through the college gates, her hat firmly pinned on her head, satchel, and books piled in the basket in front.

At first glance, there was no sign of any package. Since the house was locked, she searched the shed and the small, attached greenhouse with its rows of seedlings waiting to be planted. Nothing.

She walked back to the front garden, scanned the front of the house, and sighed. Where else could Alf the postman have put it?

The Post Office must have been mistaken. She would have to go back and speak with the postmistress when it reopened on Monday.

Stepping up to the front door, she turned the key and went inside. She paused on the threshold, feeling like an intruder. The air was very still, and the cottage felt profoundly empty.

With a brisk movement, she shut the door behind her and headed to the kitchen, determined not to wallow in sadness. Emily had asked for her help, and she must find out what it was all about. The answer might be found in her home.

She filled a kettle and got out the teapot. She had brought with her a small loaf of bread, some butter and cheese. As always, she had Reg's old Boy's Brigade penknife in her bag and quickly assembled a makeshift meal. After making a fire in the living room to take off the chill, she sat down with a cup of tea and looked around as she tucked into the food. Where to start?

The cottage was small but comfortable. Under a low beamed ceiling, the kitchen and one large main room took up the ground floor, while upstairs, two bedrooms were tucked under the eaves. Gwen sat in one of the comfortable chintz-covered chairs in front of the large fireplace, facing its empty counterpart across a small table where Emily had served tea and scones on her visits. Living alone had given Emily the luxury of arranging things exactly as she desired, and it was clear how her work and her life were seamlessly intertwined. The room was dominated by a large desk, a wall of shelves, and a tall cabinet, all crammed with books and neatly organized boxes of journals and papers.

Her papers were the obvious place to start. Gwen pulled out the letter. She had read it so many times that she had it off by heart, but she read it over once again.

...there is a long and shaming story behind all of this...

The line haunted her. What could Emily have to be ashamed of?

* * *

It took her hours to go through the contents of the cabinet. They told the story of Emily's professional life; manuscripts for books, scholarly papers, bound reports from myriad archaeological digs over a forty-year career, from England to Mesopotamia.

On the shelves stood a row of yearly diaries with a page for each day. Before tackling them, she made another pot of tea. Taking a stack of diaries over to the armchair, she settled in to read, starting with the book for 1887.

In a tidy, clear hand, the young Emily referred to a happy upbringing as the only child of a country vicar, ranging the fields and woods, exploring the natural world. Her joy at being accepted to the new University College in London was followed by brief impressions of her classes and teachers and her archaeological enthusiasms. As the years went on, Gwen realized, to her disappointment, how little of Emily's personal life was recorded in these diaries. What about love and romance? Had she ever been courted, or lost her heart?

She had just started on the diary for 1904, when a sudden knock on the door made her jump. "Oh, bother!"

A reference to a dig at her native town of Corbridge had excited her interest. With a sigh, she put down the book and opened the door to Alf the postman, short and tow-headed, and looking rather shame-faced. He held a neatly wrapped parcel the size of a large biscuit tin.

"Miss Armstrong?" He stared at her in surprise. "Why, what are you doing here?"

"It's a bit complicated, Alf, but I'm...I'm getting things sorted out. Did you know that Miss Temple..."

He nodded his head vigorously. "Aye, aye, indeed I just heard yesterday that she died in foreign parts, God rest her soul." He looked down at the package in his hand. "I didn't rightly know what to do with this as was supposed to be delivered afore now."

The parcel was wrapped in brown paper, sealed with gummed tape and, for good measure, securely wrapped with string.

This had to be it. Tempted to snatch it from his hands, she reached out encouragingly.

19

"The thing is, Miss, there's been a mistake." Alf hugged the package to him and didn't quite meet her eyes. "This here parcel should have been delivered last week, but with no one home and me living just up the road and with such an 'eavy load all the time…well, I sort of accidentally left it in me shed. Then today I sees the smoke coming out of yon chimney and I thinks, well, here's my chance to make amends. If I take it back to the post office now, that postmistress will be wanting to know why it didn't get delivered afore, and there'll be hell to pay. Rightly speaking, it should go to next of kin, I suppose, but…"

"I'm looking after things for the College. And I've got a note."

She showed Alf Emily's letter of authorization and he visibly relaxed. Trying not to look impatient, she reached out again for the package. "Don't worry, I won't say anything about the mistake." Alf placed it into her hands with relief.

His bicycle stood by the gate, and Gwen suddenly noticed the long shadow it cast over the grass.

The sun hovered not far above the distant hills, and the light had turned warm and rosy. "Why Alf, what time is it?"

"Nearly seven, it be. And a real fine evening."

She had missed supper. A pang of guilt gave way to a sense of righteous justification. They had to learn to manage on their own sometime, and there was plenty of cold food in the pantry. She turned to go inside, then hesitated and looked back at him. "Alf, can you do me a favour?"

She scribbled a hasty note and handed it to the postman. "Can you ride over and give this to my father?"

She watched him peddle back down the lane, then closed the door. Dad would be furious at the notion of her staying here overnight alone, but it couldn't be helped. She turned to examine the parcel.

Inside a sturdy cardboard box were nested smaller wooden boxes. Inside those, freed of their protective layers of cotton wool, a disparate collection of objects lay spread out on the table, glimmering in the light of the oil lamp: Several strings of richly-coloured beads that looked like semi-precious stones, garnet, turquoise and amethyst. A small hoard of coins, mostly silver, bearing crude profiles of ancient rulers, and worn inscriptions that looked like Latin. An array of copper beakers with incised designs.

Beautiful things, and probably very valuable.

Most impressive of all, was a curious object of gold metal. Gwen picked it up. It felt cool in her hand. Only three or four inches across, but very heavy for its size—at least three or four pounds. Could it actually be gold? It took the clearly recognizable shape of a rider on his mount, an upright little figure with an eerily blank face. Somewhere over the centuries he had lost his arms and lower legs, but not his mount. The horse had rings through its ears and an object dangling from its bridle.

She had never seen anything like it. The little horseman both fascinated and repelled her. She noticed that the bridle decoration had a face. It was a severed human head.

With a shiver, she put it down abruptly. The figure seemed like the embodiment of something very old and pagan. Something disturbing. Telling herself not to be silly, Gwen sat for a long time looking at the precious objects in the lamplight. They were clearly very old, and probably very valuable, especially the horseman statuette.

Words from Emily's letter came back to her *... It is vitally important that it be concealed and protected...* Concealed and protected from whom? Where had this collection of ancient artifacts come from, and what should she do with them now that Emily was gone? She could take them to the Dean or Miss Henderson. Perhaps they should go to the British Museum and let them sort it out. But something made her reluctant to tell anyone that Emily sent these items, with the intention of concealing them.

Relics like these could only have come from a dig or a museum. How could she find out where they belonged? Did they come from Spain? Most countries now had arrangements that gave the authorities control over dig finds, while allowing a proportion to be given to an associated museum.

She couldn't get that phrase from the letter out of her head, *a long and shaming story...* Surely Emily hadn't been involved in anything...her mind shied away from the word *criminal.*

Emily had been a passionate believer in ethical archaeology. She had nothing but contempt for the likes of Schliemann who smuggled Priam's treasure out of Turkey and draped his wife with the golden spoils of Troy.

The coal fire had mostly turned to ash when Gwen looked up at the mantel clock to see that it was now past eleven. She sighed, thinking of how early she would need to get home and make sure her brothers were properly turned out for church, not to mention prepare Sunday dinner and, of course, make amends to her father.

She had still found nothing to answer her myriad questions, just more mysteries. Hoping an answer might lie in the more recent diaries, she took the volumes for the past five years off the shelf, picked up the oil lamp, and went up the narrow stairs.

Away from the residual heat of the fire, the air struck chill as she sat down on the narrow bed and slipped off her shoes. A small bookcase on one wall held fat tomes on various historical subjects. She took out one titled *The Celts* and found it filled with large, detailed photographs of artefacts discovered across a huge swath of Europe, from Ukraine to the Orkneys.

Pulling off her wool dress, she dove under the covers in her petticoat, shivering at the touch of chilly cotton sheets on her bare arms. The down quilt would warm her up in a minute or two. She burrowed into the covers and started to look through the book. It was a dim hope, but she might find something that would help identify the objects in the parcel.

On impulse, she jumped out of bed, hurried down the stairs, and picked up the gold horseman from the table. Only the dull glow of the fire's embers lit the room.

She stood still, suddenly aware of the darkness and the silence. No, not silence. A gentle waft of cool air came from an ill-fitting window, carrying the rustling of last year's leaves in the woods, as nocturnal creatures scurried about their business.

The surrounding trees stood out like a black paper cutout against the starlit sky. Gwen shivered. If Emily's spirit still walked the earth, surely it would be here, in the place she loved. The thought was unsettling, but not really frightening.

Gwen pulled the window closed and latched it, drew the curtains, then made sure the front door was locked. She picked up the little horseman again. The fading firelight flickered on the little statuette, making it seem to grimace and come to life. She shuddered. "I wonder…. What kind of world did you come from?"

Suddenly cold, she hurried back upstairs. Slipping under the covers, she opened the book and immersed herself in Celtic history.

Sometime in the night, she came instantly awake, staring wide-eyed into the darkness. The recollection of a noise hung on the edge of her consciousness. Just as she grasped it, she heard it again from downstairs. The crash of shattering glass.

Chapter Four

Gwen lay paralyzed for what seemed like an eternity, her senses straining to catch every little sound. Her pounding heart throbbed in her ears. With agonizing slowness, she slipped from between the sheets and flinched at the cold floorboards on her bare feet. She crept toward the door, desperate not to make a noise. From somewhere below came a creak. Was that a tread on the stair? She looked around wildly for a place to hide. The tiny room with its low slanted ceiling offered no refuge.

Desperate for some kind of weapon, she grabbed the heavy oil lamp from the night table, accidentally knocking a book to the floor with a resounding bang.

She froze, hardly daring to breathe. After a brief pause, a series of muffled thumps came from the room below, and for a sickening moment, they seemed to be coming up the stairs. Then the sounds receded, and she heard what sounded like a casement being thrown open below.

She rushed to the window, peeked through the curtain, and saw the bobbing light of a torch playing wildly across the garden, carried by a dark figure which ran toward the woods. A door slammed, an engine roared to life, and headlights lit up the rutted lane. A small, closed car pulled out from under the trees and sped off toward the village.

Trembling, she pulled on her clothes, then crept quietly downstairs, listening intently and praying there had only been one intruder. She turned up the oil lamp and gasped to see that the main room was in a shambles.

There were papers scattered everywhere, so that at first, she didn't notice that the shelf where the row of diaries had stood was now empty, and the box of artefacts was gone.

$$* * *$$

"What on earth were you thinking?" Her father's face was chalk-white and gaunt in the early morning light, his eyes red-rimmed. She hadn't told him about the break-in when she walked in at six a.m. to find him sitting bolt upright beside the dead kitchen fire, having evidently not been to bed the night before. "A young woman alone, spending all night in that cottage. It's improper, not to mention dangerous. Some tramp might come by, or God knows what…" he gave a choked gasp and struggled for breath.

Sick with guilt and pity, Gwen sank down beside the chair and put a hand on his knee. "Dad, for Heaven's sake! I was perfectly alright." It was a white lie, but after all, nothing had actually happened to her. "I know you aren't happy about it, but it's only right to look after Dr. Temple's things."

"I can't rely on any of you." He gestured wildly toward the back door. "Your brothers made themselves scarce when I needed them. Disobedient louts!"

Wracked with worry about his raspy breathing, she wrapped him in a blanket and made up the fire to take the chill off the room, then began to prepare breakfast.

She'd been so caught up in worry about Emily, it had made her thoughtless. She should have known how badly he'd be upset by her absence, and by his own powerlessness. For the rest of the morning, she tended to her father with extra care, trying to make amends. But as she worked, her thoughts whirled repeatedly through the previous night's events.

What should she do?

After Sunday dinner, she gave her father the small dose of morphine, which allayed the worst of his pain and eased the cough. He seemed to breathe more easily after that. By the time she settled him for his afternoon rest, he spoke to her kindly and seemed calmer. When she was sure he was asleep, she put on her coat.

* * *

Heaving a sigh of dismay, Gwen looked around the cottage living room. The carpet glittered with shards of window glass, among the bits of string and brown paper from the parcel. The contents of the empty shelves lay scattered in random piles, loose papers strewn everywhere. The wooden box, and its artefacts, carefully wrapped in cotton wool and newspaper had all gone. Except…

She dashed upstairs to the small bedroom. The stack of diaries still sat on the bedside table and the reference book still lay under the quilt, where it had slipped from her hands as she fell asleep. Beneath the book lay the golden horseman.

She cradled the heavy metal object in her hand and stepped to the window, staring at it intently. It lay quietly in her cupped hands, gleaming in the sunlight.

"Where did you come from?" she whispered. The stylized figure sat firmly upright in the saddle. In daylight, she could clearly see the horse's plaited mane and tail cleverly suggested by punched-out circles and decorated with an incised design. The abstract features of both the rider and the suspended head looked somehow modern and as ancient as the earth itself.

Gwen sank down on the bed and looked at it. What made the thing so compelling? Because it was so old? If it really was Celtic, it could have been made as long ago as 1000 BC. What kind of world produced art like this?

She shivered. An utterly alien world, in which enemy heads were taken as valuable trophies.

As frightened as she had been the previous night, Gwen felt an additional weight of guilt and discouragement. Emily trusted her, and she had failed. With most of the artefacts gone, what chance did she have to find out what had been going on? Even if part of her was afraid of what she might discover. And yet…

She looked at the diary that lay open on her lap, at the entry for the previous November; it began with an itemized list in Emily's clear, rounded script.

Notes for 1928 tour:
   Bilbao, Senor Ochoa at Casa Antiguedades, Eduardo at Sala de Ventas
Lopez, Don Alfonso Alvarez collection?
   Santiago, Fr. Suarez, perhaps the Bishop?
   Corunna, meet with Dr. Hunt prior to excursion

The list of places and names continued, a random aide-memoire, as anyone would jot down thoughts to collect them before they fled. The back pages of the 1927 diary were filled with names and addresses, including the people noted in the list. Nothing in the diary seemed to have any connection with the hints of worry in Emily's letter, but Gwen couldn't suppress the sour, anxious feeling in her stomach. She couldn't ignore the conviction that something was really *wrong* about Emily's death.

There were four more diaries to go through; she could only hope they might contain something useful.

Hugging the book to her chest, she looked out the window at the fresh green treetops that Emily would never see. If she felt so sure that something was wrong, shouldn't she do something about it? The obvious answer presented itself. Emily had died in the cathedral at Santiago de Compostela. Somehow, she had to get there and find out the truth.

Chapter Five

"Absolutely not!" Dr. Bridgeman glared up at Gwen over her pince-nez. "It would be highly irregular. Dr. Spenser does not need a secretary on this journey; she has her graduate student to assist her, and quite frankly, you are much more useful here."

Gwen challenged her across the vast oak desk, as if storming a citadel. "That's unfortunate, then. Because I intend to give my notice." She gulped. Where did that come from? She improvised recklessly. "I'm sure I can be useful to Dr. Spenser, but if not, I want to join the tour like any other traveler."

"Good Heavens, Miss Armstrong! That would be neither appropriate nor, indeed, possible. This is a very exclusive group, all of whom booked their places some time ago. Aside from that, it would be quite beyond your means."

"I beg to differ. The fee is a hundred pounds, is it not?" Gwen asked. "I have the funds."

She must be crazy. All she had in the world was her post office savings of 116 pounds, the product of years of careful scrimping.

The Dean stared at her in perplexed silence, then finally said. "Why on earth you are behaving in this way is quite beyond me. Ultimately, it will be up to Miss Henderson. But you must speak to Dr. Spenser first.

* * *

"Are you mad?" Amanda Spenser regarded her as if she really were insane.

Gwen had found her in a classroom, standing at the lecturer's desk, tall, slim, and sleek, paging through a sheaf of test papers. Looking down from the platform, Amanda regarded her with impatience. Backlit by the late afternoon sun, her blonde curls became a golden halo. Gwen felt at a severe disadvantage.

"I'm not sure why you say that," Gwen said. "After all, Dr. Temple was thinking about taking me along." She crossed her fingers behind her back. She'd been intending to ask Emily about going on the tour, with no serious expectation that it would happen.

"Really." The word carried a wealth of sardonic disbelief. "Well, I must disappoint you, Miss Armstrong. There is absolutely no need for your services on this trip."

"I know you are taking a graduate student, but I doubt he can provide secretarial expertise." All Gwen had heard was that he was a young German from the venerable University of Heidelberg. It seemed a safe bet that he didn't take shorthand.

Amanda swept up the papers and walked quickly across the platform and down two shallow steps. Her high heels clicked loudly on the parquet floor. "My student will be quite adequate, thank you." She paused at the door and turned a withering stare on Gwen. "You've got nerve, I'll give you that." Without another word, she slipped through the door and marched smartly down the corridor.

* * *

When Letitia Henderson founded Seathorne College in 1891, she had been an energetic thirty-five-year-old, fired with reforming zeal to make things right for women. At seventy-one, she was scarcely less vigorous. Tall, spare, and brisk, her iron-grey hair was shingled in the latest style, and she wore a jersey two-piece in French navy that Gwen suspected might be an actual Chanel.

Miss Henderson had received Gwen in the drawing room of Uplands, the small Georgian house to which she had moved when she turned Seathorne

Towers into a women's college. Pale spring sunlight streamed in through the tall windows behind her as she stood by the Adam fireplace.

"I'm not sure I quite understand, Miss Armstrong." Miss Henderson moved over to the couch and gently subsided onto the chintz cabbage roses. She nodded toward the bergère chair opposite the couch, and Gwen sank down on a seat decorated with needlepoint shepherdesses.

"Emily Temple was a dear friend of mine. Her death was a dreadful tragedy, but you seem to think there was something…something untoward about it."

Gwen knew she must choose her words carefully. She didn't want to show Miss Henderson the letter with its murky implications, and she didn't mention the artefacts for the same reason. "I can't be sure of anything. It's just there are some questions I think should be answered. Some uncertainties…" Gwen paused and took a breath. "Dr. Temple was a friend of mine, too. She went out of her way to help me. Now I feel I have a responsibility to her." Gwen leaned forward earnestly. "I think someone from Seathorne should ensure that the authorities have given us the whole story and that she has been properly laid to rest."

"I see." She gave Gwen a meditative look. "Tell me, Miss Armstrong, have you ever been abroad?"

Gwen shook her head. "No."

"Do you speak Spanish?"

Her spirits sank. "I know some French." It suddenly struck her how totally unsuitable she was for the job she was trying so hard to get.

Miss Henderson gave an exasperated sigh. "You did talk to Dr. Spenser, I believe, but she declined your offer to act as her secretary."

Gwen nodded. That had not gone well.

"Hmm…" Letitia Henderson gave her a long, piercing stare. "You are remarkably stubborn, Miss Armstrong. A quality which can be an asset at times." She paused consideringly.

"Emily Temple was a brilliant scholar who became a dear friend of mine." Emotion lent a harsh edge to her voice. "She had an offer from Cambridge, you know. But she joined us here because she believed in what we were doing. She believed that young women deserved a place where they weren't second class, a place where they could be given an excellent education.

"In her work as an archaeologist, she was respected at the highest levels. She brought this college great prestige, and for that alone, I am grateful to her. Her death is a terrible blow. However, your…suspicions about this event are rather far-fetched. After all, it seems impossible that it could have been anything but an accident."

Gwen sensed she was about to be turned down and made a swift decision. After all, she had to trust somebody. Reaching into her bag, she handed Emily's letter to Miss Henderson. "I think you should read this."

Letitia ran her gaze quickly over the letter, then lifted a swift frown up to Gwen's face. The frown deepened as she scanned the pages.

Finally, she looked up. "This parcel…"

"It did arrive. I had it…briefly." Gwen haltingly explained about the parcel's contents and then the subsequent break-in and theft. It seemed better, not to mention the item that hadn't been taken. The fewer people who knew about the Golden Horseman, the better. For the moment, it lay hidden in a locked drawer in her wardrobe.

"You should have called the police!"

"I know that." Gwen leaned forward urgently. "But don't you see what the police might make of this letter and the parcel of artefacts? We both knew Emily. We knew how honest and ethical she was. But to someone who didn't know her…"

"Are you suggesting…. Good Heavens, you're not talking about theft, I should hope? That's preposterous!" Miss Henderson flung down the letter on a low table.

She stood up and went over to a little marquetry table near the fireplace. Extracting a cigarette from a delicate wooden box, she flicked a silver lighter and took a deep inhalation of the blue smoke. "Emily was spotlessly honest."

"Of course, she was," Gwen said. "But we knew her. It sounds as if she felt threatened. What if…." She hesitated.

Miss Henderson gave her a sharp look. "Surely you don't think her death was not accidental."

"I know, it sounds far-fetched, but…"

"Colonel Fairlamb assured me there was a thorough investigation." Miss Henderson sat back down on the couch, looking uncertain. At Gwen's questioning look, she went on. "Colonel Fairlamb and his wife organize and run the tours. They are old friends of mine. They were in Santiago at the time of the accident and made sure things were taken care of properly. The burial and so forth."

Letitia Henderson shook her head. "I'm not sure what you expect to find out there. Or, indeed, what good it will do." She gave Gwen a speculative look. "However, I can see why you found this letter concerning. Although there is undoubtedly a prosaic explanation." Sounding as if she were trying to convince herself, she picked up the letter and read it over again with a frown.

Gwen held her breath. Miss Henderson folded the paper and handed it back to her.

"I shall speak to Dr. Spenser. Since you are so determined on this crusade, you will go with the tour as secretary."

The swiftness of her decision left Gwen startled. "Thank you," she said hesitantly. "I don't suppose Dr. Spenser will be very happy. She was quite adamant that she didn't want me."

Letitia's face hardened. She brushed aside the question of Dr. Spenser's preferences. "On due consideration, you will be invaluable. Colonel and Mrs. Fairlamb make all the practical arrangements. As you know, Emily…Dr. Temple…handled the lectures and tours of the historic and archaeological sites. Her contacts were extensive. She is impossible to replace, but Dr. Spenser is certainly a worthy successor, and of course, Emily had confirmed all of the arrangements before she was struck down. However, Dr. Spenser may have underestimated the challenges."

Miss Henderson got to her feet in one decisive movement, with a speed belying her age. Gwen automatically followed suit.

"You haven't much time to familiarize yourself with all the material, but I'm sure you're more than capable. I will alert the Fairlambs that they need to adjust the arrangements to add another person. We depart in two weeks, from Le Havre."

Chapter Six

Her father did not take it well. No matter how much she explained about the arrangements for Mrs. Robson down the street to take care of the cooking and cleaning, he made it clear that, in his eyes, she was abandoning her family.

"It's pure selfishness," he told her after breakfast, a few days before she left. "Gallivanting off to the continent, shirking your responsibilities."

"It's not gallivanting; it's part of my job, Dad," The dirty plates clashed as she stacked them beside the kitchen sink with unwonted carelessness. That wasn't strictly true about her job, but she'd taken on this task from a sense of responsibility. "Don't worry; they're going to deliver my pay packet to you while I'm gone." The moment the words were out of her mouth, she could have bitten her tongue.

His knuckles whitened as he gripped the arms of the kitchen chair. "How dare you imply that this is about money!"

"I'm sorry, Dad, that was inexcusable of me." She plunged the crockery into the hot, soapy water. "But I've done everything I can to make sure you're taken care of, what more do you want from me?"

She scrubbed hard at a perfectly clean plate, unable to look at him. A lump rose in her throat, with the painful conviction that he was right. She did want to get away, to escape from the burden of this house, of her family and their demands. Get away, most of all, from her father.

She felt desperately guilty the moment she admitted it to herself. What kind of daughter could behave this way? Weary of the battle, she heard the letterbox rattle and jumped at the opportunity to escape the kitchen. Of course, the boys had disappeared the moment they ate the last morsel of porridge.

Gwen scooped up the letters from the mat and flicked through them, then stopped abruptly at the sight of her own name and shoved the envelope into her apron pocket.

After finishing the washing up, she put on her hat and coat and hurried out with a basket over her arm to shop for dinner and supper. But instead of heading for the butchers, she took the narrow leafy lane that led down through a wooded dene and, in fifteen minutes, brought her to a small sandy cove on the seashore.

Perching on a rock, Gwen stared out across the sparkling water. The fresh breeze smelled of salt and seaweed and lifted the fine hairs on her brow. Gulls screamed in the distance. The horizon was a navy blue line, as crisp as if drawn by a pencil. As the small waves rolled in, she could hear the faint chinking of pebbles being pushed up the beach and rolling back with each successive green-blue surge. She realized that her whole body clenched painfully, and her head ached as if wound around with a tight band.

She rubbed her temples and tried to breathe more slowly. Gradually, she felt the peace of this place seep into her. A place of refuge when everything got too much.

Digging into her pocket, she pulled out the envelope. The creamy paper was a thick, heavy stock bearing a Durham address under the name of Pargeter, Pargeter and Venables, Barristers and Solicitors.

What on earth could this be? Anything to do with the law meant trouble and expense, her mother had always said.

She opened the letter and had to read the page three times before it sank in. Shaking her head, she read it once more.

You are invited to attend at our office at three o'clock, on the 20th inst. of the fourth month of 1928, for the reading of the will of the late Dr. Emily Elizabeth Temple, wherein you are a named legatee.

* * *

The offices of Pargeter, Pargeter, and Venables, in the ancient city of Durham, occupied a building not far from the cathedral and seemed indeed to share its ecclesiastical atmosphere. Through mullioned windows set into Gothic arches, the late afternoon light illuminated a halo of fluffy white hair framing the head of Mr. Venables. At the other end of a vast oak table, Gwen shifted on the hard leather chair and found herself thinking that the elderly lawyer looked rather like a shy parson. Or a kindly sheep.

In the distance, the cathedral bells began to chime. Mr. Venables cleared his throat. "It is now three o'clock, and I think we may begin." He paused, picked up the sheet of paper in front of him, and began to read. "I will now read the last will and testament of Miss Emily Elizabeth Temple, late of this parish..."

After a lengthy preamble in which the testator declared her sanity and that her attestation had not taken place under duress, the lawyer stated, "I hereby leave all of my worldly goods to Gwendolyn Doris Armstrong, to do with as she sees fit, with the hopeful request that she will use this legacy to pursue the education she so fervently desires and is so well-fitted to undertake."

Gwen sat in stunned silence, struggling to comprehend what he had just said. At last, she managed to choke out, "But... but why? What about her family?"

"Ah..." He cleared his throat and polished his glasses. "Here is indeed the rub. You see, Miss Armstrong, the will is quite explicit and certainly legally sound, however it would be remiss of us, as trustees, to execute the inheritance without confirming that there are no other potential claimants. That is, who might launch a suit challenging your right to inherit."

"So, you think there are relatives?"

He tapped a thick folder of papers at his elbow. "There is, in fact, some indication of a second cousin who may have gone to Australia. His claim would be tenuous to say the least, but we are duty-bound to rule it out."

"I don't know what to say." She felt dazed. "I mean, what do I do now?"

"Nothing, at present. Wait for us to conclude our investigations. But I would advise you to prepare for a significant change in your circumstances." He peered at her intently over his half-moon glasses. "You do have a solicitor of your own, I trust?"

Still stunned, Gwen could only shake her head.

He made a disapproving noise. "My dear young lady, very soon, you may be the owner of quite a substantial estate. I would advise you to engage a good solicitor."

"Can't you be my solicitor?"

He raised his eyebrows. "It would be most improper to suggest that you engage the trustee. However..." He coughed discreetly. "Should you request our assistance, I could certainly arrange for one of our younger partners to give you advice."

A question formed in her mind. A dreadfully crass question.

Seeming to read her thoughts, the lawyer gave another dry cough and went on. "You will, of course, be curious about the nature of the estate that you may have inherited. There is the primary residence, Dene Cottage, of which Miss Temple held the freehold. The parcel on which the cottage stands extends to something over fouracres. It includes extensive woodland and even a trout stream. In addition, Miss Temple held a portfolio of excellent securities, gilt-edged bonds, that sort of thing...yielding an income of some ten thousand pounds a year."

* * *

As the train rattled back along the track from Durham to Seathorne, Gwen stared out at the sheep-dotted fields without really seeing them. She could barely remember leaving the solicitor's office and making her way to the station.

Ten thousand pounds a year! Her head swam with thoughts of what that could mean. Buy a comfortable home for Dad and the boys, get a housekeeper to look after them. Perhaps some new clothes. With a sigh, she smoothed a hand over the rough, grey wool skirt that had been her mother's. Wouldn't it be lovely to afford smart suits like Dr. Spenser wore?

Most of all, it meant freedom to chart her own course in life. A sudden vista opened before her, like the thrilling view she had seen as a child from the highest point in the Eildon Hills. Standing on top of the world as the land below rolled away to the sea.

With an impatient noise, she shook off the vision. "Ridiculous!" she said out loud, startling the man in the opposite seat dozing over his newspaper.

Ridiculous to build these castles in the air until she knew for certain. Mr. Venables had indicated that it might take one or two months at least to conclude their inquiries into Emily's family, but that he would keep her abreast of their progress.

However, one stark question nagged at her incessantly. Where had Emily's money come from?

Nothing she had read in the diaries contradicted the few mentions Emily had made of a modest upbringing. Were there wealthy relations? Perhaps some kind of inheritance? Darker possibilities were unthinkable. And could she accept the legacy in all good conscience if she didn't know its origin?

A sudden shudder and squealing of brakes recalled her abruptly to the present moment as the train drew into the small station at Seathorne. Bracing herself against the lurching of the slowing train, Gwen stood up in readiness to get out. The whole issue of the will remained academic for the moment. She had more pressing things to worry about.

The trip to Spain was less than a week away. At this moment, Emily's most important legacy was her reputation. A surge of fierce determination swept through her. Whatever it took, she had to defend that reputation by finding out the truth.

Chapter Seven

Gwen leaned on the rail of the S.S. Isabella and watched stevedores swarming over the line of grimy cargo ships moored along the quayside. Creaking boat cranes swung out over the cobbled wharf and lowered massive rope nets to be filled with tea chests and barrels, then sent swinging back to be lowered into the hold. Across the decks, crewmen shouted at each other in a harsh, incomprehensible French dialect bearing no resemblance to the polite Parisian exchanges she had learnt at school.

Here she was in Le Havre, the furthest she had ever been from home and about to set out even further on a real sea voyage. The thrilling prospect almost banished her exhaustion.

At the last minute, she had discovered that she'd be travelling alone, responsible for shepherding a very heavy trunk filled with Dr. Spenser's books, papers, and lantern slides to be used for her lectures.

It had taken two days to get here and felt like a week. Seven hours on the train from Durham to King's Cross in London. Then, getting the luggage across the city to Waterloo Station for another three-hour journey to Portsmouth.

After the mad rush of changing trains on the long journey south, she had collapsed onto a hard bed in a cheap but respectable hotel near the ferry dock. Only to rise early for a rushed breakfast, before dealing with the luggage in preparation for the three-hour ferry trip across the Channel. After reading so many tales of its legendary roughness, she'd been surprised and relieved when it had been as smooth as a millpond. Thank heaven for small mercies. After a few hours sleep in a Le Havre *pensione*, a rattletrap taxi brought her to the right quay.

Under the direction of the purser, she had gratefully handed off her own suitcase and the precious corded trunk, after affixing the ship's labels that specified WANTED ON THE VOYAGE, and seen it carried off on the broad back of a burly Lascar crewman.

A stiff breeze had sprung up, whisking little whitecaps across the harbor and making her shiver in her thin mackintosh. Rain threatened from the low grey sky, in the dull light of late afternoon. Oily water beat against the hull in choppy waves. She felt a curious mixture of excitement and apprehension.

The *Isabella* was a medium-sized ship, as far as Gwen could tell, looking around the harbor, where craft of all sorts bobbed at anchor. She was primarily a cargo carrier with accommodation for a modest number of passengers.

The Fairlambs had engaged her exclusively for the trip from Le Havre, around the coast of France, and across the Bay of Biscay to Bilbao. Gwen looked toward the misty horizon, hoping those stories about the legendary roughness of Biscay were exaggerated.

The tour officially started here in France, as many of the group were already in Europe. In the flurry of boarding and getting things organized, she had seen some of them, but now, as evening approached, she nervously anticipated formally meeting the tour guests. She pushed herself upright from the rail. Time to dress for dinner.

She had been so unsure about what to wear on the trip that she'd even bought a little book, *The Manners and Rules of Good Society*. From this invaluable source (authored by 'a member of the aristocracy'), she had learned that no one 'dressed' for the first night on board. But what did that mean, exactly? Her best navy frock would be the safest choice, she decided.

Hurrying down the deck, she negotiated the heavy door that led to the narrow companionway down to her cabin. Because she had been a last minute 'add-on' they had put her in the only spot left, Amanda Spenser's cabin, which had two narrow beds.

Gwen squeezed past Amanda's large cabin trunk and was relieved to see the small space was empty. The professor had not been pleased at having to share.

After changing her dress, she paused to dig deep into her suitcase and pulled out the small but heavy amber velvet bag slipped into the toe of one shoe. She took a quick look inside, then tucked it away again.

She still wasn't sure it had been wise to bring the horseman with her, but she couldn't have left it behind. It seemed the last tangible connection to Emily.

Chapter Eight

The Isabella got underway just before six. The engine rumbled under Gwen's feet as she made her way down the corridor in search of the passenger lounge, swaying a little as she adjusted to the ship's movement.

She smiled at her first sight of Captain Burton, Master of the Isabella. He looked so exactly like every ship's captain she'd ever seen on a tobacco tin, or a cigarette packet. Indeed, with his full white imperial, he bore a strong resemblance to old King Edward, and, more worryingly, to Captain Smith of the Titanic.

"Good evening, ladies and gentlemen." He accepted a small sherry from the steward and gave a genial nod to the nine people standing or sitting in the lounge. "I look forward to joining you at dinner tonight, though I must make my excuses before the cheese course as I'll be needed on the bridge."

He began conversing with the small group around him, with the air of someone doing their social duty while longing to be elsewhere. Gwen found a seat in the corner, beside Dorcas Bellamy, Miss Henderson's companion.

"Quite a commanding presence, is he not?" Miss Bellamy murmured at her side, with a nod in the captain's direction.

Dorcas was a small, fair woman of indeterminate age who twittered incessantly with determined good humour. Gwen had known her slightly, as the intermediary between Miss Henderson and the Dean, but in the past two weeks of preparing for the trip, she had discovered that Dorcas managed the social minutiae of her employer's life with surprising efficiency and intelligence. A woman one might easily underestimate.

Now, she was giving Gwen a little sketch of each of the passengers gathered in the room. "The couple over there, that's Marion and Brett Sloan. Americans from New York. He's something in stocks and bonds. Very wealthy and cultured people."

The tall, silver-haired man now talking to the captain had a tangible aura of power about him, and the elegant woman in green silk at his side bent her perfectly coiffed head in rapt attention.

"He's taken this tour many times, claims to be an ardent amateur historian. But he is also acquiring a stellar collection of antiquities. The introductions to museum directors and archaeologists prove invaluable. Cutting out the middleman, I believe it's called."

The acerbity in her tone made Gwen give the older woman a startled look. This genteel English rose had hidden thorns.

The steward was coming around with a tray of coupe glasses filled with bubbling golden liquid. They both took a glass and sipped. "Mmm…" Miss Bellamy murmured appreciatively. "An excellent vintage. Pre-war, I should think."

Gwen sipped tentatively and rolled the bubbles around on her tongue. So this was champagne. She took a bigger sip, and the crisp, tingling wine slid down her throat. Delicious.

"Champers all round for our first night, eh?" The plump man standing beside Miss Henderson gave a cheerful smile and raised his glass with a gesture that encompassed the whole room. "Here's to a splendid adventure. Cheers."

With sidelong glances and a few raised eyebrows, everyone in the room raised a glass in his direction. "Oh, dear." Miss Bellamy murmured to Gwen. "I do hope people will be nice to the Dixons." The couple had already introduced themselves effusively to Gwen as 'Alice and Jim', their Lancashire origins proclaimed by their broad accents.

"They seem like very nice people," Gwen said defensively, her hackles raised by the snobbish implication that they somehow didn't fit.

"Indeed, they are. He owns several cotton mills, quite a vast fortune, I believe. And very generous. You can be sure that champagne will be only the first of many magnanimous gestures." Dorcas Bellamy heaved a sigh. "There's something rather sad about it. A careless quality, as if he's trying to dissipate all that wealth, he spent a lifetime accumulating."

Her wistful tone made Gwen curious. "Why do you say that?"

"They had three sons, all killed at the front within a single month. Dreadful." She shook her head. "No one to carry on the family name or inherit the family business." She sighed again and said bitterly, "That wretched war. No one should have to pay such a price. And for what?"

Gwen wondered what price Miss Bellamy had paid. It was hard to judge her age, but she'd guess somewhere in the forties. Was she one of the 'surplus women' the papers had made a fuss about after the 1921 census? So many men had died that a whole generation of women had seen their hopes of marriage blighted.

She caught sight of a small, young blond man hovering on the edge of the group, looking anxious. "Oh, there's Mr. Heider."

Dorcas' expression hardened. "I don't know why Miss Henderson would put up with that man."

Gwen sighed. "It's been a long time since the war, surely—"

"As if that makes any difference!" Dorcas' face was flushed.

"Franz was a child then. It's not his fault he's a German." If there was one thing she longed for, it was that the world could get past that terrible conflagration and start anew. "He's Dr. Spenser's graduate assistant and we have to treat him as we would anyone else."

But she could tell that Dorcas Bellamy might never feel that way, and somehow, she didn't think the Dixons would either, even though they had been scrupulously polite when he had introduced himself a few minutes before.

A rush of cool sea air and a sudden turning of heads focused everyone's attention on the doorway that led out to the promenade deck. Amanda came sweeping into the lounge in a shimmering gold-beaded frock that barely covered her knees. Gwen felt an unworthy pang of pure envy, followed by a stab of annoyance. What was that rule about not dressing for dinner?

Amanda scooped a glass of champagne off the tray and made a beeline for the captain as a buzz of excited chatter rose around her.

"She certainly has a way with her, that young woman." Dorcas gave a wry smile, watching the tall, slender Amanda slouch diplomatically and bend her head to converse with the rather less tall Captain Burton.

Gwen glanced around the room to see if all the tour members were present. Aside from the Fairlambs, the only couples were the Sloans and the Dixons. Otherwise, it was a predominantly female group: Miss Henderson and Miss Bellamy, Dr. Spenser and herself. Then there was Father Garrick, a priest from Liverpool.

Gwen smiled. "I see Father Garrick has no religious qualms about champagne."

Clad in a sober cassock, glass in hand, he stood conversing animatedly with Miss Henderson. Dorcas nodded. "He's very sociable. Quite charming, in fact."

"It's rather surprising to see a priest on a tour like this."

"I suppose you might think so, but apparently, the main attraction for him is Santiago de Compostela. He's interested in the history of the pilgrimage and St. James himself. Also, the conversion of the pagan Celts and Romans."

He looked relatively young and quite approachable. Perhaps Father Garrick could tell her more about the cathedral.

Only one passenger remained unseen. Gwen decided she might as well consult the oracle and turned to Dorcas. "Michael Greville doesn't seem to be here, yet. Do you know anything about him?"

She gave a little shake of the head. "I've never met him myself, but I understand he's a dealer in rare, ancient coins. Quite a specialty. Of course," she added, with an embarrassed little laugh. "I'm not suggesting for a moment that he's in trade."

Why shouldn't he be? Gwen wondered.

Looking over to where her employer stood, Dorcas said in an undertone. "Letitia knows his relations. She tells me he's connected to the Cornish Grevilles, quite a good old family. Second cousin to the Earl."

Gwen nodded, as if this explained everything. Clearly, it meant a great deal to Dorcas. Her clipped 'county' accent indicated a genteel upbringing.

How had she come to be a paid companion to the wealthy Miss Henderson? Did her subservient position ever rankle?

Earlier, Gwen had stepped into the ship's dining room and looked at the place cards. They told an eloquent story. Everyone had been assigned a seat in what she presumed was a careful gradation of status. At the Captain's table sat the most important passengers: Miss Henderson, with her indispensable Dorcas, Dr. Amanda Spenser, Colonel and Mrs. Fairlamb, and the Sloans. They were American, which put them outside of British calculations of class, but they were also extremely wealthy.

The Dixons might be equally wealthy but were clearly not 'our sort' in the estimation of the upper classes. They were seated at the First Officer's table, along with Gwen, Franz Heider, and Father Garrick. Michael Greville, too, despite his aristocratic credentials. Presumably, because he had been another late addition to the tour group.

"Is this the typical sort of group that Dr. Temple would have led?" she asked Dorcas.

"I would think so. Miss Henderson used to go on all the trips before the war. We have attended several since I became her companion, though not many in recent years. It's generally about this number, and it tends to appeal to the sort of people who have the leisure and can afford the fee. I believe the Sloans went on the Egyptian trip three years ago. We usually have some scholars as guests, but not this time."

She lowered her voice and bent closer to Gwen. "Miss Henderson has told me of your concerns about Dr. Temple. I do so admire your spirit in making this journey to ensure her affairs were properly taken care of."

Miss Henderson had suggested that Gwen's mission to visit Dr. Temple's grave and inquire into her death should be explained by putting it about that Miss Temple was an old friend of Gwen's family. Having died with no known relations, Gwen was taking on the responsibility that might have been assumed by a niece.

"As Miss Henderson's confidante, do let me offer any help that I can."

"That is very kind of you. I'd rather not say too much about it at the moment..."

"You don't want people making a fuss." Dorcas nodded. "Quite right, too. It shows a ladylike sense of discretion and reticence. A quality sadly lacking nowadays." She sent a withering glance toward Amanda Spenser, who was hooting with laughter at something the captain had said.

"Miss?" The steward was making his second round of the room and once more proffered the tray of champagne.

At the risk of being unladylike, Gwen delightedly scooped up another glass, got to her feet, and said to Dorcas, "I think I should meet everyone properly."

Dorcas gave an anxious little start. "Would you like me to introduce you?"

"Nowadays, I think it's acceptable to introduce oneself."

"Well...that's very, um...modern of you." She gave Gwen a doubtful look. Taking a fortifying sip of the delicious bubbly, Gwen headed toward the Sloans.

At that moment, a man stepped through the door. Tall, lean, and dark-haired, in a well-cut grey suit, he glanced quickly around the room. Not exactly a handsome face but quite arresting, with intense blue eyes that seemed to take in everything around him with one glance.

Gwen caught Amanda's swift assessment of the newcomer and her purely physical reaction. In one sinuous, subtle movement, she straightened her spine, put her shoulders back, and shifted her weight onto one hip in a delicately provocative stance. Had she been a cat, she would have purred.

"Ah, Mr. Greville!" Letitia advanced toward the man. "At last."

He nodded politely, looking a little bemused. With a hand on his arm, she drew him into the group clustered around the captain and managed to insinuate herself next to him.

Suppressing a smile at this blatant maneuver, Gwen turned her back on them to find Marion Sloan right behind her.

"You must be Miss Armstrong." Mrs. Sloan offered her elegant hand with an air of *noblesse oblige*. Gwen had the satirical urge to curtsey but behaved like a respectable young woman and shook her hand. It was so encrusted with rings that she had to be careful not to squeeze too hard, lest the sharp-edged gems cut into her palm.

"So nice to meet you, Mrs. Sloan." She took in every detail of the other woman's immaculate appearance. 'Looking like she'd stepped out of a bandbox'—wasn't that the American expression? Whatever a bandbox might be! She had only met wealthy Americans on the cinema screen, or between the pages of a novel, but this couple were exactly *it*.

Beautifully made-up, with her brunette hair in a perfect Louise Brooks bob, Marion Sloan certainly lived up to the image of lacquered perfection most English people would expect. Close to, however, fine lines around her eyes and mouth revealed that she was older than the first youthful impression.

"I'm delighted to be here." She glanced around the room. "And pleased to see so many ladies on this trip." Her voice had a lilt that softened the superior manner. "Back home, we women are making great progress, but in Europe..." She shook her head with some disgust.

"England isn't Europe. And what do you define as progress?" Gwen was genuinely curious.

"Why getting our rights, of course. Taking our full share in public life. Those poor European women don't seem to care how downtrodden they are. Back home, we got the Nineteenth Amendment passed back in 1920." She answered Gwen's quizzical look. "That's when women won the vote. I read in the newspapers that English women are still waiting."

Gwen felt duty-bound to defend her country, despite her own frustration at the long struggle for British women to achieve democratic fairness. Besides, she didn't like Mrs. Sloan's air of pitying condescension.

With a defiant lift of her chin, she said, "There's an act in Parliament right now that we hope will get passed this year. It gives the franchise to all women over twenty-one."

Marion took a breath as if preparing to genteelly demolish Gwen's spirited riposte.

"Ladies, please! Can we skip the politics?" Mr. Sloan strode in carrying two brimming cocktail glasses. He handed one to his wife. "Your Gibson, my dear."

Brett Sloan looked like a captain of industry who wanted to be a cowboy.

He had the expensive tailoring and manicured hands of a plutocrat that didn't quite match the broad-shouldered, beefy physique and the florid face that belonged under a Stetson—or perhaps a gangster fedora?

"What can I get you, Miss Armstrong?

Startled out of her flight of fancy, she said, pointing at the drink in his hand. "Oh, one of those, I think!" She noticed a little white sphere at the bottom of the glass. "Ummm, what was it, again?"

He grinned. "It's called a Gibson. And yes, that is an onion."

Her amused chuckle sounded alarmingly in her ears like a schoolgirl giggle. Right! No more drinks until she had something to eat.

* * *

A glass of water and a cold lemonade restored her more or less to sobriety. By the time they sat down to dinner, Gwen had met all the tour participants, except Michael Greville. For some reason, she had deftly avoided the introduction. Something about him made her feel nervous, which was ridiculous. Yet no matter who she talked to, wherever she stood in the room, she remained aware of him, tuned in to his voice, deep and smooth. He had the sort of upper-class accent she'd expect, but not as obtrusive as she might expect. And he seemed to say very little about himself, always turning the conversation so that the other person would talk about their own interests.

What the cocktail gathering did reveal was her own deep antipathy toward the Fairlambs. Affecting a pukka sahib manner, the colonel regaled her with tales of his days in the Raj, which all seemed to end with him getting the better of 'the natives.'

In conversation, he fixed her with an unblinking stare from his pale, gooseberry-coloured eyes. With his gaunt features and thick military moustache, he reminded her of some fanatical medieval knight in modern dress. Mrs. Fairlamb was a fitting consort, a tall, angular woman with the demeanor of a disdainful thoroughbred.

At some point, she would need to ask him about and thank him for the arrangements he had made for Dr. Temple's grave, but since he didn't raise the subject, she gratefully decided to leave it until they arrived in Santiago de Compostela.

Just before they went to dinner, Gwen noticed an odd little interchange. She saw Amanda having a quick, murmured conversation with the steward that ended with her pressing something into his hand. Money, Gwen assumed. But why? She had her answer when they took their seats.

"Oh. but I'm sure I was seated here..." At the captain's table a chair scraped the wood floor as Dorcas rose awkwardly to her feet.

"You really must check the place cards, Miss Bellamy." Amanda gave an impatient sigh. The others at the table bent their heads to study their menus. Dorcas shot a pleading look at Letitia Henderson that was ignored.

In a flurry of confusion, she picked up her shawl and evening bag and moved uncertainly out of the way as Amanda took her seat. Over at the first officer's table, Father Garrick rose swiftly to his feet, followed by the other men.

He swept an arm toward the empty space beside him. "Please do us the honour of dining at our table, Miss Bellamy." His soft Irish lilt added warmth to the invitation.

He pulled out the chair, and Dorcas sat down, her back stiff and two bright spots of red burning on her cheeks. At the Captain's table, Amanda Spenser was now sitting directly across from Michael Greville.

What a dirty trick. She had obviously bribed the steward to rearrange the place cards. The better to exercise her practiced allure, Gwen supposed.

Her heart ached for Dorcas. The older woman picked at her meal and kept sending venomous glances toward the other table. Fortunately, Father Garrick turned out to be an entertaining conversationalist, regaling them with stories of his Liverpool parish, and by the time the cheese was served, Dorcas seemed to have forgotten her humiliation.

The cleric appeared to be in his thirties, with a boyish face, thick brown hair, and engaging humour in his eyes. Quite good-looking, although it seemed rather shocking to think that way about a priest. He glanced over toward Amanda. "Dr. Spenser must be a very accomplished young woman. I understand she is the academic expert on our tour."

"She's already had quite a glittering career." Dorcas' comment was edged with ice. "A First at Oxford and stints working with some of our foremost archaeologists. Of course, she does come from a brilliant family. The Spensers moved in the same rarified circles as the Huxleys and the Darwins. Her father did important work in Natural History, and her elder brother was just making a name for himself in Physics when the war broke out. Lost at Passchendaele, I'm afraid." She shook her head.

"It's remarkable to find someone of her calibre at a small college like yours," Father Garrick said.

Gwen darted a look at Dorcas and saw her affronted expression. "Seathorne is a first-class institution, for its size." Miss Bellamy was fiercely protective of her employer's interests. "I believe Dr. Spenser considers this to be something of a favour on her part. Miss Henderson is an old friend of the family." There was no doubt now of a steely undertone of sarcasm to Dorcas' words. Gwen wondered if there was more to her antagonism than just the dinner table demotion.

"She is replacing an even more eminent scholar," Gwen said quickly. "Dr. Emily Temple."

"Yes, of course." The priest nodded. "I read about Dr. Temple in the prospectus, and I had looked forward to discussing with her the cult of St. James. Her, um... her absence seems to be a sensitive topic." He looked from Dorcas to Gwen with an inquisitive expression. "I did not know until now that she had passed on."

A letter had gone out notifying the tour guests that Dr. Spenser would now be the scholarly expert in charge, but not of the reason for the change.

After an awkward pause, Gwen said, "It was thought that the news might cast a pall over the trip, particularly the time we'll be spending in Santiago de Compostela."

He shook his head. "Discretion is no match for human curiosity. Back on the dock, while we were waiting to board, I heard Mrs. Fairlamb telling the Sloans, the sad tale, so undoubtedly, all the passengers know by now. I'm afraid that terrible accidents like that have a strange fascination for many people."

Dorcas gathered her shawl more tightly around her shoulders and stood up. "That may be so, Father, but I would appreciate your help in repressing such discussions. They would cause great distress to Miss Henderson, as Dr. Temple was an old and dear friend." She turned to Gwen. "If I might have a moment of your time, Miss Armstrong, can we just go over the schedule for shipboard events?"

Gwen rose to follow her. Repressing discussion was the last thing she wanted. She needed to discover what the Fairlambs knew before they found out more about her purpose in going to Spain.

Chapter Nine

After dinner, most of the passengers returned to the lounge, where two tables of bridge were quickly set up. Amanda contrived to be Michael Greville's partner against Miss Henderson and Dorcas Bellamy, while the Fairlambs maneuvered the wealthy American couple to their table.

Gwen watched the play for a while. She knew the basics of the game. Might that be a way to engage the Fairlambs in conversation? However, as time went on, an air of intense competition developed, which made it clear that neither couple considered it a place for idle chatter. Besides, they were playing for money, and that was out of the question for her.

With a shrug, she turned to scan the ship's library, which consisted of a small bookcase in one corner, holding a stack of out-of-date magazines and a motley selection of books clearly left behind by previous passengers. Amid exotic travel tales and books of sermons stood a depressing number of novels that were simple variations on *The Sheik*.

She shoved them back on the shelf in disgust. It might have made Valentino's career, but Edith Hull's tale of desert passion had a lot to answer for, encouraging female readers to equate violent kidnapping with erotic pleasure.

Attracted by the pristine dust jacket, she found a detective novel by an unfamiliar author, intriguingly titled *Whose Body?* She settled into a comfortable armchair and smiled to herself, suddenly conscious of her own hypocrisy. After her self-righteous condemnation of the 'sand and sin' genre, here she was wallowing in the aristocratic sleuthing of Miss Dorothy Sayers' hero. Hardly more elevated reading, was it?

An hour later she closed the book and went down to the cabin for her warm coat. It might be May, but if she wanted to take a stroll on deck before turning in, it meant wrapping up, as the sea air would be chilly. Stepping out through the bulkhead onto the deck, she paused for a second to let her eyes adjust to the darkness.

Silhouetted against the dark sea and sky, a slender figure leaned on the ship's railing, her flimsy gown rippling in the breeze beneath a dark fur wrap. Amanda stared out into the night. The mass of stars made a glittering roof that darkened to ink at the horizon, as the ship lifted and fell beneath them on the unseen waves. Far astern, a faint, misty smear of light marked the distant coast of France.

As Gwen approached, Amanda looked around, with a slight frown that quickly faded. Turning back to her contemplation of the sea, she said quietly, "There's nothing so exciting as the start of a journey, is there?"

Uncertain how to respond to her unexpectedly friendly tone, Gwen said, "I'm afraid I haven't made many journeys, and none by sea."

"Well then, it's past time that you did." Amanda glanced up at her sideways with the hint of a smile.

Gwen leaned on the rail beside her, unsure how to respond. During the past two weeks of preparing for the trip, Amanda's initial arrogance had sometimes given way to a warmer attitude, especially when she asked Gwen about her friendship with Emily. But this overt friendliness set Gwen a little off-balance. However, that was no reason to miss an opportunity to get things on a pleasanter footing. She genuinely wanted to know more about this impressive woman.

"You must have been to so many foreign places. Do you have a favourite?"

Amanda gazed out into the starry void and smiled more broadly. "Oh, I can't choose just one. Greece, of course. The Aegean Islands. Schliemann's Troy. The Acropolis…Egypt…naturally." The look on her face held a kind of dreamy wistfulness Gwen would never have expected to see.

"And Spain?"

"Ah, yes, Spain. Particularly Galicia, the northwest, where we are going, close to Cabo Finisterre. That's the westernmost point in Europe, jumping off place for the unknown." Her expression became somber. "The end of the world… that's what the ancients called it."

"Sounds rather sinister." Soft glowing lamps had come on behind them along the deck, and far below, a gleam of phosphorescence tipped the glassy swells.

"It's very Celtic," Amanda's voice still held a wistful note. "All craggy seashores and heavy mists. Green as Ireland and just as full of ancient secrets. That's the area of Spain I'm really interested in," She took an onyx case from her small, beaded evening bag and extracted a cigarette. "Galicia is simply littered with Celtic remnants."

Once more, she became the cynical sophisticate, but for a moment, a very different Amanda had emerged. Gwen gazed out into the dark. "It sounds as if you know the area very well."

Amanda held the cigarette loosely in her long fingers, gesturing in that elegant way that betrayed her aristocratic forebears. "I've travelled around there a bit."

"Do you know the dig site we're visiting?"

"Castro de Carballo. It's right on the coast. Cedric Hunt is digging up a Celtic fort there, and he's found some marvelous things."

That must be the Doctor Hunt that Emily had mentioned in her letter and the diary.

Gwen couldn't clearly see Amanda's face, but the suppressed excitement in her voice was unmistakable. In the short time Gwen had known her, she'd discovered a woman of confusing contradictions.

As soon as she thought she had Amanda pegged as a vain, self-centred snob, she'd begin talking about her work and turn the picture upside down. History and archaeology were her consuming passions. And yet she looked the epitome of modernity, in her Persian lamb coat and the beaded chiffon dress underneath, as if she were on a cruise to Bermuda, not a scholarly mission.

She fished in her bag again. "Oh damn, I've forgotten my lighter." She heaved a sigh. "I won't even bother asking you for matches. How tiresome of you not to smoke. It's that damned Methodist upbringing, keeping you on the boring straight and narrow."

Delivered with the hint of a smile, for once, the little jab didn't bother her. Gwen smiled back. "Very tiresome, I'm sure."

Amanda turned to her. "Could you be a darling and get my lighter from the cabin." The faint lamplight caught her clear blue eyes and the appeal in her pretty face as she gestured toward the lighted windows of the lounge. "I'd go for matches, but I can't bear to see those dreadful people in there. They'll try to make me play bridge again or something equally ghastly."

Gwen couldn't help but smile and nod like the efficient assistant she aspired to be. "Certainly, I'll be right back."

"Don't worry if you can't find it," Amanda called after her.

She hurried down the deck, then paused outside the bulkhead. Just before she stepped through the doorway, something made her turn and look back. Up by the bow, she could just make out the dark figure of a man against the faintly glowing waves and the deep navy sky.

A tiny dot glowed cherry red, then moved in a slow arc down to the railing. A cigarette. Perhaps she could save herself the trip to the cabin after all. Amanda must have seen him, too.

As she watched, Amanda straightened from the railing and walked languidly towards the male silhouette. Lingering in the shadows, Gwen suddenly felt like a fool. She'd been sent away on purpose.

Not much doubt who that man would be. For some reason, she felt her cheeks begin to burn. It was no business of hers what Dr. Spenser got up to.

She slipped in through the metal door, turned right, and followed the corridor down toward the lounge. In the faint haze of cigarette smoke, she scanned the scattered card tables, sofas, and chairs.

Several of the passengers had already disappeared. Including Michael Greville.

"Miss Armstrong, this is capital!" Colonel Fairlamb had already half risen from the nearest table. "I just said to the padré before he disappeared that he should pray for another fourth to take his place."

"Hardly a fit subject for prayer, Colonel." Mr. Sloan gathered in the cards and shuffled expertly, with a sympathetic grin in Gwen's direction. "Since my wife is heading to bed, it seems we've also lost our third, so it seems rather pointless to recruit Miss Armstrong."

The pale eyes blinked rapidly. "Perhaps Miss Spenser would…"

Gwen shook her head a little too emphatically. "I really don't think so."

Time for her to go to bed, too. She had no interest in bridge, and whatever game Amanda was playing was obviously a game for two.

Chapter Ten

Gwen lay for a long time listening to the distant rhythmic throb of the engines. The gentle rolling motion should have lulled her to sleep, but an hour later, she was still awake when the cabin door opened. A dazzling shaft of light from the corridor pierced the darkness for a moment. Then she heard the rustling swish of silk.

"Sorry about the lighter," Gwen said quietly.

There was a quick exhalation. "Gwen, I thought you were asleep." With a click, the lamp between the beds glowed to life.

Amanda slipped off her shoulder straps and stepped out of the beaded gown, revealing a brief satin chemise. She flung the dress carelessly on top of her cabin trunk. "And never mind the lighter, I told you it wasn't important. I got a light from someone."

She turned away and sat down on the bed to roll off her stockings, admiring the shape of her legs as the corners of her mouth curved in a secret, amused smile.

"Anyway, you must be tired." She pulled off the chemise and tossed it on top of the dress, then sat on the dressing table chair, picked up the hairbrush, and dragged it through her short curls as she regarded her naked reflection. Through the mirror, she met Gwen's eyes.

Clearly, she enjoyed shocking people, and Gwen was beginning to weary of it, along with the gibes about her supposedly strait-laced northern upbringing.

The brush clattered on the table. Amanda dipped into a pot of cold cream, and began spreading it over her face, then wiped it off with a pad of cotton wool. "I had a fascinating chat with Michael Greville. Apparently, he knows Spain quite well and even speaks the language. Anyway, since my Spanish is rather rusty and yours non-existent, I've persuaded him to help us once we get to Bilbao."

"Surely the Colonel speaks Spanish."

She turned and gave Gwen a pitying look. "Honestly, darling. You're too good to be true!" Her voice sharpened a little. "You did send off that letter to the Cardinal's secretary, didn't you? Or there'll be trouble getting access to the library."

"Of course, I did." By now she should be used to Amanda's lightning changes of mood. For a moment up there on deck, she'd felt a fleeting human connection. What role was she expected to play right now, girlish confidante or loyal, efficient secretary? Amanda seemed to expect her to be both, and to know instinctively when to slip back into her 'place'. "I also wrote to The Pilgrim's Office and the…Hostel de los Reyes Catolicos," she pronounced carefully. Amanda wiped the cold cream off her hands, then dug into her evening bag.

"Good to know you're so conscientious." She pulled out her cigarette case and tossed the beaded purse onto the table between the beds. "I can see that you'll save me all sorts of work. Perhaps the Dean was right after all when she forced me to bring you along."

"I'm so glad you've changed your opinion." The acid comment slipped out unintentionally.

Amanda didn't seem to notice. "Well, I have." She reached for the small lamp. "Do you mind?"

Gwen shook her head, and Amanda flicked it off, plunging the room into darkness, then with a rattle of curtain rings, the dim circle of the porthole took shape, and faint milky starlight showed the dark outline of Amanda reclining on the bed and leaning back against the headboard, one knee raised. The lighter flared, and for a brief second, her face glowed like a fiery cameo against the darkness, a beautiful, hard mask. "I suppose I've been rather beastly to you about this."

It seemed better to say nothing than make some polite denial that neither of them would believe. "But now that I know you a little better, I can see that you're not..."

Amanda hesitated, and perhaps the darkness made her bold, but Gwen couldn't resist the urge to speak frankly. "The Dean's little sneak? A sour old warden with a face like grim death?"

Amanda groaned. "Oh God, you heard?"

Gwen had to laugh. "It wasn't difficult, I was right outside the Dean's office at the time." And even if she hadn't been, their flaming row was all over the College before luncheon.

"I don't know who that woman thinks she is," Amanda said. "Lecturing me like a first-year girl about the dangers of the Continent. Me! I'll swear she's never been out of England, while I've travelled on my own for years. To places that would have her begging for a British gunboat to take her home." The glowing tip of the cigarette burned more intensely as she took a furious puff.

Standing outside the Dean's door, listening to the argument, Gwen had actually sympathized with Amanda. She could only assume that the Dean's insistence on propriety had been Letitia Henderson's idea of a plausible reason for Gwen going along.

"It seems someone on the Board of Governors told her that the Spanish regard a young, unescorted single woman as practically a whore. Apparently, the presence of my graduate assistant makes it even more scandalous."

"Then what good is it to have another single woman along? Perhaps they'll take us for a traveling brothel."

Amanda gave an astonished laugh. "Well, well, you may have unexpected depths." She drew on the cigarette again, and the tip flared in the dark. "We might do quite well at that, actually. A redhead and a blonde. You know, a bit of exotica."

Gwen felt her cheeks burn. It must be something about the darkness, about being so much out of her usual element, that had her saying so boldly whatever came into her head.

Amanda chuckled again. "Anyway, the Dean's solution to this scandalous state of affairs was that I had to take you along."

"The sour old warden."

"Yes, sorry about that. You're not old, or the least bit sour. Actually, you're very pretty."

The compliment astonished her. "I…um…so are you."

"I know. And I like to have beautiful things around me," she said matter-of-factly. "So, once I got over my pique, I decided that we could actually have some fun on this trip."

Gwen was too stunned to reply. Part of her admired and envied Amanda's confidence and independence, and even her arrogance. But she knew it would be foolish to trust such a mercurial personality, despite being flattered by her sudden friendliness.

"I can't say I'm looking forward to dealing with the wrath of God every day, in the person of that creaky old Colonel," Amanda went on.

With a sudden shiver, Gwen slipped down under the covers. "I find him a bit frightening. He reminds me of a painting I once saw in a book. One of those conquistadores who burned natives alive for the good of their souls."

"Pfff…" The cigarette waved dismissively to and fro. "He's just a man. Most of those fanatical types are secretly obsessed with sex and scared to death of it at the same time. You must have noticed how he looks at me." There was a note of gleeful satisfaction in her voice. "And you too, for that matter, but I'm more obvious."

"Maybe he's really afraid of you. In the lounge I heard him telling Father Garrick how strongly he disapproves of the 'new woman.'"

"The 'new woman'!" She gave a snort of disgust, and a bitter tone crept in. "I'm fed up to the teeth with this 'new woman' rot. A lot of good it's done us. All it means to men is free sex. When it comes to what really counts, they keep all that in the old boys' club. I'm a damn good scholar, but I'm not even in the running for any of the jobs that a man with my qualifications would have in a snap. I just don't have the right equipment between my legs."

Then came the sound of a cigarette grinding hard in the ashtray. "It's just the way it's always been. A woman has to make her way the best she can, using all the weapons at her disposal. The old school tie isn't worth a damn to us, except perhaps as a noose…"

Chapter Eleven

The next day Gwen suspected that Amanda regretted her frankness of the night before. She was positively frosty when Gwen helped her and Franz set up for the first lecture, a presentation on the tradition of pilgrimage to Santiago de Compostela.

The tour guests sat around the darkened lounge, looking at the glowing image projected by the lantern slide. In Rembrandt's portrait, an ascetic, pious Saint James stood with his hands clasped in prayer.

"You can see here two symbols associated with the pilgrimage to Santiago," Amanda pointed out. "The scallop shell on his shoulder and the pilgrim's staff in the background."

"There is no biblical evidence that James ever visited Spain," she went on, "But medieval sources asserted that he was assigned to spread the Gospel to the Iberian Peninsula. He apparently reached as far as Galicia but seems not to have had much success. He gathered all of seven followers." Her dry delivery sent a wave of laughter round the room.

As always, she looked immaculate. Today, she wore a coat and skirt in fine grey tweed. On anyone else it would be severe and scholarly, but on Amanda, the exquisite tailoring was perfection.

She nodded to Franz at the projector, and another image clicked into place. This one showed a silver casket set into a stone niche. "Every story about Santiago is steeped in mystery and myth. This beautifully worked coffer reputedly holds his relics in the crypt beneath the main altar of the cathedral. How they got there is a much-disputed tale."

The next slide showed the baroque exterior of the cathedral. "So how did the remains of one of Christ's disciples who was martyred in Jerusalem in 44 AD ended up in what was then an obscure village in the isolated and primitive North West of Spain, so far removed from the Holy Land? And why did St. James become so revered that his resting place grew to be one of the principal pilgrimage routes for Christians during Medieval times, surpassed in importance only by Jerusalem and Rome?"

She perched one hip on the desk and leaned forward confidentially, telling the story. "My favorite tradition has it that two of James's disciples took his remains in a stone boat which, although having no rudder, oars, sails, or even sailors, miraculously carried its precious cargo across the Mediterranean and up along the coast of modern Portugal to Galicia. The boat landed at Iria Flavia, a Roman hamlet now known as Padrón, a name said to be derived from *pedrón* which means 'big stone' in Galician.

"According to legend, St. James's body suddenly soared into the air and flew east, pursued by his disciples, until it landed in its current location. As you can see, the tale is notable for its lack of historical confirmation and its dependence on miracles and tradition."

Gwen caught sight of Father Garrick sitting at the back of the room, looking unamused by Amanda's derisive tone.

There followed further slides illustrating the glories of the Santiago cathedral while Amanda talked about the history of the building. She went on to sketch a survey of the rich history of northern Spain, from the ancient Celts, through the Roman settlements, to the Moorish occupation and the gradual re-conquest by the Franks.

Amanda managed to make the dry topic not only interesting, but often amusing. Once again, Gwen could see that Amanda might be unconventional, but she undeniably knew her stuff. Even if she could be bitingly sarcastic about the Church, an institution for which she clearly had little respect. It wasn't surprising that the priest left before she had finished.

When the presentation concluded, and she and Franz were left to pack up the slides, Gwen took the opportunity to talk to Amanda's graduate assistant. She was curious and more than a little sorry for him. It was ten years since the armistice, but the dreadful legacy of the war still infected every aspect of life.

"I hope people haven't been too nasty to you," she said quietly. "It must be difficult, still."

She couldn't help comparing him to her brothers. Franz was a few years older, but in comparison, the boy looked so beaten down. He wore the same baggy, brown tweed suit as the day before, and his frayed shirt cuffs were inexpertly darned. He had a habit of not looking people in the eye but would just give them a quick furtive glance from under his blond brows, then look down at his worn brown boots.

He did this now, then nodded. "Yes, indeed. It has been hard, but on this boat, the people have been not so bad. Mr. And Mrs. Dixon have been actually very kind."

Such generosity of spirit impressed her and relieved some of her anxiety. The Dixons, of all people, had every reason for bitter resentment of anything German.

He nodded in the direction of the tall couple just leaving the lounge for the deck. "The Colonel, though. I do not think he likes me at all. He makes comments about the Bosch and the Hun. How the reparations should have been even more harsh. As if they have not been driving us all to desperation and despair!" His voice sharpened and cracked with emotion.

"I'm so terribly sorry. Have your family been suffering?" Gwen felt helpless and awkward.

"They are ruined. Once we had a fine house in Berlin. Now they live in a tiny apartment, crammed into three small rooms. My mother sold her jewels to pay my fees for the gymnasium and the university. I am their hope, you see." He gave her another quick upward glance and she saw his eyes were wet.

Desperately, she searched for a less emotional topic. "You like your work with Dr. Spenser?"

"Jah, indeed, I love it!" He nodded with enthusiasm. "She is quite brilliant, Fraulien Doktor Spenser. She guides me in my research."

"What is your research?"

Now he looked her directly in the eye, with a sudden burst of excitement.

"It is most important. Important for my country, for our self-respect. You have heard of *Nordische Gedanke,* of course.

Gwen could only shake her head, as he went on earnestly, his voice ringing with enthusiasm. "The great Hans Gunther has shown conclusively that the Nordic race conquered Europe in the Iron Age. As a dominant warrior race, they became a natural aristocracy and, in fact, were the founders of European civilization."

"I, uh… I see…" Although she didn't really. Nothing like this had come up in her reading about European prehistory. "And how does this relate to your research, exactly?"

"My intention is to demonstrate the Bronze Age connection between the Celts and the Aryans. Look at the material culture; study skeletal remains for bodily traits such as the characteristic long dolichocephalic skull shape…"

He went on and on with increasing vehemence as Gwen tried to follow his convoluted explanation. As far as she could understand it, this theory was intended to prove that modern Germans were the natural heirs to a dominant warrior culture that could be traced back to the prehistoric Celts.

"So, you see why I must complete my thesis!" he ended breathlessly.

Gwen nodded, dazed by the torrent of words. It sounded to her like a crazy mixture of myth and history designed to soothe wounded national pride, but she could hardly say so. "It sounds fascinating," she said faintly.

Right now, all she wanted was a brisk walk around the deck. And a few minutes of blessed silence. Poor Franz couldn't be blamed for seeking solace for his misery, but the hectic tone of his outpouring made her uncomfortable. Still, it had also given her an idea.

In her cabin, she pulled her small suitcase out from under the bed and took out a brown envelope. She slid out a stack of six photographs onto the lilac satin counterpane, selected the best close-up, and tucked it into her pocket. One of the skills Emily taught her, had been simple photography, and the college had a well-equipped darkroom. The golden horseman was safely hidden away in her case, but it had seemed prudent to take some photos, and now she thought of a useful way to use them.

All the books she had consulted led her to believe the piece was Celtic, but it might be helpful to have an expert opinion. The logical person to consult was Amanda Spenser, but not without saying where the object came from. And that opened a Pandora's Box of consequences.

One thing had emerged from Franz's elaborate disquisition after the lecture, he clearly knew a lot about Celtic archaeology.

Avoiding the lounge, where tea was now being served, she found Franz alone in the small cabin that did service as the ship's library and writing room. He sat hunched over the notebook that occupied whatever waking moments were not employed in dancing attendance on Dr. Spenser.

Startled at Gwen's entrance, he jumped up and gave a formal little bow. His old-world mannerisms still caught her by surprise. "Oh, please..." Feeling awkward, she sat down at the table and pulled the photograph from her pocket. "I wonder if you would mind taking a look at something for me?"

Franz took the print. His eyes widened, and he stared at it for a long, silent moment. "Where did you get this?" he asked at last, in a choked voice.

"At the college...it was loose in one of the filing cabinets." It sounded pretty thin, but she couldn't think of a better story.

"Dr. Temple's cabinet? Is it hers, perhaps?"

The intensity in his question unnerved her. "I'm not sure..."

"Have you seen the original?" he asked breathlessly.

She shook her head, already regretting the decision to show it to him.

He stared intently at the image. "This is a Celt-Iberian fibula," he said at last. "A brooch to fasten the cloak, yes? It represents a rider. You see this round shape hanging off the bridle," he pointed to the detail, with feverish excitement. "This is a cut human head. You know, of course, how the Celts prized the heads of their defeated enemies. These kinds of fibulae are an emblem of elite warriors. The very best, most rare ones are made of gold. Unfortunately, in a photograph, one cannot tell the colour."

A chill went down her spine. She was no expert, but Gwen was fairly certain the lustrous and heavy object in her luggage might very well be just such a rarity. It would be worth an absolute fortune.

Franz stared at her with alarming intensity. "Dr. Spenser must see this!"

"Oh, no! I mean..." Gwen didn't have to try hard to look anxious. "You know how particular Dr. Spenser is about organization and precision. I do so admire that about her. But to be honest…. Well, I'm a bit scared of her. I want her to think that I'm doing a good job. She can be quite…demanding, can't she?"

She had no particular reason to mistrust Amanda Spenser, but the risk to Emily's reputation was too great. Gwen had been determined not to reveal the horseman to anyone unnecessarily, not until she knew what this was all about.

Now she had the awful feeling that she'd just made a big mistake. Had she gambled too much on Franz's sympathy for her and their shared situation as Amanda's vassals? "Now that you've told me what it is, I'll know where to file it. Please don't tell on me."

At her pleading tone, he stared at her for a moment, then gave a faint smirk, sat taller in his chair, and assumed an expression she'd never seen on his face before—a masculine attitude of superiority and condescension. "Don't worry. I won't say a word."

Now, she just had to pray that he wouldn't.

Chapter Twelve

Miss Henderson had invited Gwen to join her, Dorcas, and the Fairlambs for drinks before dinner in her cabin. Cabin was a bit of an understatement. The suite included two bedrooms, a bathroom, and a fair-sized sitting room.

Dorcas handed round the sherry, while Letitia Henderson gave the Fairlambs an edited version of Gwen's task.

"Dr. Temple had quite taken Miss Armstrong under her wing, so to speak, and now Miss Armstrong would like to represent the college in ensuring that Dr. Temple's memorial arrangements are suitably taken care of."

"My wife and I made certain she received a respectable Christian burial. All the proper decencies were observed." Colonel Fairlamb looked a little affronted, as his gooseberry eyes maintained their glacial stare. Gwen had the unaccountable feeling that he knew she was concealing something.

"I'm sure your care was exemplary, Colonel," Miss Henderson bowed her head in his direction, "But there is the matter of a headstone, and I imagine a provision for ongoing care of the grave."

"Well, naturally—"

"And, of course, the college will be reimbursing any expense you have so far incurred." The Colonel looked offended by this reference to base matters of money.

"I understand that you and Mrs. Fairlamb knew Dr. Temple quite well." Gwen ventured. This could be an opportune moment to probe for more information.

"Indeed," Mrs. Fairlamb answered, her long equine face conveying not just regret, but real sadness. "As you know, we have organized these tours for Seathorne College for many years. There were several Mesopotamian and Egyptian trips before the war, and we resumed not long after the Armistice.

Emily...Dr. Temple, has been our academic expert since then. Was our expert, I should say." She sighed. "Such a sad funeral. The English Cemetery in Santiago is rather woebegone, and there were few mourners."

"You were in Santiago at the time?"

"Oh, yes. We were making preparations for this tour. The Colonel and I deal with the domestic arrangements. Emily was consulting with the ecclesiastical authorities for special permissions and getting in touch with those archaeologists with active digs in that region."

"Damn glad we were there," the Colonel's gruff bark cut in. His wife shot him a glare of reproof at the profanity. "Lord knows what kind of dago palaver would have ensued if I hadn't gone straight to the top, to the *Alcalde*. That's the Mayor, you see. They run the show in these Spanish towns."

"What kind of... *palaver*, do you mean exactly?" Gwen asked.

"Officious policemen strutting around. Damned little peacocks in their gold braid and tricorn hats. Jabbering on about the accident." He glared at no one in particular.

"Did they think there was anything, well...suspicious?" Gwen couldn't help but ask. He turned the glare on her. "Nonsense. Sheer self-importance. There was nothing to investigate. Hook came out of a wall. Crumbling mortar. Happens all the time in old buildings, and that one's been there since the thirteenth century. Bad luck it was holding that censer, and that Emily got in its way. Freak accident of the worst sort."

His mouth set in a thin line that implied nothing more need or could be said. Gwen shivered at the nightmare image of a heavy metal censer slamming into Emily. Clearly, the police had not been fully satisfied. She needed to speak to them, as soon as possible. "Did she have friends there?" she asked urgently. "Who came to the funeral?"

The Colonel looked insulted at her peremptory tone. "That Oxford chap who's digging out at Finisterre, Hunt is his name. Some people from the hotel. As I said, very few mourners."

"Don't forget her friend from Bilbao." Mrs. Fairlamb added.

"Oh, yes. The Scott woman." The colonel's face stiffened. In reply to Gwen's questioning look, he added unhelpfully, "Mrs. Scott."

"This friend lives in Spain?"

The Colonel's wife shot an anxious glance toward her husband, before answering.

"I believe Mrs. Scott is married to an English marine engineer who runs some of the shipbuilding works at Bilbao. She had just come to town, and they were going to have luncheon together the following day. She was terribly upset. A friend from university days, I think."

Someone else Gwen needed to talk to. But the conversation also made something else clear. Elsie Fairlamb was evidently more upset by Emily's death than her husband. Did she know more than she was saying? The only way to find out was to talk to Elsie alone.

* * *

Her effort to talk to Elsie Fairlamb alone was destined to frustration, for the rest of the evening. Was it her imagination that the Colonel stayed purposefully glued to his wife's side? Next day, there were no opportunities before lunch, or afterwards until the moment Amanda swooped in and virtually frog-marched Gwen to the ship's library.

"I need my notes compiled for this evening's lecture." She indicated the pile of books and papers stacked on the desk. "I found some new material on Lugo, which I need you to extract and summarize."

Gwen sat down and quickly surveyed the bookmarked pages, then riffled through the presentation outline. There was certainly plenty of new material about the old Roman city of Lugo. Before she had the chance to ask a question, Amanda waved casually at the material on the desk. "Use your judgment about where to insert the new information," she said and whirled out of the room.

Gwen stared after her at the empty doorway, then shook her head. She turned her chair to the typewriter table at right angles to the desk and rolled a fresh sheet of paper into the machine. To look on the bright side, she should take this delegation as a vote of confidence.

An hour later, she rubbed her eyes and looked out of the porthole at the bisected blue circle of sea and sky. She heaved a sigh.

"Is it that bad?" A deep male voice made her head spin around to see Michael Greville standing in the doorway.

Her heart leapt and began to pound. She took a deep breath and quickly got it under control. He had taken her by surprise. "Oh, it's just work, you know."

He stepped into the room, and it suddenly felt uncomfortably crowded. He held out his hand. "I must apologize. Somehow, we have not been introduced. Most remiss of me."

She shook his hand. It felt warm and firm and disturbingly pleasant. She let go abruptly. "I haven't had much time for social pleasures. I have a lot of work to do."

"Yes, I can see that. Amanda keeps you very busy." He leaned a hip against the desk and picked up a weighty book from the stack. "Looks like you've brought the whole library with you."

"They're invaluable. We need to have reference material for the talks."

"You mean she doesn't have it all by heart?" There was a satirical note in his voice that she didn't quite know how to take.

"There's so much material…" She knew she sounded stiff and awkward and that the question wasn't serious. "No one could possibly…"

He smiled apologetically. "Of course not. Pardon my poor attempt at humour. So how long have you been in Dr. Spenser's employ?"

"Actually, I work for Seathorne College. I've been there for a year and a half." She felt intensely conscious of him looming above her, his intensely blue eyes never leaving her face.

"You knew Dr. Temple quite well, I believe."

"How did you…?"

"Letitia told me." His expression softened. "I was sorry to hear about the accident. It must have been a shock."

She nodded, her voice sinking to a whisper. "It was." She cleared her throat and strove to sound more detached. "Did you know her?"

"Not well, but archaeology is a rather small world. I ran into her on the Continent a few times over the years. She was quite a traveller," he said with a faint smile. He flipped idly through the pages of the book in his hand. "Did you ever travel with her?

"No. But I would love to have had the opportunity. Did you meet her at digs?"

"Sometimes." He put the book down. "You must have been a great help to her, back in England."

There was a faint undertone of cynicism in his voice that she didn't understand. "At the college, you mean? I do hope so. It was my job, after all."

He gazed at her silently for a long moment, then stood upright. "Well, I've interfered with your work long enough. Though it's been a pleasure to talk to you." He stepped out of the door and turned to smile at her. "I'll see you later."

She stared after him with a frown. Now, what was all that about?

* * *

"As Professor Spenser informed us yesterday, Santiago de Compostela is an ancient place. Goes back much further than the 13th-century building of the cathedral." Father Garrick leaned back in his deck chair and stared across the Bay of Biscay toward the misty blue horizon. His voice softened. "What did you think of the legend of Santiago? Or Saint James, as we call him."

Gwen said, "I was intrigued, of course, but... and don't tell Professor Spenser...to be perfectly honest, I'm not clear as to which Saint James it is. I know there was more than one."

"This one was the Apostle James. James the Greater, son of Zebedee, brother of John. One of the first disciples to join our Lord and one of the first to be martyred. Put to the sword by Herod Agrippa."

The cool breeze made Gwen shiver and nestle further into her tweed jacket. "That would have happened in the Holy Land, in Judea. So, if it really is him buried in the cathedral, how do you think he *actually* got there?"

Father Garrick smiled. "I see you share the Professor's skepticism."

"I don't want to offend you, Father. That tale of stone boats and flying Saints is a wonderfully colourful myth, but as an archaeologist, I quite see why Dr. Spenser couldn't take it as fact."

"Believe it or not, the Church shies away from such stories. We don't condemn them, They're just folk tales, that are ways of explaining the unexplainable. However Santiago may have got there, Spain is not an impossible resting place for him. He lived in the glory days of the Roman Empire. Iberia was known as Hispania, a thriving province of Rome in the time of our Lord. It's not so farfetched that he may have preached the Gospel there and converted many to Christianity. Probably more than seven," he added dryly.

Gwen smiled. "I imagine that people commonly traveled around the Empire fairly easily."

"And in comparative safety," he added. "From the accession of Augustus to the end of Marcus Aurelius' reign, there were two hundred years of relative calm around the Mediterranean. They called it the *Pax Romana*."

"But from what Dr. Spenser said, the shrine at Santiago doesn't go back that far, just to the 9th Century."

Father Garrick nodded. "Of course, there's a story about the discovery of his grave. In the year 811, a luminous star caught the attention of a hermit, who followed it to a funerary monument on Mount Libredon. He found an altar and the tomb of a beheaded man with his head under his arm, and beside it, a sign indicating: "Here lies James, son of Zebedee and Salome."

"Well, that's pretty clear." She couldn't think what else to say.

He smiled. "I know. Yet another fanciful story, but there is certainly biblical precedent for following a star. And the episode gave its name to the town and the cathedral. The name Compostela is derived from the Latin *Campus Stellae*, meaning 'Field of the Star.'"

Gwen sighed and looked up into the fathomless cobalt sky. The morning haze had burned off, and the deep navy blue of the Bay of Biscay spread to the horizon.

"You know so much about Santiago de Compostela. Is that why you left the lecture partway through?" She turned her head to look at the priest.

He lay relaxed upon the steamer chair, arms crossed. Beneath his flat-brimmed black hat, he returned her gaze. "There's always something new to learn, but I didn't care for the professor's brisk dismissal of the stories told by simple people to make sense of the world."

"She is a scientist."

"I don't object to science. But I do object to that hard, fashionable cynicism that disdains anything it can't explain. Dr. Spenser embodies the notion that those who believe in nothing, will believe in anything." A hard glint of anger sparked in his eyes.

"You really don't like her, do you?"

The anger vanished, and he gave a brief smile. "Forgive my rudeness. I don't know the lady well enough to dislike her. I just object to her type. Which is no doubt a very shallow and unchristian attitude for me to take."

The ship had slightly changed direction, catching a brisk wind from the east. Gwen sat up. "I'm getting cold, and I need some exercise. Would you care to walk, Father?"

Setting off at a fast pace, they walked the length of the deck, buffeted by gusts and fine spray.

When they reached the lee side, Gwen stopped to lean on the railing. "I need to catch my breath!"

Father Garrick paused beside her. "About the lecture. I'm curious to know if she went into the legend of Santiago Matamoros. It's rather a favorite of mine."

"What is that?"

"It means 'Saint James the Moor Slayer,'" he said. "There's a reason that James is the patron saint of Spain. In 711, the Moors stormed out of North Africa and invaded most of Iberia. The Christians barely hung on in the north. Not long after, they built the first chapel to Saint James. At the beginning of the Christian reconquest of Spain, they fought a desperate battle at a place called Clavijo. Legend has it that a heavenly champion led the charge, slaying every Moor in his path. You'll see a rather garish statue

73

in the cathedral depicting Saint James on horseback, trampling the enemy, and hacking off their heads."

Gwen shuddered. "How gruesome. But why would it be a favourite legend of yours?"

Garrick stared out to sea. "They were struggling to survive. The vision of Saint James inspired them to fight back and reclaim their land." His boyish face held no trace of his usual good humor. "They needed a champion and found one. The statue may be gruesome, but it reflects reality."

A flicker of raw pain crossed his face. The ship lifted and fell beneath their feet. Gwen looked down twenty feet below into the glassy green swells and said quietly. "You were in the war."

"Wasn't everyone?" His attempt at lightness held a biting edge.

"It must have been dreadful," she said and inwardly winced at the inadequate word. "Were you a priest then?"

"Fresh out of the seminary," He stared out at the horizon, his face grim and his words a harsh staccato. "Full of exalted notions and…" He stopped abruptly and gave a brief bark of laughter. "That was another world, thank the Lord. And not one suitable to talk about with a young lady."

"It seems that no one who was there wants to talk about it," Gwen said reflectively. "My dad won't. Nor will any of the other men in the village. The ones who came back." She thought of the stone tablet in the village church with its list of names. "But it changed them. Everyone knows that. Some families want to understand, And some would rather not know."

"They're better off not knowing. Because it did change men, in ways most of them would rather not think about."

"Did you question your faith?" Gwen asked quietly, shocked at her own frankness, putting such a question to a virtual stranger. But he was so easy to talk to and treated her like a serious, intelligent person. She already felt as if he were an old friend.

Father Garrick turned to look her in the face. His blue eyes were filled with tears. "Of course, I did. I struggled through many dark nights of the soul, or should I say nights of blazing explosions and searing phosphor shells. With men in agony and dying all around me, I begged the Lord for help. He led me to a ruined church in a village with barely a house left standing. It had been taken by both sides in succession as the front line advanced and then retreated. The old priest had somehow hung on there, waiting for the villagers to come back."

He shook his head. "Poor man. We prayed together. He was living in the crypt and showed me proudly how he had hidden the statues of the crucifixion and the Blessed Virgin, along with the vessels for the sacrament. Waiting for the day, he could once again celebrate the Mass with his flock. That was my moment of revelation. My time in the wilderness came to an end. I suddenly knew my purpose." His face shone, and he gave her a slow, compassionate smile. "I left that church as if newborn, certain of my path and filled with newfound zeal."

"Did you ever know what happened to the priest?"

He looked away out to sea again and gave a deep sigh. "Not a day later, the Germans advanced again. The church took a direct hit, blown to smithereens."

"Oh, no."

"I prayed for him, of course, but in a strange way, I think the old man died as he would have wished. Martyred while defending the faith against barbarism."

He fell silent, apparently lost in thought, looking out toward the far horizon, where a faint smudge promised the sight of land.

It seemed wrong to ask him any more questions. His story made Gwen wonder again what experiences her father had endured, and if the damage caused by such memories could ever be healed. Her heart ached, and she felt a deep pang of guilt for her own selfish anger and frustration.

From further down the deck came the melodious chimes announcing luncheon, and the cheerful sound made her spirits lighten. Gwen had been charmed the first time she watched the steward tapping out the four ascending tones on what looked like a miniature xylophone.

Father Garrick shook himself, as if deliberately shedding the painful moment they had shared. "Ah, the most welcome sound on shipboard!"

They had started walking toward the dining salon when the priest said,

"Miss Henderson has told me about your special mission while in Spain."

"Oh?"

"This dreadful accident that occurred to your friend, Miss Temple. I understand you are making sure that she has been properly laid to rest. Was she a friend of your family?"

Gwen hesitated. That was one thing she was definitely *not*. But it seemed best to be consistent in her story, even though Father Garrick was someone she was tempted to confide in. "An aunt of mine went to the same university." That at least was true, although they actually never met. "I didn't really get to know her until I started work at Seathorne."

He nodded, then said hesitantly, "I didn't mention it earlier, but as it happens, I had heard about this tragic event before I left home. I correspond with Father Ignatius, who serves in the cathedral. We both studied in Rome before the war, and we've stayed in touch."

Gwen stopped and looked at him. "Was he there when it happened?"

"No," he shook his head. "But he was very distressed. A dreadful accident but, alas, not unprecedented. There have been three or four such occasions over the long history of Santiago de Compostela."

She longed to ask him more, but the Dixons were approaching from the opposite direction, clearly intent on conversation. What else might Father Garrick's friend know that might help her? Frustrating though it was, she would have to wait to find out.

Chapter Thirteen

I n the lounge, the passengers were gathering in animated conversation when Gwen went in search of Amanda. She found her deep in conversation with Michael Greville, their heads close together as they sat in adjoining chairs in the corner.

Gwen hesitated as she watched Amanda hold his gaze and raise a cigarette to her lips. Greville slid a gold lighter from his pocket and ignited the flame. For some reason, the sight made her deeply uncomfortable. After all, she'd seen Amanda flirting with every man on board and the woman delighted in scandalizing the deeply religious Fairlambs. If she was honest with herself, Gwen secretly rather enjoyed seeing a woman with such enormous confidence. So why did Amanda's blatant pursuit of Michael Greville get under her skin?

He was certainly a very physically attractive man, tall and lean. He dressed with the kind of discreet elegance, that indicated custom tailoring and the money to pay for it. He came from the same class as Amanda; they literally spoke the same language.

He reminded her too much of Sidney, she suddenly realized. Was that what bothered her? Taller, better-looking, but with the same supreme confidence conferred by money and private education. Sidney had been several rungs lower on the social ladder than Michael Greville, his family being 'in trade,' but still son and heir to an industrial fortune.

He had swept her up, and she willingly enjoyed the whirlwind. Delirious and infatuated with her first love affair, it had taken weeks until she woke with a cold shock. Quite by accident, she had seen him leaving the small

Durham hotel that she had thought of as their own secret trysting place. Of course, he wasn't alone. She recognized the dark-haired beauty on his arm. It seemed that Sidney treated the typing pool as his own well-stocked pond.

How could she have been so naïve? How could she have actually thought he was in love with her? Crushed and heartbroken, she vowed never to let herself be that vulnerable again. Men of his sort might dally with someone from the lower classes, but it could never be more than that.

Her cheeks began to burn. She suddenly realized Amanda had turned to look at her with a frown.

She shook herself and hurried toward them, careful not to look in Greville's direction. "Sorry to disturb you, Dr. Spenser. I need to discuss our plans for debarkation tomorrow."

* * *

Next morning, she was on deck before breakfast, searching the low hills on the horizon for signs of their destination. They were headed for Bilbao, but the purser informed her that the city itself was three miles deep in the estuary of the Nervion River. They would be docking in Portugalete, a village near the mouth of the river.

As they got closer, the arms of long concrete moles seemed to open wider as they approached. The pitching motion of the waves calmed as soon as they passed between the piers. Growing up near the coast, Gwen found the scene familiar but, at the same time, excitingly strange.

Small boats clustered along the wharves, and she could hear the distant cries of fishwives hawking the day's catch. On the right, between the hills and the shore, lay streets lined with rows of tall, narrow houses with enclosed balconies on each floor. In the distance, to the south, smoking chimneys indicated the steel mills and shipyards that made Bilbao the industrial heartland of modern New Spain. There'd be no orange trees and flamenco here.

The most striking sight on the river lay ahead where two iron structures, like twin miniature Eiffel towers, rose on either side of the river. From the connecting struts fifty feet above, a car slung on cables traversed from side to side. A transporter bridge!

She remembered Dad taking her to see the one in Middlesborough when she was young. These clever devices allowed tall ships to pass down the channel while ferrying traffic across at regular intervals. There was something comfortably familiar about the sight.

On the deck around her, the Colonel had organized everyone in military fashion, ready to transfer to shore, with a small mountain of luggage stacked beside them. Men in small boats gathered in a shouting cluster around the ship, but he dealt with them brusquely, and soon, the entire party had checked in at the *Gran Hotel Portulagete*, a small, classically styled building located right beside the massive bridge. Whatever her opinion of the Colonel's personality, he did a good job of managing the chaotic scene.

Mrs. Fairlamb had arranged for afternoon tea. "Though frankly, I advise having the coffee," she told Gwen with a frown. "In fact, I would advise drinking coffee for our entire time in Spain. I'm afraid they don't understand about tea and the need to steep it in boiling water." She leaned forward as if imparting a secret. "I don't have it unless I can make it myself."

Gwen glanced around to ensure they were alone in the small dining room, whose red velveteen drapes and gilt cherubs emanated a faded Edwardian glory.

"Do you have a moment? I've been hoping to speak to you privately, but there hasn't been an opportunity till now."

Elsie clasped her hands in agitation and didn't quite meet her eyes. 'I can't imagine why you'd want to talk to me privately."

"About Emily—"

"We've told you everything we can about Emily!" Her voice rose an octave, and her hands gripped each other tighter.

"That's curious." Gwen frowned. "Because you're telling me there's more to know." Elsie looked distractedly toward the stairs.

"I think perhaps you're afraid of your husband," Gwen said softly.

"What nonsense!" Elsie's attempt at brusque denial fell flat.

"Please believe me, I don't want to cause you any grief. But I'm sure there's something about Emily's death that you're not telling me. Please, please tell me. Perhaps your husband didn't like Emily, but I think that you did."

"Yes, Yes I did." The sound of footsteps on the landing made her look upward. There was real fear in her eyes now.

"Then tell me what you know," Gwen begged.

"Albert will be here any moment," Elsie said in an agonized whisper. "I'll talk to you after dinner." She broke away and hurried toward the bottom of the staircase.

Chapter Fourteen

After taking Elsie Fairlamb's advice about the coffee, Gwen ate a few crusty ham sandwiches and unfamiliar little cakes from the hotel's offering, then set out to visit Emily's friend, Mrs. Scott. Pointedly, in front of her husband, Elsie had given Gwen the address and telephone number, leaving Gwen wondering about the couple's differing reactions to her inquiries. It made having a private talk with Elsie even more imperative. But it wouldn't be easy.

For now, it was a relief to be outdoors. The day was cloudy and mild, with a fresh breeze that carried a faint tang of the sea and a definite undertone of fish. From the hotel, she took a hired pony cart and was soon jouncing up a steep cobblestoned hill toward a street of larger houses that looked out over the wide estuary.

Gwen anxiously scanned the facades. On the telephone, Mrs. Scott had warned her of the lack of house numbers and given very specific instructions to look for a second-floor flat with a blue-curtained balcony and geranium-filled flowerboxes. Gwen sat back on the worn leather bench and hung on to the side of the carriage, feeling dazed and anxious. The woman had sounded friendly enough, if a little guarded.

"Blue curtains!" She pointed upward, and the cart lurched to a stop.

"*Esta eso a qui?*"

She got the gist of the grizzled cab driver's question.

"Si, si. Here."

She jumped from the cart on wobbly knees. Her head felt a little wobbly, too. Probably still getting her land legs. Not to mention adjusting to being surrounded by people speaking a language she didn't understand. And perhaps feeling anxious about what this woman might tell her.

The feeling did not improve when a taciturn maid ushered her into a spacious room with massive carved wood furniture and red plush upholstered settees and chairs. A deep bow window faced the harbour, dotted with the multi-coloured sails of fishing boats.

"*La Senora estará contigo en unos minutos.*"

Gwen nodded as if she understood and sat down to wait. After five minutes, a pair of double doors on the opposite side of the room opened, and an extraordinary figure stepped through; A tall, strongly built dark-haired woman dressed in green mechanic's overalls smeared with oil, and tools of various kinds protruding from her pockets.

She strode toward Gwen with an outstretched hand. "Don't worry. I've washed." She shook hands vigorously, ushered Gwen into a chair, and sank down onto the sofa. Gwen noticed that the seat was draped with rough canvas. Presumably, to protect the furniture.

"I'll have Isabella bring in the tea. Unless you'd like a cocktail, perhaps?" Her fresh, rosy features looked like that of a country woman, and her blue eyes were just as keen. "We're a little behind the times here, but I do like a cocktail myself now and again. I understand they're all the rage back home." She rang a bell on a small side table.

Gwen smiled, warming to her friendly attitude. "I've just been introduced to them. They're not exactly common in my part of the world."

She chuckled. "I suppose the north is still more strait-laced than the south, at least it was in my day. Of course, I've lived here so long I've quite lost touch with things back home."

The maid came in and Mrs. Scott gave her instruction in rapid Spanish. As she left, her mistress looked down at herself and sighed. "I really should have changed. I hope you don't mind. I'm afraid I do look a sight." She leaned back against the canvas-draped sofa cushions. "I'm overhauling our car. The suspension is loose again thanks to these dratted roads, and Tommy is much too busy at the works."

"I'm impressed. It's unusual to find a woman who can repair cars."

She chuckled. "Oh, I go back to the early days, the real horseless carriages! Emily and I both picked up a great deal on those early digs with Dr. Petrie." Gwen could imagine them excavating a trench, the birdlike Emily, contrasting with Mrs. Scott's tall, solid frame. Emily's friend had the same vibrant force about her, her brunette hair barely touched with grey and caught up in a straggling bun. "Had to fend for ourselves in some pretty dodgy situations." She laughed again, then her smile suddenly faded. "I still can't believe Emily's gone."

Gwen leaned forward in her seat. She had warmed to the woman immediately. "Tell me about her, Mrs. Scott."

"Call me Hildy, dear." She reached out and patted Gwen's hand.

At that moment, the housekeeper entered and placed a tray on the table between them, laden with a silver cocktail shaker, two glasses, and a plate of small sandwiches.

"Do help yourself to the sandwiches." Hildy took the lid off the cocktail shaker and poured two drinks.

"How long have you lived here? And what brought you to Bilbao?" Gwen asked with genuine curiosity.

"I've been here twenty years. And as for what brought me here." She chuckled. "It was love." Her broad, lined face suddenly lit up. "I suppose that sounds hopelessly sentimental to a young modern like you, but it's the truth. I came to Bilbao for a conference. I met Tommy on a ship from Plymouth. It was a wretched crossing; Biscay was heaving, and all I could do to stave off seasickness was walk the deck endlessly. Going below was deadly. On my walks, I realized I had a companion, a young man who kept trying to talk to me. I was anxious to preserve my dignity, and of course, we hadn't been introduced, but after one particularly terrifying plunge of the ship, I lost my dignity and my breakfast in no uncertain terms." She gave a shy smile and a flush mounted in her cheeks. "I suddenly became aware that a pair of strong arms were holding me from going over the side. Well, at that point, an introduction seemed superfluous."

Gwen smiled, not just at the vivid picture, but the touching warmth in Hildy's voice and manner. "When was that?"

"1908, May 12th, at 10 in the morning. Indelible…" Hildy's smile faded, and sadness crept into her expression. "But you asked me about Emily before, and I should be talking about her, not my silly old stories." She briskly topped up Gwen's glass. "We met at University College, in Flinders Petrie's first year teaching Egyptology. I imagine she spoke to you about that."

"Yes," Gwen remembered other conversations, in the cosy firelight of Emily's cottage. "A little, but she didn't really talk about herself that much."

"That was Emily. A very private person. What do you know about her background?"

"She came from a village near Hastings, I believe."

"Yes, the only daughter of a very forward-thinking vicar. He actually believed in education for women. Proper education, I mean. Not just pianoforte and needlework. He taught her Latin and Greek and gave her a thorough grounding in the classics. She quite outshone us all that first year."

She stared out the bow-fronted window at the harbour beyond, with a distant expression in her eyes. "University College was revolutionary. It had no ties to religion or ancient privilege and was established to allow ordinary people to get a good education." She turned her gaze to Gwen with a smile. "Did you know that the Oxbridge crowd were such snobs they used to call it 'Cockney College'!" The smile turned to laughter. "But the best thing at UC was the Archaeology department. You've heard of the great Amelia Edwards, of course?"

Gwen nodded. The novelist was a fervent advocate for protecting Egyptian history and had amassed a famous collection of antiquities.

Hildy went on, "She left a legacy which founded the Chair of Egyptology at UC. Flinders Petrie was the first to lead it, and we were among the first lucky students. At that time, any woman interested in archaeology had an uphill battle. It was all very well for Gertrude Bell, but her family had a lot of money."

The famous writer and traveller had died two years ago, after taking part in the post-war Cairo Conference that established new borders in the Middle East following the collapse of the Ottoman empire.

"Still, give the woman credit, her exploits have inspired many of our young women."

She paused for breath and laughed again. "Sorry dear, I do get on my hobby horse, but it's hard to convey how unprofessional it all used to be. For years, the British Museum had been sending out quite unqualified men to Egypt and the Near East to collect artefacts. Gentleman amateurs looking for treasure and stories of exotic adventure. They did untold damage and contributed little to scholarship."

"So, you and Emily became archaeologists?" Gwen tried to steer the conversation back to the subject she dearly wanted to know more about.

"We were the first generation of women to earn degrees related to our work in the field. We were quite impressed with ourselves, I can tell you!" she chuckled. "That is until we started looking for work. Dr Petrie actually employed many women for fieldwork in Egypt—he was carrying out excavations at Saqqara and Thebes—but there were more students than places. Our dreams of digging mummies in the desert heat were rather dashed when we ended up that first summer staying in damp and dreary England. Dr Petrie persuaded Leonard Woolley to hire us for a Roman Fort excavation, which actually turned out to be fascinating and led us both to an interest in European ancient history."

"Dr Temple... Emily seemed to know about so many different places and eras. It seems she travelled everywhere, judging by her correspondence."

Hildy nodded. "She impressed Woolley so much—and he was a hard man to impress—that he invited her to the British School at Athens, and from there, her connections multiplied. I saw her seldom after that, though we wrote to each other regularly. Every letter from her had some colourful stamp from another exotic locale. It's funny to think she almost didn't make that trip to Athens."

If only Emily had told her some of these stories. "Why not?"

Hildy shrugged. "Cold feet, I suppose. She hadn't been out of England, of course. But still, she had a lot of dauntless confidence. After a freezing start, that summer had turned warm and lovely. We were both fit and healthy, brown as a berry from being outdoors. I remember how beautiful she looked at that time, with a kind of glow about her. She told me about Woolley's invitation, but she seemed very uncertain what to do, which wasn't like her at all. A day later, she told me she'd accepted, but it was strange..."

"Yes?"

"There was a kind of fatalistic air about her, as if she didn't really care. There was some trouble with her parents, I think. Perhaps they didn't want her to go. As it turned out, she fell ill and had to postpone the trip for a few months. I never really knew the details. By then I had taken up a teaching position down south. We wrote to each other, of course, and remained good friends, but neither of us did much girlish confiding."

Gwen suppressed a smile. If this conversation was anything to go by, Emily would have trouble getting a word in edgeways.

"When did you see her last?"

She paused and gave a sad, pained sigh. "It should have been last month in Santiago. We had arranged to meet there and travel to Corunna, but the morning I arrived, the hotel manager told me what had happened the night before." For the first time, her brisk, jolly facade cracked. Tears sprang into her eyes, and she struggled to speak. "I had to identify her, you see..." Her voice dropped to a whisper.

"How awful."

The full horror of that moment showed in Hildy's face, and the tears spilled over. She pulled a large white lace-edged handkerchief out of her pocket and dabbed at her face. "I'll never get that image of her out of my mind. It's hard to see her as she really was. I suppose that will get better with time."

"I'm sure it will." Gwen reached out impulsively and put a hand on her shoulder. She searched for something else to say, some word of comfort, but none seemed adequate as the silence stretched between them. Through an open window came the sounds of the street, the clop of hooves and clattering cartwheels. From farther away, a distant tram bell and the bellow of a ship's horn told of the world going about its business, heedless of all the everyday tragedies that filled people's lives.

Gwen awkwardly withdrew her hand, as Hildy wiped her face again, blew her nose, and squared her shoulders in a visible effort to get herself under control. "Now. Let's ring for some proper tea. If I have another cocktail, I'll just get maudlin, and I want to hear all about the Emily you knew."

Despite the healthy number of sandwiches she'd eaten earlier, Gwen drank several cups of proper English tea and ate an equal quantity of Isabella's featherlight teacakes. Through their conversation she had come to trust this woman. She told Hildy the whole story of her own friendship with Emily and all the events that had followed, including the arrival of the package and the break-in at the cottage.

Finally, she told her of the scene at the solicitor's office. "The thing is, I just don't understand her leaving me...well, everything."

Hildy sat back on the sofa, stirring her tea and looking at Gwen for a long moment. "All I know of her in recent years is what she told me in her letters, I knew she'd come into some money when she moved into the cottage, but I had no idea of how much." She gave a helpless shrug. "I gathered it came from some distant relative, but more by inference than anything she actually said. She was so reticent about personal things. Probably didn't want to seem boastful." She shook her head. "As to leaving it to you, I can't think of anyone else in her life who deserves it more." She hesitated, then seemed to reach some decision. She put down her cup on the table. "I haven't mentioned this because, to be blunt, I wanted to get to know you a little for myself, but Emily did talk about you quite often in her letters."

"She did?"

"She said nothing about her will, of course. Our generation was taught that discussing money was terribly vulgar. But she wrote often of how impressed she was by your intelligence and thirst for learning. I don't think she had many other close friends. Many friends in the profession, of course. But not just as a woman." She patted Gwen's hand. "I can't say I'm terribly surprised at her decision. After all, she clearly intended to enable you to gain a good education and all of the opportunities that would open up to you."

"Yes, but...all that money." Gwen's brow creased in a troubled frown.

"I don't expect she foresaw that you'd inherit so soon." Hildy gave her a wry look. "Besides, who else that she cared about could use this good fortune? She knew *I* was well provided for, and she wasn't the type to leave it to a cat's home or a donkey sanctuary." She shook her head. "No, I'll tell you what does concern me, this robbery. And... and Emily's death." Rising to her feet, she shoved the handkerchief into her pocket. "This may sound melodramatic, but what you've told me gives rise to troubling thoughts." She moved toward the door. "Just a minute. I'll be right back."

She returned with a folded sheet of paper in her hand and a pair of spectacles perched on her nose. "This was posted the day she died, so I didn't read it until I returned home after the funeral. I was so upset that I hadn't looked at it since, but she said something..." Her gaze ran over the closely written page. "As you can see, it's very short, and it didn't even occur to me till now how odd it was that she should write the day before we were due to meet. Ah! Here it is." She pushed the spectacles firmly on her nose and read, "Some things have been happening lately that I must talk to you about. I keep thinking about that line from Marcus Aurelius that Professor Petrie always quoted. About seeking the truth." Hildy frowned.

"What did she mean?"

She gave a helpless shrug and said plaintively, "I've been wracking my brains over that! It was so long ago, and Emily was the literary one, not me. Petrie was fond of classical tags, which meant nothing to me, but of course, Emily understood Greek and Latin. Mind you, he usually translated for the rest of us." She glanced toward a bookcase on the back wall, well filled with a careless arrangement of leather-bound tomes and stacks of paperback novels. "It's not here, but Tommy has a collection of the classics in his study. Marcus Aurelius must be in there. I'll take a look and see if anything jogs the old memory. But it really bothers me. What on earth could she have meant – seeking the truth?"

"You don't think..." Gwen hesitated to voice her deepest fear. "You don't think that there was something wrong about her death?"

"Oh no!" Hildy said categorically, with a shake of her head. But then she sank down on the couch, looking much less certain. "How could there be something wrong? It was an accident. The authorities looked into it. They had the equivalent of an inquest and confirmed it was an accident."

It sounded to Gwen as if Hildy was trying to convince herself.

She handed Gwen the letter with a shaking hand. "You must know how Emily always played down any emotional display. But reading between the lines, she sounds deeply anxious, even despairing."

Dear Hildy,

I cannot wait to see you tomorrow. I had been so looking forward to this trip, but some things have been happening lately that I must talk to you about. I keep feeling that the world has turned upside down and will never be the same again. If only I could keep you out of this, but I must talk to someone, and you are the only person whose trust and loyalty I can count on. I only hope that after we have talked, you can still retain a good opinion of your old friend.

I keep thinking of that line from Marcus Aurelius that Professor Petrie always quoted. About seeking the truth. There are times that fill us with doubt as to whether we really want to know, and more importantly, whether we want others to know, the truth about ourselves. I can't possibly explain all this in a letter, but I needed to start the conversation somehow.

Your most devoted friend, Emily

Gwen lifted her gaze from the page in dismay and said in a whisper. "This is terrible."

Hildy nodded. "If I didn't know how it happened, I might have thought she..." Her voice faltered. "That she did away with herself," Gwen said bluntly.

Hildy shook her head. "I know she would never have done that. But you see what I mean about her emotional state. And there's another thing." Her voice hardened. "I'm not one to cast aspersions, but I do think I should tell you about Colonel Fairlamb."

"What about him?"

"Tommy would call this vicious gossip, but he's not here, and I think you ought to hear it. Emily had mentioned Fairlamb in her letters from time to time, when she took part in these tours, which started before the war. I'd never met the man until he turned up and began taking over Emily's funeral arrangements. I was quite stunned to recognize him, though I don't think he recognized me."

"Recognized him from where?"

"Egypt, 1915. I was a sort of secretary for a chap attached to the diplomatic..." She flapped her hand. "It's a long story, but the thing is, I had seen Fairlamb in Cairo where he got into a spot of bother. The whole thing was very murky and hushed up, but it had something to do with smuggling. He narrowly escaped prison. They stripped him of his rank and sent him to Blighty, from whence he was destined for the Front. It was a shock to see him in Santiago, but amid all those other shocks, it didn't seem all that important. But now..."

Somehow, this revelation didn't surprise her. "Why do you think I should know this?"

"Because I don't think you should trust the man. In the East, he got himself entangled with some ruthless, violent people, and though the authorities didn't have enough for a court-martial, it was clear the man had no scruples."

Gwen hesitated to voice her own instinctive distrust. She tried to be rigorously fair. "I admit that I don't find him terribly congenial, but I don't know any ill of the man. After all, he did take care of the funeral arrangements..."

"With indecent haste." Her sardonic tone gave Gwen pause. "By the afternoon of the day after she died, he had already found an Anglican priest and inquired about a spot in the cemetery. Don't you think that's, well... odd?"

"Not necessarily," she said slowly. "He's used to organizing things, after all." But her sense of unease only deepened. The silence stretched between them, as a welter of conflicting impulses flooded Gwen's mind.

"Let me get you the cemetery details and a list of people you might want to see in Santiago," Hildy said at last and rang the bell for the maid.

"Yes, I must be getting back." Roused from her troubled thoughts, Gwen suddenly came back to reality as she thought of the duties that awaited her.

They parted company at the front door as Hildy wrung Gwen's hand with a fervent air of worry. "You must keep in touch," she insisted. "The telephone system here is not always what it should be, but persevere, and you should get through."

"We're returning to Bilbao a fortnight from now. I'll come and see you before I leave for home."

Hildy nodded distractedly. "If I find out anything useful, I'll write to you care of the Gran Hotel, would that be the best thing?"

With that agreement, Gwen secured a horse-drawn cab, and jounced on down the hill, waving to Hildy, who stood in the doorway seeing her off. Everything she had learned today had only bolstered her feeling that Emily's death was not an accident. Or at least, that it was shrouded with suspicious and troubling circumstances.

Chapter Fifteen

The next morning, a gleaming motorcade fit for an Emperor stood parked in front of the hotel as Gwen ushered the tour group into their respective cars: a Hispano-Suiza, a Rolls-Royce, a Duesenberg, and a Bugatti.

The tour would begin in Bilbao with a trip to the country estate of Don Alfonso Alvarez. The amateur antiquarian had devoted a great deal of his fortune to exploring Spain's archaeological heritage, but clearly had enough left over to accumulate an enviable collection of luxurious motorcars.

In the lead Hispano-Suiza rode Letitia, Amanda and Michael Greville. The massive Rolls carried Mr. and Mrs. Sloan, and the Fairlambs. Franz, the Dixons, and Father Garrick followed in the Duesenberg. Bringing up the rear, the scarlet Bugatti carried Gwen and Dorcas. The cars pulled away and moved at a stately pace as they took the coast road out of Portugalete.

Gwen settled back into the red leather upholstery of the Bugatti to see Dorcas pressing against the window as she tried to get a better view of the waves crashing on the rocky shore below.

"What a splendid view!" Dorcas exclaimed,

"It's certainly spectacular. Is Don Alvarez's estate on the coast?" Gwen asked.

"Part of it is." Dorcas turned her head reluctantly from the panorama. "It stretches quite far inland. Though I believe the house is on a clifftop."

"Tell me about him." She imagined someone out of a Cervantes novel, or the *Tales of the Alhambra*. "Is he a nobleman of ancient lineage?"

"Not by our standards," Dorcas said loftily. "More like a Lord Guinness or Baron Kenilworth. A captain of industry. Apparently, most Spanish noblemen of ancient lineage disdained the thought of stooping to invest in dirty industries like steel, rail, and shipbuilding. The Alvarez family bought into them all. Then they bought the title."

"I see." Gwen looked ahead, past the liveried chauffeur, whose expert handling of the great motorcar took them smoothly over the uneven road. Up ahead, the lead car turned in between two massive gates. "It seems we are here."

They passed through gardens ablaze with flowers, drifts of blue, purple, and white, then she caught sight of the house through the trees; a vast brick and stone neoclassical palace gleaming in the sunshine.

She gave an involuntary gasp. "My goodness!" A sudden wave of unreality washed over her. She'd stepped into another world.

* * *

The feeling stayed with her as they were welcomed in a cavernous entrance hall by their host. A man of small stature, Don Alfonso Alvarez, wore a neat Van Dyke beard and black hair pomaded to a shiny cap. He had greeted all the women by kissing their hand, which drew a sharp intake of breath from Letitia Henderson and a positive look of horror from Dorcas.

They were served luncheon in a majestic mirror-lined salon that reminded Gwen of photos she had seen of Versailles. Above her, the distant ceiling hosted a vibrantly-coloured panoply of sporting gods and goddesses, lit by tall windows opened to a stone terrace dotted with statuary. The name cards on the lavishly decorated table clearly followed the same order of precedence as their shipboard ranking, Gwen noticed.

After a delicious luncheon, their dapper host led them to the East wing, which housed his collection. They entered through elaborately carved ebony doors. Ahead of her, Amanda stopped dead on the threshold and stared down at the floor beneath her feet. It was the first time Gwen had seen her genuinely astonished. She gazed open-mouthed, clearly lost for words. When Gwen saw what she was looking at, she understood.

Don Alfonso smiled and stroked his neat little beard. "You like my stone carpet, I see."

Spread out beneath their feet lay an exquisite mosaic. A series of borders looped and twined around a tessellated floor at least twelve feet square. The central motif portrayed Diana in superb detail, surrounded by hunting scenes with leaping stags and hounds in hot pursuit.

Amanda found her voice at last. "It's magnificent. I've never seen one so fine and yet so complete."

The rest of the group crowded into the room and ranged around the mosaic, staring down at it and excitedly commenting in a sudden babble of voices.

Don Alfonso stroked his beard again with a complacent smile. "Rather... nice, isn't it? It's second century, from a villa complex near Seville."

Gwen looked around the lofty space to see marble statuary interspersed with large glass cases holding all sorts of ancient treasures. The group drifted apart, strolling around the displays and exclaiming at the rare and precious objects.

She stood looking down at a display of spectacular gold objects from some warrior's grave. Glittering armlets and a massive torc of twisted strands, with beautifully rendered beasts adorning the rounded terminals—a magnificent neck ring likely worn by some Celtic chieftain.

A movement behind her made her look up to see Michael Greville's face reflected in the glass.

She turned her head to look at him directly. "This place is quite overwhelming."

"Indeed." His gaze went from the display of gold to meeting her eyes. She turned back to the treasure, feeling an acute need to fill the silence that fell between them.

She waved a hand toward the vast room of treasures. "Franz should see this. It's exactly his area of interest. I wonder if Don Alfonso allows scholars access?"

"Do I sense doubt in your tone?"

She certainly sensed something negative in his. "I haven't seen many museums, but I'll wager this is one of the most beautiful in the world, with an astonishing collection..." She faltered and saw him smile. A cool, mocking smile.

"But?" he added.

"But I can't help being acutely aware that the only people who can see these historically important relics are the few whom Don Alfonso deigns to invite." It had come out more cutting than she intended.

"People like us, in fact." The cool smile lingered.

"I'm only here by luck, really." Something in his expression got under her skin. "I was thinking of people like my father. People with a genuine interest and knowledge, who can only see these things if they're publicly accessible."

"So you don't think private collections should be allowed? I believe the Bolsheviks think exactly along those lines."

"Please don't put words in my mouth," she said impatiently. "I'm not talking about dictating what people are allowed to do. I just think it's an important principle." It sounded priggish, but she meant it.

A peal of laughter came from behind her, sending a wave of heat up into her face. She turned to see Amanda smiling with what seemed like malicious glee. Her gaze went over Gwen's head to meet Michael's, and her smile took on a conspiratorial edge.

"Good Heavens, Gwen. I knew you northerners tended to be radicals, but I never took you for a Bolshevik!" Amanda stood a few feet away, looking around at the group with an infuriating grin.

Gwen felt her cheeks burn. Mortified and furious, she searched fruitlessly for a sharp retort. "That's an unfair stereotype," she said at last, wishing everyone would stop looking at her with sophisticated amusement.

In a moment, most of them had turned away except for Franz, who stood behind Amanda, looking deeply uncomfortable. Gwen grasped at a straw. "Franz, have you seen the La Tene cauldron over there?" She waved toward a case on the other side of the room, stepped over to him, and took his arm. "I think it might fit into your Ur-Aryan theory."

She practically dragged him away from the others toward a very large glass case holding an ornate silver cauldron. "The label says circa 150 BC,

95

do you agree with that?"

He nodded. "This is typical La Tène style of Celtic art," he jabbed a finger at the unyielding glass. "See the intricate repousse work! That means it's hammered out from the inside. The style seems to emanate from Ancient Gaul and Thrace, but much of this silverwork has been found in Scandinavia and Germany."

"It doesn't say where this comes from." Gwen read the scanty labels. "Just the approximate date."

"I am surprised by the dearth of information. Without the provenance, there is no context for dating," Franz said. "But this cauldron would certainly fit into the late European Iron Age which goes from about 450 BC to the Roman Conquest around the 1st century BC."

Still conscious of Amanda and Michael, who now stood looking at the gold torcs, Gwen moved around the glass case holding the cauldron, tracing the lively figures around the bowl. "Look at this amazing decoration!"

Franz nodded rapidly, his face alight with excitement as they looked at the ornately worked surface. "See the antlered male here. That is likely the Celtic God *Cernunnos*, holding a horned serpent. Also, the stag here echoing the figure of the god. See, he's surrounded by canines, perhaps hunting animals." He beamed with pleasure.

Caught up in his enthusiasm, Gwen pointed to the other side. "There's a female figure, too. And look, they're both wearing torcs! Perhaps like those ones over there." She pointed back to Amanda and Michael, who had been joined by Don Alfonso and Brett Sloan, their heads close together in deep conversation.

They were clearly discussing the gold torcs in the case, Alvarez and Sloan looking particularly intense, the Spaniard making impassioned gestures.

Gwen couldn't tear her gaze away and strained to hear what they were saying, but despite their forceful conversation, they clearly did not want to be overheard. "I had a question about this casket." She edged back toward a display case closer to the other group, indicating that Franz should follow and hoping the others were too engrossed to notice.

She just caught Sloan say something that sounded like 'temple', then the conversation abruptly stopped. Turning her head slightly, Gwen saw Amanda and Brett Sloan looking at her with vague alarm.

Amanda quickly assumed her usual hauteur. "Gwen, I think it's time to gather the group for my lecture. Would you please get my attaché case with the notes?"

Gwen had seen the case handed off to a manservant when they arrived, so she hurried off, hoping the man spoke some basic English, and trying to remember the Spanish for 'case'. Her first challenge was finding the servant.

By the time she returned, the group was seated in two semicircles of delicate gilt chairs, and Amanda stood in front, already speaking. "First of all, our profound thanks to Don Alfonso Alvarez for extending us the privilege of seeing his unparalleled collection of antiquities." With a slight frown, she indicated that Gwen slip into a seat close by. "Before I start our guided survey, Don Alfonso would like to share a few words."

She sat down beside Gwen and held out her hand for the notes, as Gwen scrambled in the case, trying not to make a sound.

Don Alfonso began with a noble bow and fulsome praise for his distinguished guests before his voice took on a mournful tone. "I cannot let this moment pass without mentioning the sad loss of our beloved Dr. Elizabeth Temple. The accident which took her from us was a heavy blow, not just to the world of scholarship, but to her friends and colleagues, among whom I would count myself and many of the people in this room." He surveyed the group in front of him, and Gwen wished she could see the expressions that his words evoked.

"My little collection which you are seeing today owes much to her depth of learning, to her counsel, and to her fruitful connections with the indefatigable archaeologists whose labour extracts the past from the earth and enables us to preserve and care for it in the pursuit of knowledge."

He bowed again. "Now I would like to invite her esteemed colleague, Dr. Amanda Spenser, to share some of that wealth of knowledge as she takes us around my collection,"

As everyone rose to their feet, Gwen quickly scanned the group to gauge the response to the speech. Most appeared suitably solemn, but Dorcas seemed troubled, and when Brett Sloan caught her eye, he swiftly looked away. Michael Greville's brow contracted in a frown. She wondered at his reaction. Then she saw Amanda's face and was shocked to see her blue eyes like chips of ice, arctic cold with anger.

Chapter Sixteen

Gwen pulled her notebook from her bag, ripped out a page, and copied down the two Bilbao addresses she had found in Emily's diary. Handing the paper to the cab driver, she managed to convey her needs with the aid of a pocket phrasebook.

Hanging on to the side of the carriage as it jostled over the cobblestones, she looked around at the tall houses, with gaps every so often through which she saw flashes of sunlight on the Nervion River. Today was the first of June, and it did feel distinctly warmer. The picturesque but prosaic scene suddenly struck her as utterly surreal. Yesterday's visit to Don Alvarez's palace had felt like stepping into a fairy tale.

It would be more accurate to say that, since the day Emily's letter arrived, she had been catapulted into a dream. A dark dream, which sometimes seemed that it might shade into a nightmare.

After taking the tram down into the old town of Bilbao, she was glad to get a cab. The streets were getting narrower and more confusing. It wasn't so different from the oldest parts of Durham or Newcastle but, with street signs being scarce or non-existent, and being surrounded by a crowd babbling in a language she didn't understand, gave her an uneasy feeling of helplessness that she hated. She shook off her distracted thoughts, checked her notebook, and focused on looking for promising shop windows.

The cab pulled up by a dilapidated frontage with a faded sign reading, *Sala de Ventes Lopez*. The driver waved at the battered wooden door. *"Cerrada, Senorita."*

She jumped down and took a closer look at the dusty window. A hand-lettered sign and her phrasebook confirmed the driver's verdict.

"Closed." She sighed. With only a few hours off this morning, it would be a challenge to find time between her secretarial duties to follow up the addresses in the diary, before they left tomorrow for Santiago de Compostela. Peering through the dusty window, she saw only a jumble of worn-looking furniture. This didn't look like the right kind of place at all.

She had better luck at the second stop. The driver reined in his horse as they stopped by a much more elegant shop front. Flowing gilt letters proclaimed it as the *Casa de Antigüedades*. "The House of Antiquities. That sounds more promising."

Giving the driver a single peseta, she said, "*Por favor, Esperame.*" and hoped to goodness she had pronounced it correctly and he would actually be there when she emerged.

A bell tinkled above her head as she opened the door and went in. The walls were lined with well-polished glass-fronted cabinets and a multitude of narrow drawers. A man with a face like a wizened but benevolent monkey poked his head out from a velvet curtain at the back. "*Momento, senorita.*"

He disappeared again, and she heard a dull thudding before he emerged, launching into a flood of Spanish that left her asking helplessly, "*Perdon, habla usted Ingles?*"

"Ah yes, you are English! I should have known at once. Please to take a seat...." He ushered her toward a small table in the corner, and introduced himself as Senor Ochoa. "Can I offer you a glass of sherry, or perhaps some tea?"

She sat down because it seemed the polite thing to do. He perched on the other bentwood chair and picked up a cut-glass decanter.

She shook her head. "That's very kind, but no thank you." She paused, suddenly at a loss for how to begin. "I believe you may have known a friend of mine, Miss Emily Temple."

"Senora Temple, indeed, yes! We have had many dealings over the years." His face brightened. "She is here on another expedition?"

"I'm afraid not." Gwen sighed and told him of Emily's recent death.

"*Caramba!* This is terrible." He looked stricken. "A very gracious lady, *muy simpatico*. A wonderful eye."

"May I ask what your…dealings were?"

He waved his arm around the crowded shop. "The antiquities I buy and sell. The Senora was always looking for the small Roman pieces, the tiny lares carried by a legionary, the broken perfume bottle of some long-dead matron. I think perhaps she had not the purse for the expensive statuary. At least not until recently…"

He seemed about to say more, but then jumped to his feet and swiftly took out an object from one of the cabinets. He cradled an exquisite piece of carved marble. "This she would have adored. It is a goddess, I think. Only the head was found."

Gwen couldn't help but reach out and stroke the alabaster cheek, then jerked her hand back. "I'm sorry! I shouldn't touch, but it's so…beautiful."

He smiled. "Oh, but these are made to be touched. And think how long it has been buried in darkness before a poor farmer uncovered this beauty. She deserves our appreciation." He gently placed the statue back on its shelf. "I paid the man well for his find. That is why everyone knows to bring these things to me. And I will be well-recompensed when I reluctantly part with her."

"Who buys this kind of piece?"

He tilted his head and gave her a quizzical look. "You would be surprised how many wealthy tourists there are passing through Bilbao. And how my name is known to the serious collectors. Since the war, the Americans have become mad for Europe, and they like to go home with souvenirs."

"What about Emily? I mean Miss Temple. When did you last see her?"

"More than six months ago, I think, because I showed her the wonderful collection I had just purchased from Don Eduardo. An elderly grandee, but sadly fallen in the world. He had inherited a magnificent group of coins. Gold sesterces from all the Julian emperors." He sighed heavily and shook his head. "Ah, they were the best I have ever seen."

"I suppose they were sold to one of your wealthy American tourists."

"Alas, no." His mouth tightened. "They were stolen."

A faint alarm bell sounded in her mind. "That's dreadful. Someone broke in?"

He nodded. "I came in one morning to find the safe open, all the contents gone. There was not so much money in there, but the coins... I think I will never see their like again." His mournful face stared into hers, and she knew this loss had been as much a tragedy to him as losing a dear friend.

What had Emily's business been here? And did it connect somehow with all the other puzzles that she had left behind? She couldn't ignore the hint that Emily had suddenly been buying more expensive pieces. It was pure cowardice, but she felt strangely reluctant to pursue the question.

Before taking her leave, Gwen told him about the tour itinerary, which led to a pleasant conversation about the archaeologists Senor Ochoa knew, including Cecil Hunt, whose dig they would be visiting.

"Senorita Temple always impressed me with her ability to stay in touch with the newest discoveries and the most brilliant young archaeologists. One of her proteges called on me last year, she said Emily had asked her to say hello. A charming young woman and so interested in my treasures."

"Do you remember her name?"

He gave an eloquent shrug. "I'm afraid I don't. But perhaps you do. She was tall, blonde, *muy elegante*."

Gwen slowly nodded. "I think perhaps I do."

On the tram back to Portugalete, she made notes of what the little man had told her. Could there be two young women archaeologists as distinct as Amanda Spenser?

She had the feeling that putting together the true story of what happened to Emily would be like assembling a mosaic as intricate as Don Alvarez's hunting Diana.

* * *

Back at the hotel, Gwen worked through the late afternoon, then hurried to get dressed for dinner, before remembering how long she would have to wait. Spanish customs were very different from those at home. It had been hard enough on the ship, adjusting to dinner at eight, when she was used to supper at six, but the news that they would not dine till ten o'clock had left her horrified. She had learned yesterday that the scanty version of English tea served at four with cakes and tiny sandwiches was not going to hold her till then.

Salvation loomed in the form of cocktails in Miss Henderson's suite. She desperately hoped there would be some type of food. Between cocktails and dinner, Amanda was giving another lecture about Santiago de Compostela, focusing on the various pilgrim routes.

With only two evening frocks, Gwen had little choice of what to wear, but she had hesitated to wear her newest, a slim column of pale green chiffon with a handkerchief hem and delicate beading that had taken untold hours to complete. She had sent away for the pattern last winter and spent the long, dark evenings carefully sewing by the light of the oil lamp. She took pride in the skills her mother taught her, and she'd been confident that the dress could stand comparison with anything sold in the expensive shops in Durham. Secretly, she had hoped it might appear to have come from the atelier of some chic *modiste*. But that had been before seeing the clothes of Mrs. Sloan, and more particularly, Amanda Spenser.

However, when she walked into Miss Henderson's hotel drawing room, she felt a satisfying reaction, as surprised glances turned in her direction.

Brett Sloan's smile had a predatory edge. He drew her toward the window, where his wife and the Fairlambs stood talking. "Well, don't you look the cat's pajamas this evening!"

Marion Sloan winced. "That silly slang expression is hardly appropriate.'" She ran an assessing look over Gwen's gown. "Your dress is charming, my dear…. Why, it looks like a Worth!"

The incredulity in her voice made Gwen smile. She avoided the unasked question and kept its homely origins to herself. "Thank you. That's a lovely compliment."

"Good evening, Miss Armstrong." The deep voice at her shoulder made Gwen turn and look up into the dark blue eyes of Michael Greville, who stood uncomfortably close behind her.

"Good evening." Her mouth felt dry.

"Can I get you a drink?" he asked. "Some sherry, perhaps?"

She nodded. "Yes, sherry. Lovely."

He moved away, to her relief, but quickly returned with a glass of amber liquid. What was it about the man that made her tongue-tied and awkward? Perhaps the fact that she couldn't stop thinking about that huddled conversation with Amanda and Sloan, at Don Alvarez's museum, and his clear discomfort at their host's praise of Emily.

Brett Sloan dominated the conversation, asking the Fairlambs about the itinerary for the following day, which led to a discussion about the political situation in Spain.

"I guess we'll have to mind what we say," Marion Sloan commented. "This De Rivera fellow seems to be taking the Mussolini line."

Mrs. Fairlamb winced and looked sharply toward the waiter who stood proffering a tray of hors d'oevres. When he moved away, she said quietly, "I would advise you to be very careful and avoid politics. There's a lot of unrest."

"Why yes, indeed, don't they keep trying to assassinate King Alfonso?" Marion's piercing tones did not seem the least bit modulated.

"Five or six times," her husband expounded. "Once even in London!"

Colonel Fairlamb leaned into the group and said in an undertone. "I should warn you that there are serious sensitivities right now." He watched until the waiter left the room. "His Majesty King Alfonso is currently hosting our Royal Family. The King and Queen, Prince George and his Grace the Duke of Wales, are in San Sebastian, not twenty miles from here."

"Why, how exciting!" Marion exclaimed.

Colonel Fairlamb frowned. "There's quite an English colony here in Bilbao. The industrial development in this region has benefited from British investment and technical advice. Certain groups would like nothing more than to poison relationships between Great Britain and Spain. They might well resort to violence to create an incident."

"We've got our Bolsheviks back home, too," Brett Sloan said. "There's only one way to deal with these seditionists—smack 'em down hard!

Michael said gravely. "It's a lot more complicated here. All sorts of rival groups are fighting each other, as well as the government. You may think, as Americans, that it doesn't concern you, but as you're part of a British tour group, you'll count as being on our side."

"But surely…." Marion Sloan looked really frightened. "Surely no one would want to harm us?"

"Probably not," Michael said calmly, "But it's as well to be aware of these things."

As the couple moved away, intent on replenishing their glasses, she heard Brett Sloan say quietly, "Don't worry, Honey. I've got my revolver."

Gwen glanced around the room and saw the waiter standing nearby with another tray of hors d'ouvres. He was young and sleek, with a Valentino-style slick of black hair and dark, hard eyes that scanned the room with a faint sneer.

She turned back to find Greville's gaze focused on her. He put a hand on her upper arm and drew her a little away from the group, who had gone to replenish their glasses. "I hope I didn't frighten you."

"Not really, but I think you were trying to frighten *them*."

He gave her a disarming grin. "Good." The gentle pressure of his hand moved her closer to the open window. The warm evening breeze made her chiffon dress flow against her body and gently flutter against her legs. Her skin tingled, and she felt suddenly breathless.

"What on earth did they do to deserve that?" Something disturbing was happening, which she must absolutely ignore. With an effort, she focused on his words.

"The Sloans are decent enough people." He didn't sound completely convinced.

Should she mention Brett Sloan's revolver?

"But they have a strange kind of naivete," he went on. "Like many rich Americans since the War, they drift through all these countries, collecting precious things like tokens in a scavenger hunt. With little understanding of the complicated politics of Europe and no real knowledge of the deep history behind them, they're heedless of the danger running just under the surface." He spoke with passionate intensity, and she wondered if he saw

105

her, too, as dangerously naïve.

He looked over her shoulder and let go of her arm. Gwen turned to see that Amanda had arrived.

Amanda wore something made of liquid silver, drawing the gaze of everyone in the room. A shimmering tunic of crystal embroidered silk, it swished and flowed with every movement. She came towards them, giving Michael a considering look, then turned on her heel and headed for the cocktails.

With a shock, Gwen realized that Amanda did not like seeing her and Michael engaged in intimate conversation. The thought sent a flush of warmth to her cheeks and gave her a ridiculous jolt of pleasure. Followed by a shiver of warning. That kind of complication was the last thing she needed.

"Excuse me," Michael said abruptly and walked across the room towards the door. He passed behind Amanda and she shot him a searing glance over her shoulder as he left. What was going on between them?

"Gwen, dear, I didn't get the chance to ask how you got on with your visit to Mrs. Scott yesterday?"

Dorcas had been circulating with a tray of cocktails. She held it out to Gwen with an inquisitive smile. "It must have been quite an adventure, exploring the town on your own."

Gwen realized that she hadn't mentioned to anyone except Dorcas about today's trip into town. After quickly finishing her work, she had slipped out while Amanda had been off somewhere with the Sloans.

Mrs. Fairlamb turned to look at her in horror. "You went out alone? My dear girl, has no one told you of the customs here?"

Beside her, Letitia gave a snort of disdain. "Good heavens, Elsie. It's not as if we're in Algiers!"

"You know as well as I do how the Spanish are about young women's behavior."

"Do I need a duenna?" Gwen asked with a smile.

"You may well laugh," said Elsie Fairlamb, "but there can be serious consequences for heedless young women."

"Come now," said Letitia, "things have changed a great deal since the war."

"In England perhaps, but not here," Elsie said insistently. "Spain was neutral, spared from the battle. They didn't have thousands of young women going into factories and driving ambulances with the VAD. They didn't have women in offices replacing men who'd gone to the front. They didn't experience those things here." The room had fallen silent around her vehement words. "It's still a very traditional society. Women are protected."

Suddenly, Gwen felt intensely sorry for her. There was something so heartfelt about her protest. As a young woman, had Elsie Fairlamb yearned for protection that never materialized?

"But I saw many young women out and about on their own," Gwen protested.

"Selling fish perhaps," said Mrs. Fairlamb with a sniff. "But not respectable young women of good family."

Good family? Apparently, she had been promoted in social rank when she wasn't looking.

"You must never venture out alone as long as we are in Spain." The older woman pronounced with finality.

Behind her, Amanda gave a peal of laughter. "Oh, my goodness, what century are you living in? Don't pay the least bit of attention. You do whatever you think proper, Gwen."

Mrs. Fairlamb gave her a venomous look. "Not everyone shares your worldly views."

Gwen took a second cocktail and sought escape in the harmless company of Franz, who stood awkwardly in a corner. He had been talking with Father Garrick.

Just as she reached them, the priest turned to Gwen and said, "I'm afraid I must take my leave, Miss Armstrong. If I don't see you at dinner, I hope we may speak tomorrow."

The lean figure in the black cassock wove his way through the crowd, nodding his farewells.

Gwen turned back to the younger man. "How are you, Franz? Do you like Portugalete?"

He nodded miserably. "It is alright. Provincial and spoiled by heavy industry. I look forward to getting on our way to the more interesting sites."

"You seemed to enjoy our visit to see Don Alvarez's collection."

To her surprise, his expression only became more petulant. "It was much too short. I didn't have any time to examine the pieces properly. When I asked if I could come back, Dr. Spenser said no. Perhaps on the way back in two weeks, but I don't believe her promises."

There was some deeper conflict going on here, but she didn't know how to explore the reasons. Could it have something to do with the provenance of Don Alvarez' Celtic antiquities? And would Franz really care about that if it supported his pet theories?

Perhaps if she got him talking about it. "And how is your treatise coming along?"

His face brightened. "That is the one good thing. I just read in the new journals about an exceptional excavation of a Roman site in Pavonia which revealed some remarkable skeletal remains…"

It was like winding a clockwork and letting it go. All she could do was nod and smile for what seemed like hours as Franz expounded on his pet topic of German anthropology. She tried to interject questions to lead him back to the objects in Alvarez's museum, but it proved impossible to divert his now familiar narrative.

At last, Dorcas tapped a little signal on a crystal wineglass, and the room fell silent.

"Ladies and Gentlemen, if you'd like to take your seats…" The group spread out and settled at the small, scattered tables. "Professor Spencer is going to tell us the fascinating origins of the various pilgrim routes to Santiago de Compostela."

Gwen hurried to Amanda's side and handed her the sheaf of notes she had prepared that morning while Franz moved an easel carrying a large map of Spain up beside her. But as the lecture proceeded, she couldn't stop thinking about Michael and Amanda. Undoubtedly, two other pieces in the puzzle. What was going on between them? Besides the obvious. And how did Don Alvarez and Senor Ochoa fit into the mosaic? Because she knew there was some kind of connection there. Michael and Amanda. Senor Ochoa and Don Alvarez.

And then there was Emily.

Chapter Seventeen

An hour later, when the lecture ended, the room had become unbearably stuffy with cigarette smoke and there was still at least another hour before dinner. Her head was spinning with a mass of conjectures and the guilty awareness that she had spent most of the time trying to make sense of her jumbled thoughts. To her relief, Amanda disappeared as soon as the talk was over.

"Franz..." she said, after tidying away the notes and maps and another twenty minutes helping Dorcas distribute typewritten copies of their itinerary. "I must get some fresh air."

With difficulty, she refused his offer to accompany her and slipped out into the foyer.

Perhaps a quick walk by the river would do the trick. Bearing Mrs. Fairlamb's warnings in mind, she looked out of the window to see pools of lamplight on the wide promenade and many local people taking the air. The creaking transporter bridge still carried little groups to and fro across the river. With so many people around, she would be perfectly safe.

She turned to go out and almost walked straight into Amanda, who was dressed for the outdoors with a pale grey Persian lamb jacket over her silver dress.

"Escaping from the gorgons?" Amanda asked, with a lift of her eyebrow.

"I'm going for a walk before dinner."

"You'd better wrap up; it's cold out there." She slipped off her fur and handed it to Gwen. "Here. Take this."

Gwen accepted it with surprise. "Thank you." The silk lining caressed her bare arms as she put it on, surprised to find it very light and butter-soft.

"Don't mention it. Just bring it back before you go to bed. It's going in the trunk that I'm sending on to Santiago. As of tomorrow, I'll be dressed so sensibly that even Elsie Fairlamb won't have anything to complain about. Unless I'm liable to be stoned for wearing trousers, which, according to her, is not unlikely," she added with a sardonic grin.

Gwen walked out of the hotel to see a few couples strolling arm in arm and the occasional carriage clopping by. She had seen very few motorcars or vans and no omnibuses down in the city, just the trams.

In many ways, it seemed that, as she walked north along the river toward the sea, despite the proximity of modern shipyards and steel mills, little had changed here for centuries.

The masts of the fishing boats that clustered along the wharves began to disappear as the cool, misty air thickened.

Turning up the broad fur collar against the evening chill, Gwen turned onto the wooden pier that projected out into the harbour and walked out along its length, to lean on the railing at the end and listen to the waves splashing rhythmically on the timbers below. A comfortingly familiar sound, but it brought a pang of homesickness as she looked out into the gathering mist.

So far from home, connected by such a slender thread. It was ludicrous to feel a quiet sense of panic, as if standing on a crumbling knife-edge.

Emily might have stood here, too. She had known this town, known the language, moved through the country with confidence. And now she was dead.

Suddenly, Gwen realized that she could no longer see the water below. Denser fog had stolen in, quick and silent, and now wrapped her in misty twilight.

Looking back toward the town she could see nothing at all, just the gold-grey nimbus of light around the oil lantern which marked the end of the pier where she stood. There was no reason to feel suddenly isolated and alone. Only a few hundred feet away lay lights, people. She could hear the clatter of carriage wheels on cobbles, the creaking of the transporter bridge, and a woman laughing somewhere in the distance. All she had to do was follow the railing back to the promenade.

She began to do just that, clutching the high-collared coat around her against the damp chill with one hand and keeping the other lightly on the wet wooden rail of the pier. This churned-up feeling shouldn't surprise her. She had willingly thrown herself into an utterly strange environment: a different language, a different culture, and a group of people who harbored unknown intentions. Add to that her growing conviction that Emily's death was not the simple accident it seemed, but that it resulted from her involvement in…in what?

Suddenly, the lamps along the pier seemed so far apart, looming up to meet her with their welcome glow, then vanishing behind so that she walked in utter darkness.

Her footsteps echoed softly, with that curious and eerie effect of fog. Like anyone who lived near the sea, she was used to it, but nevertheless, it always made her uneasy, as if someone were shadowing you, just far enough away to be screened by the mist. Her heart began to hammer in her chest. She increased her pace.

It must have been nerves playing tricks on her, but she thought she'd heard an extra footfall, out of rhythm. She stopped abruptly beneath the next lamp, and the echoes continued, one pace too many.

Her knees weakened. Someone was following her.

She must be close to the promenade by now, but the sounds of carriages and people had stopped. All she could hear was the sea, lapping ten feet below, deep and black.

She wanted to cling on to the wooden railing, as if there were some safety in the weak glow of the light. The last thing she wanted was to head into that darkness, but she forced her legs to move. It couldn't be much further. For all she knew, the other person was innocent of any evil intent, but all she could think of was the cold, dark sea below, and that even if she screamed, how could help reach her in time?

She clenched her fists. *Come on, Gwen, be sensible.* In a few minutes, she'd be safely inside the hotel, laughing at her overwrought reaction.

In the next patch of darkness, she heard the voice. *"Puta,"* it hissed, somewhere off to her right. She froze to the spot.

"Puta," came that voice again, from behind her now. And she began to run.

The wet planks thudded under her feet as she ran blindly through the fog. Something touched her shoulder, and terror pushed her to a speed she never knew she possessed.

The ground fell away, and she stumbled, then caught herself and dashed on, realizing that had been the step down onto the promenade. Her shoes now reverberated on stone and suddenly a horse whinnied, looming up out of the darkness, with a flash of huge, gleaming teeth and showing the whites of its eyes. A torrent of Spanish followed her as she darted out of its way. Just in time, she saw a stone wall ahead and collapsed against it, gasping for breath.

Heaving the damp, cool air into her burning lungs as the unseen wagon passed by, she heard the ringing of horses' hooves on the cobblestones only a few feet away. She crouched against the stone barrier, trying to get her bearings. Which way to the hotel?

Suddenly, a dark shape loomed in front of her. Fear coursed through her veins, and she tensed her muscles, preparing to leap upright. She'd be damned if she'd go down without a fight.

"Miss Armstrong?"

Her knees sagged with relief. Her voice quivered. "Mr. Greville?"

As he came closer, she could dimly make out his features as he asked, "Are you all right?"

"I'm fine." Suddenly aware of her absurd position, she struggled to stand.

Greville put an arm around her and helped her straighten up. "You seem distressed."

Now, she felt merely foolish as she stared at his coat buttons, too embarrassed to look up into his face. "I...I lost my way in the fog." Her terrified flight in the dark seemed like a hugely overblown case of nerves.

"Well then, thank goodness I found you," he said, slowly releasing her from his encircling support.

"Yes, thank goodness," she said weakly.

"Come, take my arm. The hotel is not far away."

She didn't like to admit just how gratefully she had accepted his supportive embrace a moment ago and how good it felt to put her arm in his. Beneath the damp, fine wool of his coat, she could feel hard muscle and sensed the stirrings of her own desire. She recoiled from the unwanted feeling. Aside from bitter experience warning her away from a man of his sort, Michael Greville was involved somehow in the complicated knot of suspicion around Emily, that she had vowed to untangle. She couldn't trust him an inch.

"You will get used to the fog," he said. "We'll encounter it often along the coast, but I advise you not to go wandering alone in the evening, or at any time really. A lone English woman might be seen as…" he paused, searching for the word.

"Available?" she suggested.

After a moment, he chuckled. "You might put it that way."

"Please don't tell Mrs. Fairlamb."

He laughed again. "You don't want to hear, 'I told you so'?"

"Exactly." Soon, they had reached the hotel and were walking up the steps. Not only did the sheer terror of a few minutes ago now seem like an absurd overreaction, she started to wonder if she'd actually heard that voice in the darkness, or if it was simply a product of fear. To that bracing conclusion, she firmly added the evidence of her lamentable susceptibility to Michael Greville's charms.

In the glaring brilliance of the hotel foyer, she saw Amanda emerging from the dining room. A frown of annoyance creased her brow.

"You're back finally!"

With a ridiculous feeling of guilt, Gwen dropped Michael's arm.

Amanda's gaze flicked to each of their faces in turn, then she gave him a brilliant smile. "How kind of you, Michael, to look after our little lost lamb."

Gwen was already slipping off the coat. "I'm afraid this is damp. Fog blew in rather quickly." She held out the fur.

With a look of impatience, Amanda said, "Give it to the maid. Perhaps, she can do something with it. One never knows if these people have any idea how to handle good clothes."

All at once, Gwen felt unreasonably irritated and just wanted to get away from both of them with their superior manners and upper-class accents.

"You'd better go into dinner while they are still serving," Amanda said to her dismissively, then turned to Michael Greville.

"Care for a nightcap?" Without waiting for an answer, she took his arm and moved toward the bar.

Feeling foolish with her outstretched arm still holding the coat, Gwen took it to the desk and asked for it to be looked after. Michael and Amanda had disappeared into the small, mirrored cocktail bar tucked away in one corner of the foyer.

Little lost lamb, indeed. Amanda's silvery laughter floated out to her as she turned away from them and toward the dining room.

Everyone else in their party must already have dined, and Gwen took a seat by herself at a tucked-away table. She didn't feel very hungry and picked at a plate of white fish in some kind of cream sauce. A little while later, she saw Michael and Amanda pass by the open doors of the dining room, likely headed toward the stairs. And most probably to bed.

Disgusted with herself, she dropped her knife and fork. Why should she care what they did? His relations with Amanda were none of her business. Despite that traitorous, but eminently explainable surge of desire she had felt for the man in the wake of his 'rescue' of her out on the pier.

Still, she waited a while before going to her own room, next door to Amanda's. Lying in the large bed, she dragged up the covers, afraid of hearing noises from next door. To her relief, the only sounds came through the open window, occasional footsteps from the street below and the hoot of a distant foghorn somewhere out on the estuary.

Her thoughts went back to that moment on the pier, the voice hissing at her in the darkness. *Puta.* It hadn't been her imagination.

Picking up her Spanish dictionary from the night table, she flicked through it, her finger ran down the appropriate page then stopped as she read the meaning. She flinched.

Puta: prostitute, whore.

Wasn't that exactly what she'd been warned about? After all, this wasn't

England. Women didn't have the same freedoms. It was only prudent to be more careful, in a country where men made assumptions about women alone.

Her thoughts went back to that moment, to the sound of his voice. But had it been *his* voice?

Could she be sure it was a man? If it wasn't just a random bit of nastiness, then it had seemed intended to terrorize her. But why?

Thank goodness she had encountered Michael Greville so opportunely. A sudden cold shiver raised goosebumps on her arms. It had been very opportune, indeed. The absurd thought occurred to her that it could have been Greville on that pier. But why on earth would he do something like that?

Every instinct told her not to trust the man. Almost certainly, he was not what he seemed. But perhaps her instincts were being warped by the little worm of jealousy that had taken root in her heart.

Chapter Eighteen

By morning, the fog had gone, and the sky sparkled bright and clear as a charabanc pulled up in front of the hotel with a local guide at the wheel. The Dixons, the Sloans, the Fairlambs, and Father Garrick were off on a tour of the city.

Soon after, Gwen watched Amanda and Michael Greville departing in the opposite direction in a horsedrawn cab. Amanda waved gaily at her as they pulled away. "Off for a ride in the hills, darling!"

Gwen turned to go back into the hotel, trying not to feel a little deflated. There was far too much to do helping Dorcas organize everything for their evening departure to Santiago de Compostela.

Any thoughts of following the traditional pilgrim methods of transport were firmly rejected early on in making the plans for the tour. They would be going overnight by train. No one wanted to walk the 480 miles of the Camino del Norte from Santander to Santiago, and going by horseback was a quaint medieval notion to be admired but not emulated, according to Dorcas. "Miss Henderson did ride the Camino in her youth, so she feels no need to repeat the experience." And that was that for everyone else.

In a room off the hotel kitchen, they inspected the packed meals provided by the hotel. "Even in first class," Dorcas explained. "Even on the wagons lit, you have no idea if there will be any decent food on the train. Better to be safe than sorry."

However, later that day, any fears of starvation were put to rest in the luxurious dining car of the *Transcantabrico*, and that night, Gwen went to her compartment well-fed.

The next morning, the train pulled into the tiny station of Cornes, and hired cars took the party the remaining mile into Santiago de Compostela. The spires of the Cathedral reached for the heavens above a sea of red-tiled roofs and stately buildings. By three in the afternoon, they were being conducted up the double flight of stairs leading to the main doors of the huge church by Colonel and Mrs. Fairlamb.

Gwen felt an anxious flutter in her stomach. She had been so strongly impelled toward this moment and yet dreaded having to see the place where Emily lost her life so horribly. She gazed up at the soaring Romanesque façade, trying to take it all in.

"This, of course, is the Portico de la Gloria," Mrs. Fairlamb was explaining. She took the lead as guide to all the churches and religious establishments they had visited so far. "Notice the Tree of Life carved with such intricacy..." She showed everyone the indentations worn by centuries of devout pressure on the spots where the pilgrims placed their hands on the stone-carved tree.

While she gave more detail, Amanda swirled a dramatic black lace scarf around her head and blithely walked past the group and into the building. "Do you know the form, Mr. Greville?" she boldly took Michael's arm and swept him along with her.

Everyone else studiously ignored this breathtaking rudeness, but the Colonel shot her a vicious glare, then turned stiffly back to his wife. "Please continue, my dear."

At the end of her lecture, the group proceeded decorously into the church. Gwen stopped dead for a moment, overwhelmed. Every surface seemed covered in ornate carved images, dazzling with gilt. The vast space dwarfed the small groups and scattered individuals who wandered along the side chapels and clustered near the altar.

They halted at the nave and looked up. A shining vessel hung high above their heads, suspended from a pulley mechanism below the cupola. Miss Henderson, Dorcas, and the Fairlambs all looked at each other, then glanced away in embarrassment.

They all knew this moment had to come, but clearly no one wanted to speak first.

The thing was massive. It looked about five feet tall, gleaming silver. It had to weigh goodness knows how many pounds.

Gwen felt sick. She looked at the others in turn. "This is the... the object?"

The silence stretched until Fairlamb awkwardly cleared his throat. "They load up the brazier with burning charcoal and incense, then a team of attendants set it swinging. Works up quite an arc."

Father Garrick had left them earlier, and now he hurried up with a pale young priest at his side. "Miss Armstrong, I must apologize. Father Alonzo here intended to meet you at the door."

"Please do not be distressed, Senorita." The priest reached out a hand, and she automatically took it. He drew her away from the altar. "Our most sincere condolences for the sad death of Miss Temple. She was your aunt, I think?"

"My aunt?"

Father Garrick interjected. "It seemed the simplest way to explain the relationship."

Gwen turned back to the priest. "How on earth could that thing have hit her?"

"They are blaming the *botafumiero*, but..." The earnest young cleric began. "It was late at night. The cathedral was almost empty. Just a few people kneeling in prayer. But no one saw anything. The truth is, we just don't know what happened." he said plaintively.

"The *botafumiero* was hanging a little lower than you see it now, in readiness for the morning mass." He gestured up towards the huge, silver vessel. "It seems the rope may have slipped, and the thurible was swinging very gently. There were signs that it caused the...the *injury*." He looked distressed at having to mention something so unpleasant.

"You mean there was blood on the thurible?" Gwen asked bluntly.

Dorcas gave a tiny gasp. Father Alonzo winced and nodded. "That's right. One of the other priests found the poor lady lying insensible on the floor there." He indicated a line of chairs beside a pillar. "There was some blood smeared on the thurible, and her injuries were clearly mortal." He gave a shuddering sigh and crossed himself.

119

"But how could the *botafumiero* have hit her? Wouldn't someone have to set it swinging?" Gwen looked down at the stone floor beside the pillar. There, Emily had breathed her last. She felt horribly detached, as if looking on from a distance.

Father Alonzo showed them how the rope suspending the censer was tied off on a metal staple attached to one of the massive pillars. "The rope is specially made from esparto, like the ships' ropes, very strong, like iron."

Gwen touched the massive, braided rope, as thick as her wrist.

"When the accident happened, the rope was secure, but, the censer hung lower than it should have," he went on. "The rope must have slipped, and the movement set it swinging. No one can understand why the rope slipped. The *tirobolieros* follow a strict routine."

Gwen shook her head. It *had* to have been an accident. But she found it hard to believe. What if someone deliberately swung it toward Emily? She couldn't forget that line in Emily's letter...a series of untoward episodes... which must have been written on the eve of her fatal visit. What did that mean?

"I hope for the sake of your pilgrims you have tested this contraption thoroughly before putting it up again!" said a peremptory voice behind her. Gwen turned to see a grim Letitia Henderson.

"Of course, of course, Senora. Everything has been checked and made secure."

After further expressions of condolence and solicitude, the young priest hurried away, with what Gwen thought was the relief of a junior sent to handle an unpleasant situation his superiors would rather not cope with.

Letitia gazed upward. "It's a magnificent sight – or I used to think so. But I'm not sure I could bear to see the thing in motion ever again."

"Perhaps I should see it," Gwen said quietly.

Miss Henderson gave her an odd look. "Of course, if you wish. Perhaps Father Garrick could advise you of the best time." She turned on her heel and walked away, followed by Dorcas, beetling along behind.

"I'd be glad to accompany you, Miss Armstrong. If I recall correctly, I don't think you've been to a mass." The kindness in the priest's eyes was a relief.

"Miss Henderson doesn't approve. Perhaps she thinks it insensitive of me."

He nodded. "Perhaps. But grief takes people different ways. Some want to not think about the tragedy. Some want to understand it. You would fall among the latter, I believe."

She nodded. "Yes." Not only understand how it happened, but why. Suddenly, she was convinced that among this group of people, someone knew something they weren't telling. Had someone else besides the Fairlambs been here in Santiago at the time? She needed to find out.

"I am hoping you will help me with something else, Father."

"If I can."

"I want to see the police."

* * *

The headquarters of the Guardia Civil were in a handsome nineteenth-century building not far from the cathedral. Their uniform of a dark blue coat with red facings and a three-cornered hat was both impressive and uncomfortably reminiscent of a comic opera she had seen at the Theatre Royal in Newcastle as a child.

However, the officer who received her was grave and charming as Father Garrick explained in Spanish the nature of her inquiry. His quick volley of speech in reply was accompanied by a bow, then he disappeared up the marble staircase to the floor above.

Somewhat overawed, Gwen looked around the grand reception area, with its black and white marble tiles and dark carved wood. "This is nothing like a police station back home."

Father Garrick's expression became serious. "No, and neither are the police. I must warn you to be careful. The Guardia can be difficult, they have powers we would consider arbitrary and unfair, but under the current government of Primo de Rivera, Spain is not a place to fall foul of local authorities."

"It's some sort of military dictatorship, is that right?"

"Yes, but I wouldn't say that out loud to anyone. In fact, avoid politics like the plague. Remember, you are just a sweet young woman grieving for your elderly relative. Appeal to his macho protective instincts."

"Macho? What does that mean?"

"A rather showy type of manliness. The Spanish are very big on *Pundonor*, as well. A kind of exaggerated braggadocio that used to lead to duels and feuds—perhaps still does."

"I certainly don't want to deal with that." She felt intensely grateful for the priest's presence, and his kindness. It was easy to forget the dog collar and think of him as a likable, ordinary man one could enjoy talking to.

With the clatter of footsteps on marble, the officer returned and said something in Spanish to Father Garrick, who turned to her. "The Captain will see us. Fortunately, he speaks English. That's unusual here."

As they followed him up the stairs, Garrick said quietly, "Remember what I told you. Tread carefully."

They entered an office as large and well-appointed as the reception hall downstairs. A man rose from behind a massive desk. A stocky man in a tight uniform, his dark hair glossy with brilliantine. He indicated they were to sit in the two chairs facing him.

"Buenos Dias, Senorita," he bowed toward Gwen, then nodded to Father Garrick. "Padre." Taking his seat again, he opened a buff file on his desk. "How can I help you?"

Gwen launched into her carefully prepared story about Emily being an old friend of the family, like an aunt, really. "We are terribly upset about her death, especially so far away from home. I was coming here to Santiago de Compostela as part of my job, and I wanted to find out exactly what happened."

The Captain glanced down at the papers before him with a slight frown. "I believe everything was done to inform the British Consulate and her employer about the accident. I was assured that they would give this information to her family."

"Oh, yes. Of course. They did give us the information." She could see that the pages on the desk included photographs. Perhaps more information than she wanted.

Remembering Garrick's advice, she softened her tone and conjured up a lump in her throat, which wasn't too difficult. "Please, Captain. It would mean so much to hear it from you, to feel that we had got the complete official story."

He nodded briskly. "Very well." He rearranged his papers and scanned them, then looked up at her. "We received a call from the cathedral around midnight on April 27th of this year that there had been an accident. Two of my men were dispatched immediately and examined the scene. A doctor had already arrived and pronounced the lady to be dead from a head injury. She had evidently been hit by the *botafumiero*. They examined the ropes from which it had been suspended. They concluded that it had been tied too low. Tragically, the lady was in its path."

Gwen shook her head. "But it couldn't have hit her unless someone set it swinging. They said there was a smear of blood on the thurible, but surely there would be more than that."

The captain's brow furrowed, and he gave her a cold stare. "You are an expert on accidents, senorita?"

Her cheeks suddenly felt hot. "Of course not, it's just that—"

"You think perhaps we did not do a thorough investigation, such as your famous Scotland Yard would do?"

"I didn't mean to imply anything of the kind." She drew herself up taller in the chair and tried to imagine what Miss Henderson would say in this situation. "But Dr. Temple was an important person; I owe it to her and those who cared about her to ensure that her death is thoroughly investigated. Surely, it's in the interests of everyone to make sure such a thing does not happen again. After all, many English people come here. They might think twice if they feel that their safety is in doubt."

He bristled, and his voice became harsh. "There is no question of that. Santiago de Compostela is a sacred place. This city is a site of holy pilgrimage, guarded by Santiago himself. Everyone, even English people, are blessed to be under his protection. There is nowhere safer in the entire country. But senorita, even the good Lord cannot protect us from the ill fortune which humans must endure.

"Everything proper has been done to ensure this does not happen again. The ropes have been replaced, and doubled, the knots double-checked every time. The Archbishop himself, insists that the whole apparatus be thoroughly examined every week from now on to ensure it is sound. What more would you have us do?" He glared at her.

Nothing he said convinced her that the investigation had been particularly thorough, but it did make clear that everyone—both church and state— wanted the episode tidied away quickly and kept quiet so as not to disturb the pilgrims and visitors on whom the town depended.

His thinly veiled impatience made her nervous. Who was she to question a police captain? The unlikelihood of the whole event still troubled her, but she had no real grounds to push him any further.

"You must forgive me, Captain; I have been very upset by this tragedy. I did not mean to be rude."

His expression softened. "*De nada.* Young ladies are not suited to dealing with these harsh aspects of life. In Spain, we protect and shelter our senoritas like the delicate flowers protected by the shade. I think perhaps since the Great War, too many English ladies are left unprotected. Alone and neglected, they must grow coarse and tough. We see many such ladies, driving cars alone, travelling by bicycle, smoking." He shook his head. "They set an ill example for the young ones such as yourself."

Gwen sat rigid through this insulting catalogue. He and Mrs. Fairlamb would get on like a house on fire.

"Thank you for your help." She stood and reached across the desk to shake his hand. He took hers and bent forward to plant a damp kiss on her knuckles. She gritted her teeth, and restrained a shudder.

"*Gracias, Capitain,*" Father Garrick nodded to the officer and escorted Gwen from the room.

* * *

Neither spoke till they emerged from the building into the warm sunlight of the plaza.

Gwen burst out, "That man could not possibly have been more arrogant and overbearing if he tried…" She stopped at the sound of a dry chuckle by her side.

"I must admit I've never heard that ladies on bicycles are a dire threat to civilization." Father Garrick gave a full-throated laugh. "I'd give anything to witness him deliver that speech to Miss Henderson. The poor man wouldn't know what had hit him!"

Suddenly, her irritation dissolved as they both gave in to laughter. "Look, there's a café over there," the priest pointed to the other side of the square. "Let's have a cup of coffee. Or perhaps under the circumstances, something stronger is called for."

A few minutes later, under the shade of an awning, Gwen sipped a glass of dry red wine and felt herself calming down. "You know, the captain's attitude towards women may be antediluvian, but I do think he was right about one thing."

"Oh?"

"The War changed everything for us, for both men and women. But it didn't happen here. In Spain, it's as if the Edwardian outlook still prevails. The church and the aristocracy rule society."

"Hmm…"

She gave him a sharp look. "You don't agree?"

"There are deep currents of unrest, especially here in the north. Republicans, Socialists, Communists—all arrayed against the traditional rulers, and especially the church." He twirled the stem of his glass and stared into the ruby liquid. "I shudder to think of the savagery that could be unleashed if all of that explodes."

"Like Russia?"

He nodded. "The things I saw in St Petersburg…"

She stared at him in surprise. "You were there?"

He looked embarrassed. "I was wounded at the Front in Belgium. After I recovered, they sent me to help a diplomatic mission. I have a gift for languages, you see. For a brief time, the Socialists had formed the closest thing to a democratic government Russia had ever seen. The Western powers knew the Czar was never coming back. They wanted to shore up Kerensky and the Socialists. But then Lenin came skulking in through the Finland Station, and the Bolsheviks triumphed."

He looked pained, and now his voice was harsh. "Vandals and murderers. Smashing the treasures of centuries in their brute ignorance."

"The churches?"

"Churches, palaces, the homes of aristocrats, the museums…" The depth of his disgust and anger took her aback.

They reminded her of her father's despairing fury about what he had seen in Flanders. His railing at the waste of war and bleak rage at the thoughtless sacrifice of lives.

"And what about the people?" she asked.

"The people?" He seemed to come back to himself all at once with a sad shake of his head. "The Bolsheviks claim to care about the people—with a capital P—but individual human beings are just dust beneath the wheels of history to them."

She asked quietly, "What made you so bitter?"

He sighed, then tossed back the remainder of his wine. "I saw too much. Far too much."

"How can you still have faith?"

He turned and looked her directly in the face. His sea-blue eyes held both compassion and deep sadness. He sighed. "What other choice do we have? It's that, or the abyss."

Chapter Nineteen

The headstones of the English Cemetery emerged from the morning mist like eerie grey sentinels marking the resting place of so many far from home: weary pilgrims who had gained longed-for grace, unlucky sailors foundered on the rocks of Finisterre and brought inland for burial, and those like Emily, stricken unexpectedly in a foreign land.

A wooden cross was all that marked the grave. Gwen set down a bouquet of daisies on the hummock of soil. A thin green haze of grass was just beginning to take hold. To think that all that remained of Emily lay under the ground, right here at her feet. As she stood up, a wave of dizziness and nausea struck her.

"I say, you're not going to faint, are you?" Colonel Fairlamb's grating voice startled her.

She shook her head and strove to get hold of herself. "Of course not." She turned to see an alarmed expression on his gaunt face. "I'm quite all right."

"I knew it was a bad idea to bring you here. Young females tend to get the vapours in places like this." He looked down at the Panama hat in his hand as he turned it round and round.

"I can assure you, I'm not that sort of female." She moved away from the grave and back onto the winding path.

Fairlamb fell into step at her side as they walked back toward the stone gateway. She still felt intimidated, but she was determined to use this opportunity to her advantage.

"You knew Emily very well," she said. "Please tell me about her."

He cleared his throat. "Not to say, well. More a business acquaintanceship."

"But I understood that you met her years ago, back before the war, in Mesopotamia."

"Oh, that, yes." He looked around, as if he'd rather be elsewhere. "It was Turkey, actually. Place called Carchemish. Chap called Woolley was digging up a palace, or some such thing. Consul sent me out to make sure they had the proper papers, ensure that we knew everyone on staff there, the British and the foreigners. Dashed lot of intrigue going on in that neck of the woods, even then. Tribes making trouble."

"And Emily was one of the archaeologists?"

He nodded. "Ridiculous place for a female. Heat. Flies. Disease. Not to mention the natives—wouldn't trust any of them around a white woman."

Gwen repressed a wince. "When was that?"

"They were digging for a couple of years before the war broke out. That Lawrence chap was there, you know."

"T.E. Lawrence?" Everyone knew the man who led the Arab revolt against the Turks and helped capture Damascus in 1918. A victory that turned the tide of war in the East.

He snorted. "Bloody pansy." He gave her a shame-faced sideways glance. "Pardon the language. But the man was a disgrace. Always swanning around in costume, as if he was going to a fancy dress party."

"Most people think he's a hero," Gwen said lightly. Fairlamb snorted again. She went on, "So Emily actually knew him."

"The woman knew everyone. Middle East was infested with archaeologists and adventurers. Still is."

"Sounds as if you knew many of them too."

Silence fell, filled by the crunch of their footsteps on the gravel path.

"Part of the job in those days." He walked stiffly, looking around as if he'd rather be anywhere else.

She wanted to know more, but he clearly didn't want to talk about that part of his past. She decided to change tack. "It was very kind of you to make the arrangements. Miss Bellamy tells me you have been reimbursed for the costs."

He coughed and looked away in apparent embarrassment. "Very good of the college. Not expected, you understand."

"Still, we are very grateful. But tell me, who do I see to arrange about the headstone?"

They had reached the cemetery entrance. Fairlamb opened one of the wrought iron gates with a long, drawn-out rusty creak. Gwen stepped through the stone archway onto a cobbled road.

The Colonel waved toward a small stone building tucked around the side of the cemetery, a few yards away. "There's a sexton sort of fellow lives there. He manages all that kind of thing. Not there now, I'm afraid. Only speaks Spanish, so you'll need an interpreter." He gave an awkward chortle. "Mine's not up to much beyond ordering dinner and buying a train ticket. Never got on with Spanish. The wife's got the lingo, though."

"I wouldn't like to bother her; she's so busy. I know, before we leave to go home, I'll ask if Father Garrick could help me order the headstone." How could she get Fairlamb to talk more about his connection with Emily back before the war?

The Colonel clapped his broad-brimmed Panama hat back on, and they turned to walk down the road that led back into Santiago. "I do wish that I could speak Spanish," Gwen went on. "It must be so useful to be fluent in other tongues. From what you were saying earlier, it sounded as if you spent a lot of time in the East, do you speak any of those languages?"

"Got on better with those. Picked up enough to get by in most places. Hindi and Bengali in India, Turkish, of course. Egyptian. Bit of Arabic and Farsi."

"Gosh!" Gwen was actually quite impressed but strove to look wide-eyed and awestruck. In her experience, men never failed to take female fascination without question and always preened a little in response. "Do tell me more about the archaeological digs. Did Emily actually work with Lawrence? She never mentioned it."

"Wasn't a woman given to boasting, must say that about her. Downright modest about her achievements. Not like that Arab lover." He looked about them, as if to ensure no one could hear him, then said in a low voice, "In fact, I could tell you a very interesting story about those days."

"Really?"

"Just after the start of the War in Europe, I was still stationed in Egypt. Pretty tense time, waiting to see if the Turks would come in on the side of the Hun. If so, the Suez Canal would be an obvious target. Ottomans would come straight across Palestine. Trouble was, the area had never been mapped, and the Turks wouldn't allow our military surveyors over there."

They paused to allow a peasant leading a donkey to cross the street in front of them. Gwen felt sorry for the bedraggled little creature, barely visible under huge bundles of sticks, looking like a motheaten brown blanket on legs.

"Do go on," she said.

"That's when my experience came in handy. I'd met a chap who had worked with the Palestine Exploration Fund, specialized in biblical archaeology. Perfect cover—I saw that at once. Suggested it to Newcombe of the Royal Engineers, and he took out a mapping party. Needed two respectable archaeologists. Asked Woolley, who actually wanted Miss Temple to come." He snorted. "Put the kibosh on that, of course. Couldn't have a woman out there under the circumstances. Had to settle for Lawrence. Dashed good plan though, eh?"

"So, they were spying."

He gave her an affronted look. "Military intelligence. Vital information."

"Oh, excuse me, I didn't mean to sound critical," Gwen said quickly. "I just meant it seems so exciting. Like something out of John Buchan." How sad that she'd never have the opportunity to hear these stories from Emily herself. "You said it wasn't suitable for a woman, but what about Gertrude Bell? Did you know her out there?" When the famous writer and traveler had died, just the previous year, the obituaries had praised her extraordinary talents and influence in Middle East affairs.

"Miss Bell, yes, quite the character." His tone made clear his disdain. "She and Lawrence both fancied themselves experts on the Arabs. Had a fine time creating kings and drawing up maps at the Cairo Conference back in 'twenty-one. We'll see what happens with Iraq. Letting Arabs govern themselves." He made a scornful noise. "In my opinion, it'll all end in tears."

After a moment, she asked, "Did Emily stay out there during the War?"

He looked uncomfortable and shook his head. "Came back to Blighty on the same ship as the Memsahib and I."

"So, you didn't stay out there either?" She remembered Hildy's comment about him being shipped back in disgrace.

He coughed. "Felt our place was back in the old country. Wife's people were in a bad way. They found a job for me at headquarters."

It suddenly occurred to her that Fairlamb could have no idea what she might know. "Emily told me a little about her time in Egypt." That much was true. A very little.

"Really?"

"Apparently, there was a scandal about antiquities being smuggled out of the country."

"Ah yes, sounds familiar." He said in a strangled tone. "Sort of thing that's bound to happen in places like that. Corrupt local officials, thieving workmen."

"Oh. I rather got the impression it was an English person involved."

"Nonsense! She probably got the idea from Maspero—French chap who ran the antiquities service. Didn't get on with the British museum people, you know."

That hardly sounded like a plausible reason to falsely accuse someone of a crime. And Fairlamb's obvious discomfort with the whole subject did seem suspicious.

He picked up his pace as they got closer to the Plaza Obrador. "Here we are, then. Just in time for luncheon."

Passing under the cloister arches of the hotel, it suddenly felt colder in the shade. As they stepped into the large main reception room, Gwen sensed the Colonel was suddenly anxious to part ways.

He nodded. "See you in the dining room, Miss Armstrong."

She watched him marching away as if a horde of Turks and the Hun were at his very heels. He had told fascinating stories, but she strongly suspected that the truth was even more fantastic.

Emily had been in some kind of deep trouble. And whatever that trouble had involved, she was willing to swear that Colonel Fairlamb had been in even deeper.

Chapter Twenty

"The end of the world." Amanda stood on the clifftop with her hair blowing back from her brow, her thin coat streaming out behind her, looking like some dauntless queen of old surveying her dominions.

Gwen hugged her jacket tightly against the cold, stiff wind off the ocean as it buffeted her face. Dizzyingly far below, waves frothed and creamed on the jagged rocks, and the roar of the sea echoed in her ears. "It's spectacular."

"The Romans really did call it that, you know," Amanda said. "They believed Finisterre to be the end of the known world. It comes from the Latin *finis terrae*. Pretty self-explanatory." She waved toward the horizon. "I wonder how they felt watching the sun set into the *mare tenebrosum*—the dark sea, they called it. How apt, considering they thought it connected to the underworld."

Gwen shivered, and not just because of the cold wind. She stepped back down the path, taking shelter in the lee of the hill and grasping the top of the reassuring stone wall.

Amanda remained standing on the crest. "You know that they call this the *Costa da Morte*." *The Coast of Death*."

"That's another self-explanatory phrase," Gwen said, hanging on tighter to the wall. "You can tell this is a dangerous coast. Those rocks down there are devilish. And the lighthouse tells its own story."

On a distant promontory to their south stood a cluster of buildings, crowned by a slender tower emitting a rhythmic warning flash.

"I don't envy the fishermen of Finisterre," Amanda said. "This shore is known for dense fogs, brutal winter storms, and dangerous currents. Quite the delightful climate."

"I'm going back down." Thoroughly chilled now, Gwen turned to follow the narrow track leading back toward the dig site. Up here, she felt too exposed and couldn't ignore the trembling in her knees when she caught sight of the sheer drop to the rocks below.

Amanda, on the other hand, seemed to revel in the danger. Gwen heard her laughter, then the sound of her springing lightly along the path behind her.

The Iron Age settlement known as Castro de Carballo covered a good two acres of land on a broad hilltop. Enclosed by two concentric stone walls, a series of circular stone foundations indicated where dwellings once stood. Other lumps and hummocks of grass-covered soil signaled the likely presence of more buildings, some of them dug into large rectangular pits, other areas overlaid with grids of sticks and string indicating the next targets for excavation.

A little further down the track, a large stone cottage did service as the site headquarters, with rough sleeping and dining facilities. A tall, fair man emerged from the doorway, stooping a little to avoid the low lintel. Not a young man, despite his lean and limber frame. His sun-browned face, with its web of fine wrinkles, attested to a life spent outdoors.

"Enjoy the view?" He grinned, his bright blue eyes alight with enthusiasm.

"Yes, thank you, Dr. Hunt." Exhilarated not only by the brilliant sunshine, Gwen felt excited to be at a real large-scale dig, run by a famous archaeologist.

"Jolly good, Cedric. I'll just have a poke about with Franz." Amanda said. "He can show me the areas he worked on. No need for us all to do the Cook's tour."

Amanda went inside the cottage in search of her student. Gwen had noticed Michael Greville disappear into the building not long after they arrived. Now she saw him on the other side of the Castro, in earnest conversation with a fair-haired young man.

Some of the group had stayed in Santiago. Father Garrick was visiting friends at the Cathedral, and Letitia and Dorcas preferred to stay at the luxurious hotel rather than roughing it overnight at the dig site.

With no one nearby, Gwen seized the opportunity. "Do you have a moment to talk, Dr. Hunt?"

"Of course! Can we walk at the same time? I need to do a quick check that the workmen are leaving the place tidy."

He led her on a path that ran around the inside of the inner wall. Groups of roughly dressed men were spreading tarpaulins over some of the excavated open grids. Elsewhere, young men clad in old flannel bags and tweed jackets crouched over notebooks, writing furiously. Undoubtedly, these were the English archaeology students working for Dr. Hunt. The man talking to Michael looked like one of them.

Hunt looked across the site to where a dilapidated old lorry sat on the road, facing downhill. "They're supposed to be finished in another hour, then we'll pack them back to Vigo. We're shutting down for three weeks, which is rotten timing as the dig season is just getting started." He gave a philosophical sigh.

"Why would you be shutting down?"

"Usual story," he said with a wry grin. "Money! A chance came up to do a lecture tour of the Midlands to various chapters of a very well-heeled society. An opportunity to raise funds that's much too good to neglect. We're always in need, I'm afraid."

"I thought Museums and Universities pay for the digs."

"They do, but this affords us a little extra help to hire more diggers, extend the season a bit. We always want to do more. There's always more in the ground than we can possibly explore."

"Do you have private sponsors, like Howard Carter had Lord Carnavon?"

He smiled. "I wish! I'm afraid Bronze-age Celts aren't nearly as glamourous as gold-masked pharaohs and hidden tombs filled with treasure."

She looked around the barren, wind-swept cliff top. "I suppose so." To her, this place looked as dramatic and full of portent as any desert shrine. "But the Celts had their treasures too, didn't they?"

"Oh yes. Over the past few years, we've found a few pieces of gold jewellery.

Unfortunately, the best pieces we ever found were stolen."

"Stolen?"

He nodded, his mouth compressed with bitterness. "Just thinking about it still makes me angry." He pointed to a spot near the south wall. "Last year, over there is where we found it. We were so excited. The grave site of a high-status woman who had been laid to rest with all her finery. Brooches, necklaces, and a very fine gold fibula."

"Fibula?" A chill trickled down her spine.

"A kind of cloak pin. As with all of their jewelry, these objects were often finely decorated with elaborate and beautiful interlace designs, often with animal motifs. The Celts were highly artistic, despite their warlike propensities."

They paused beside one of the open excavations. Gwen could see the striations in the soil, the different colours marking off the passage of time. Her mind was racing, wanting to ask questions but afraid to learn more about the stolen hoard.

"I think you knew my...my friend, Emily Temple."

He looked a bit taken aback at the sudden change of subject." Dr. Temple? Oh yes, an old friend. Such a sad loss. Of course, you must have known her at Seathorne." He gave her a penetrating look. "But clearly, you knew her as more than just a colleague."

Gwen nodded. "I understand you were at her funeral."

He slowly shook his head. "Such a terrible thing to happen. I had only seen her the week before, when she came up to visit the site. We talked for hours about our old adventures in fieldwork." With a wistful expression, he began walking again.

"You had known her for a long time?"

"We met in Athens, at the British School. Around Nineteen-Nine, I think. She'd just come out from England. I remember her looking rather wan and thin when she got off the boat. They assigned me to meet her, you see. Looked as if she'd had a rough passage." He chuckled softly.

"In those days, I was rather a pompous ass, I'm afraid. Ragged her a bit about being six months late. There was some mix-up, can't remember now about what. Anyway, I didn't believe women belonged at the school. Assumed she got her place as some kind of special favour to Flinders Petrie. And, of course, she came from the Cockney College." He glanced at Gwen. Beneath his tan, he flushed. "Sorry, that's what we called UC."

"Yes, I've heard that. From Hildy Scott."

"Ah, you've been to see Hildy." He held her gaze for a moment, as a grimace of wry amusement crossed his face. "Quite a character."

Gwen nodded. "I like her."

Cedric paused and leaned an elbow on top of the stone wall. "Hildy and I had a good talk at the funeral. Discovered we'd met once before, a long time ago in Egypt. We knew many of the same people. Small world, archaeology. Anyway, we'd known Emily at different times in her life, but shared a great affection for her."

They had stopped at a spot where the stone wall had tumbled down, leaving a wide gap. "Watch your step here," Cyril warned her.

On the other side of the wall, the cliff edge was only inches away. Gwen looked over to see the jagged black teeth of the rocks in the cove a hundred feet below. She jerked backward. Heights always turned her knees to jelly.

"That's another reason we need to dig this site as quickly as possible," Hunt explained. "Erosion. The settlement would have been quite far back from the cliffs when it was originally built. Some of the suspected grave sites are very close to it now. One fierce storm could wash away irreplaceable finds."

She drew a deep breath, knowing she had to ask. "Like the ones that were stolen?"

His lips tightened. "Damned workmen. We'd hired an itinerant crew. Claimed to have experience in the South. Turned up with what looked like a bona fide letter of recommendation. Right near the end of the season, we found this marvelous grave hoard. Then, a week later, the crew vanished in the middle of the night, along with every valuable item we'd discovered."

"How terrible," she said faintly. She repressed the thought that Emily could have had any connection with the theft.

"It was indeed. Ask Franz. He was set to write his thesis on it. Poor chap was practically heartbroken." A hint of embarrassment crossed his face.

"Don't know if you've noticed, but he's dashed emotional for a German."

"I can't say I know any other Germans. Did you meet many during the war?"

"At the point of a bayonet, do you mean?" He winced. "Sorry, that was in shockingly bad taste. Actually, I served in the Middle East. When hostilities broke out, a lot of German archaeologists got caught out in the field, blissfully unaware that they were at war. They sent me out to find them. Arranged to ship them out of harm's way to some neutral country. After that, it was up to them to get home. Most of them just wanted to stay put, of course. Once the Ottomans came into the war on the Huns' side, I heard that a few of them managed to find their way back."

"Colonel Fairlamb told me that Emily actually worked with T. E. Lawrence."

"Oh yes, Fairlamb. I notice he didn't come on this jaunt today."

Something about the way he said the name made her look at him more closely. "Pardon me, but I get the impression you don't care for him."

"That obvious, is it?" A wry grin deepened the creases around his eyes. "Didn't take to the man when I met him at the funeral. And, of course I had to talk to him about this visit which Emily had arranged." He gave an irritated sigh. "I found him officious, overbearing, the very image of the posturing official acting as if this country were some benighted colony. I couldn't imagine how Emily could stand working with him, but I imagine he's an excellent organizer for this kind of junket." He sighed. "Perhaps that's what was getting Emily down, last time we met. The prospect of having to work with him again."

"Emily was unhappy?"

"Not to say unhappy, more like worried about something. The more we talked, the more anxious she seemed to be. She was terribly upset about the theft, especially since she was actually here when we found the grave site. I don't think she wanted to believe it had been the workmen. She always had a soft spot for the diggers, especially the locals in Greece."

"She was one of those people who always see the best in everyone," Gwen said softly. And perhaps that generous good nature had got her into trouble.

"She knew such a wide range of people, "Hunt continued. "It was a shame her funeral happened so quickly. I'm sure there are many who would like to have paid their respects." He nodded toward Greville, still talking to the young student. "That coin chap was at the cemetery. He left before I had the chance to speak to him, but he must have known her."

She gave a swift, startled glance toward Michael Greville. Michael was *there*. Why hadn't he said anything?

"And there's another thing." He hesitated, then added. "I told you that I met Fairlamb at the funeral, but that isn't strictly accurate. Of course, it's been a very long time. But I recognized him. In Cairo, one of my mundane duties was making sure questionable characters left the country. Nothing was ever proved against him, but Captain Fairlamb, as he was then, had got himself involved in some dubious company. Before the war broke out, he made quite a routine of palling up with tourists, who ended up buying pricy souvenirs from some of his other friends—who happened to be the most prominent forgers of antiquities in Egypt. Nothing proved, of course. But enough to get him shipped home, pronto."

Still surprised by the revelation about Greville, she said faintly. "That's pretty much what Hildy told me."

He sighed. "Shouldn't judge a chap. Perhaps he's mended his ways. Still, having someone like that connected with this kind of business…rich travelers touring the historic sites. I must say, it raises an eyebrow. And I did tell Emily that."

A distant shout drew their attention. Franz waved from the door of the cottage as the Sloans and the Dixons stood behind him.

Cedric Hunt drew himself up and waved back. "I'll be right there!" He gave her a rueful smile. "Time to put on the show. With any luck, your rich Americans or the Midlands millionaire may decide to follow in Carnarvon's footsteps and become our patrons. Only wish I had hopes of turning up an Iberian version of King Tut."

Gwen followed, lagging behind him, as a tumble of contradictory thoughts and impulses raced through her mind. She needed to know why Michael had kept quiet about being at the funeral. She desperately needed to find out more about the stolen finds. It would be reassuring to find that they bore no resemblance to the antiquities in the parcel Emily sent her. But in her heart, fear lay like a block of ice.

When Hunt talked about the missing gold fibula, she wanted him to stop, in case he told her what she didn't want to know.

Chapter Twenty-One

T he group of travelers sat around the rustic oak table in the cottage, eating a dinner prepared by the expedition cook, a broad-beamed local woman who unceremoniously dished up the meal, then set a basket of coarse bread in the centre of the table.

The sun had not yet gone down, but the small windows made it very dark inside the cottage, and already the oil lamps were lit.

The group chattered around her, but Gwen stared into her bowl of hearty stew without really seeing it. Her thoughts were deeply troubled. Two episodes hardly made a pattern, but all she could think about were the thefts that had followed shortly after Emily's visits to the curiosity shop and the dig site. She hated her own cowardice in shying away from asking Dr. Hunt for more details about the stolen artefacts. But really, the gold horse fibula could hardly be unique.

She comforted herself with the thought that it made no sense for Emily to be involved. Apart from being totally at odds with her strong moral code, Emily had no need of ill-gotten gains to judge by her will. Despite her apparently modest way of life, she had a great deal of money.

Feeling suddenly sick, Gwen put down her spoon. A great deal of money, but from where? After all, Emily was the daughter of a vicar, and Gwen could distinctly remember getting the sense that it had not been a wealthy household. In fact, she now recalled Emily telling her about having to work as a governess while she waited for acceptance to University College.

How could a life of scholarship and teaching have earned her a fortune yielding an income of ten thousand pounds a year?

This train of thought appalled her. How could she be so disloyal to a person who had treated her with such kindness?

She looked up to meet the dark blue eyes across the table. For a terrible moment, she felt Michael Greville knew every thought that crossed her mind. He held her gaze for a long moment.

"You're very quiet," he said at last. "What do you think of this place?"

"It's... magnificent. I can't quite take it all in." She needed to ask him about being at the funeral, or was it better to keep that knowledge to herself for the moment?

He nodded. "In a place like this, one feels the presence of the past very strongly." He reached into the basket between them and took a slab of coarse bread, gesturing to the dim space around them. "Three thousand years can seem like the blink of an eye. One almost expects armored horsemen to come riding up the hill, laden with trophies." He tore a piece off the bread and took a bite.

"Trophies? You mean like treasure? Loot? That kind of thing?"

He chuckled. "Heads, my dear Miss Armstrong. Heads." He put down the bread and gave her a considering look. "I hate to shock your delicate sensibilities, but the Celts took the heads of their enemies and prized them above mere treasure."

"I'm quite aware of the Celts' propensity for decapitation," His patronising attitude irritated her. "And I'm more than able to cope with the grim realities of history, I can assure you." Gwen sat up straighter, trying to look assertive. "Tell me more about these heads."

He laughed again, this time without condescension. Down the table, she saw Amanda dart a look in their direction.

Michael caught her eye, then turned back to Gwen. "The Celts liked combining their passions, so horses and heads featured in much of their art— often stylized horses carrying stylized heads. Remember that cauldron in Don Alvarez's collection? The decoration included a warrior on horseback, carrying a string of heads."

A clear image of that sinister gold horseman hidden away in her case appeared in her mind's eye. Not to mention, the even more sinister object hanging from the bridle.

She looked down at chunks of pale meat—was that mutton?—and stirred her spoon through the hearty bowl of stew. The facts were staring her in the face, but she didn't want to accept them. Hadn't Emily taught her to think logically and not be swayed by emotion toward the conclusion she wanted to be true? She took a deep breath and steeled herself to face facts.

First, gather the data. What was the evidence? She needed more details about the stolen hoard.

* * *

The mellow lamplight caught the burnished glow of bronze as Dr. Hunt laid out a collection of artifacts on a large, scrubbed wood table. At one end lay an assembly of swords and daggers.

A staccato chorus of indrawn breaths emerged from the group in the storage room. Brett Sloan stared down greedily at the largest sword. The swooping line of the blade ended in a stylized hook for a handle, beautifully engraved in the shape of a bird.

"Now that is something special."

"Indeed, Mr. Sloan, you are correct," said Dr. Hunt. "This type of sword has not been found in this area before."

"That curving blade—it almost looks like a scimitar."

Hunt nodded. "Many authorities believe it may be a precursor. It's a southern Celtiberian style that is known as a *falcata* blade. Named after its supposed resemblance to a falcon."

Franz stared down at the weapon silently, his face a rigid mask. Amanda gave him a sideways glance of startling contempt, then quietly excused herself and left the room.

Not for the first time, Gwen wondered at the relationship between them. Far from being his mentor, Amanda acted more like an imperious employer toward Franz, treating him as her dogsbody. It was very different from the collegial academic ideals that Emily had taught her to expect.

"Have you found any jewelry?" Alice Dixon asked, hopefully.

Gwen's attention focused instantly. Would Dr. Hunt mention the theft?

"Well…." Hunt hesitated. He turned and opened a large cupboard, with shelves that pulled out, to reveal many small finds, from pottery sherds to small metallic objects. He removed a small tray and put it on the table. "We found these just last week."

A dark cloth lined the tray, on which lay a cluster of roundish beads. "Are they glass?" Mrs. Sloan inquired.

"Coral and Amber."

"They're lovely," she said, clearly being polite.

Hunt looked uncomfortable. He needed to cultivate potential benefactors, and spectacular finds undoubtedly helped. "We hope to find more like this, but we get a great deal of important information from the more mundane objects of daily life." He lifted out a bronze basin, aged to verdigris and engraved with graceful animalistic patterns.

"Eee, that's lovely," Alice Dixon's round face softened into a smile. "What do you do with all of this? Does it go to the British Museum?"

Dr. Hunt shook his head. "Every dig is unique. The way it works in most countries is that you must get a permit from the appropriate authority, and you negotiate some general guidelines so that a portion of the finds go to the government. The rest go to the expedition funders. In my case, it's the University."

"Why should the government get any of it?" Brett Sloan shoved his hands in his pockets with a derisive shrug. "They don't shell out the money; they don't put in the work or take the risk."

Dr. Hunt looked offended. "This is the country's heritage. If I had my way, it would all stay here. In my opinion, it belongs to the people."

"The people?" Sloan's voice rose, and red patches sprang up on his cheeks. "You know what happens when the people get hold of artistic treasures. Just look at Russia. Those Reds ran roughshod over a thousand years of culture. They've got no respect for history."

Tension sizzled through the group, clearly shocked by the unexpected outburst of anger.

From the doorway came a peal of laughter. "Oh please, Dr. Hunt, don't tell me you're another Communist!" Still laughing, Amanda stepped toward the table. "Next thing you'll take to wearing those dreadful hats."

Some people chuckled uncertainly, but the lighthearted jibe did succeed in breaking the tension.

"Now, Professor Hunt, I'd like to know more about the running of a place like this." Jim Dixon made an obvious effort to change the subject. He drew Dr. Hunt toward the large wall-mounted map of the site. "As a businessman, I'm interested in how you get the staff and organize it all."

As Dixon engaged the archaeologist in conversation about the practical side of the work, Mrs. Dixon picked up the bronze bowl and examined it distractedly. "How old would you say this is, Dr Spenser?"

Amanda took it from her and gave it an assessing glance. "Fourth century BC, I'd say. As are the beads."

Gwen noticed the Sloans had moved away and were having a tense, muttered conversation. Marion Sloan did not look pleased with her husband.

The evening concluded with a subdued gathering in the main room for a nightcap of sherry, or whisky and soda. If Amanda had intended this side trip to gain support for Dr Hunt's expedition, it had clearly not been a success. Gwen didn't understand Brett Sloan's anger, but sensed it had something to do with his purpose in being there. Perhaps Dorcas's barbed comments had been accurate, and Brett Sloan's bargain-hunting for artefacts had so far been a failure.

* * *

The cook-housekeeper showed them to their spartan rooms, where they could experience firsthand the accommodations of the expedition staff. Each small room had bare stone walls and two camp beds, made up with linen sheets and, thankfully, down-filled quilts. The small window had no glass, but a wooden shutter to keep out the rising wind. With no source of heat, the room was glacial. After removing only her outer garments, Gwen dove under the covers.

Shortly after, Amanda entered and did the same. "Ready?" she reached out to the knob on the oil lantern.

Gwen nodded. With a twist of Amanda's fingers, pitch darkness fell.

For a long time, Gwen lay awake. They were leaving after breakfast tomorrow, and she had failed to get any useful information about the stolen artefacts. Since their walk, there had been no further opportunity to speak with Dr. Hunt alone, and even then, she didn't know how to get the information without raising his suspicions about Emily.

The dinnertime conversation with Greville had left her wary of him for the rest of the evening. What was his game? For no good reason, he made her feel that he knew her secrets, but how could he?

Eventually, she must have dozed off and then woken again to realize that her face was cold. About to burrow deeper into the quilt, she noticed a flash of light from the other bed and realized it was a thin beam of torchlight. A creak of the canvas and wood frame told her Amanda must be getting up.

Gwen shuddered. The expedition house lacked the luxury of plumbing. She didn't envy Amanda the trip to the outdoor privy.

But hadn't the housekeeper indicated the chamber pots under the bed? Surely, even someone as fastidious as Amanda would take advantage of that option.

Not exactly sure why, Gwen decided to follow her. She slid from under the covers and put her feet in her shoes, glad she had kept on her heavy lisle stockings. Her coat lay at the foot of the bed. She found it by touch and put it on. A faint light from the hallway showed that the door now stood ajar, and she stepped through it.

A low-burning oil lamp on the dining table gave enough light to get her bearings. The torch beam bobbed and flickered at the end of the corridor, illuminating the door to the storage room as it opened.

Gwen crept up to the open door and could see the torch beam playing across the shelves of potsherds, and then stopped at the filing cabinet in the corner, with Amanda's face illuminated by the reflected light. She had the lower drawer open and was flicking through the files, then pulled out a folder and shut the drawer.

Gwen fled back down the corridor and was able to slip under the covers scant seconds before she heard Amanda come back into the room. She watched Amanda put the folder into the satchel holding her papers, then get back into her own bed.

What could be in those files? Somehow, she had to find out.

At breakfast the next morning, she looked for an opportunity. The cook had just slapped down a plate in front of each of them, with three overcooked eggs and some kind of greasy sausage, when Gwen got to her feet.

"Excuse me, I'm a little cold. I'll just get a cardigan."

Beyond desultory nods, no one paid her much attention. She hurried back to the room, relieved to see that the satchel still sat on the chair by Amanda's cot.

Listening hard for any sound of someone approaching the room, she unfastened the strap with a trembling hand. Lifting the buff folder halfway out of the case, she opened it wide enough to see that it held a sheaf of photographs. She started to flip through them, but a noise from the hallway made her drop the folder and its contents back into the case, fasten the strap, and buckle again with fumbling fingers.

She had just stepped over to her own bed when the housekeeper entered the room. "*Disculpe, señorita. ¿Puedo llevar tus maletas al auto?*"

The woman gestured toward the satchel and Amanda's travel bag on the bed. Gwen realized she must be asking about putting the luggage in the car.

With a helpless shrug, she indicated incomprehension. The woman gave her an impatient look and went out, probably to seek out someone who could understand her.

Gwen headed for the door, then hurriedly turned back and got a cardigan from her carpet bag, the ostensible reason for her absence. She had better eat some breakfast, even though her appetite had deserted her. Her glimpse of the photos had been brief, but long enough to reveal images of some of the items in Emily's parcel. Including the Golden Horseman.

Chapter Twenty-Two

The drive from the coast back to Santiago de Compostela took them over rugged hills and into deep green wooded valleys along rough roads that appeared to be little more than cart tracks. Their chauffeur was plump and cheerful, bumping over obstacles with abandon and seemingly oblivious to the sheer drop always so perilously close to the rear wheel.

It would have been lovely to see, but for entire stretches, Gwen had to squeeze her eyes shut and hang on to the door handle for dear life.

Her only relief lay in the fact that she was in the third car. For long stretches, they lost sight of the first two, except for the clouds of dust in their wake. Brett Sloan and Amanda Spenser drove the open-topped hired cars as if they were competing at Brooklands, and the Spanish chauffeur driving their motor followed suit. She had only read about hurtling juggernauts tearing around a track vying for supremacy. Now she knew what it must feel like. Except that race cars didn't take terrified passengers.

By the time they crested a hill and saw the cathedral spire in the distance, she was ready to kiss the earth in gratitude for their imminent deliverance.

When she wasn't praying to survive, Gwen had been thinking obsessively about the items stolen from Castro da Corbello. Honesty compelled her to tell Dr. Hunt what she knew, but she hadn't had the courage to do it. After all, everything was gone, except for the gold horseman.

So many questions swirled through her mind. How did Amanda fit into all this? Were the Sloans and Greville knowingly involved? What really happened to Emily? And how could she possibly be some kind of criminal?

Her head ached with contradictory impulses. What she needed was a quiet half-hour to think.

The motors ahead pulled up at the side of the hotel. Amanda jumped out of her Hispano Suiza with a grin of triumph. Brett Sloan emerged more slowly from the Duesenberg. Their chauffeur, in a more modest Austin, drew in behind as a hotel porter hurried out and began to unload the baggage.

The Dixons emerged from the back seat of Sloan's vehicle with pale faces and shaky legs. Mrs. Sloan had a set, grim expression, but Mr. Sloan pulled out a cigar, lit it with élan, and gave Amanda an exuberant smile. "My God, little lady. You sure as hell can drive!"

Amanda laughed. "You are an *automobiliste par excellence*, yourself, sir. What do you say to a cocktail?"

"I would say, lead on, my dear. And, make that two cocktails!" He offered his arm to Amanda, who took it as they sailed into the hotel. Franz trailed behind like a disconsolate puppy while Greville got out of Amanda's car and looked after her with a speculative frown.

Gwen caught a look of pure, cold fury distorting Marion Sloan's face for a brief instant, replaced by a worldly roll of the eyes. "Boys do like their toys, don't they," she murmured to no one in particular.

Did she mean the car, or the woman?

The Dixons stared after her as she followed the others into the hotel, then looked at each other in dismay.

Alice Dixon shook her head. "I must admit, I would have expected better from a high-toned woman like that."

Jim Dixon turned to Gwen and shook his head. "Argued like cats and dogs all the way; meanwhile, the man was driving like the devil."

"And the *language*!" She frowned and shook her head again. "I'm a broad-minded woman, but to hear a wife abusing her husband like that...." It was the first critical comment Gwen had heard from Alice, who seemed the type who always wanted to pour oil on troubled waters. But not this time.

Mr. Dixon watched the others disappear into the hotel, then turned to Gwen. "Call me an old prude, but it seems like ever since the War, standards of behaviour have dropped like a stone."

"I know a lot of people feel that way," she began hesitantly, "Young people especially. They think they might as well live for today, because no one has faith in the future." The thought emerged without conscious analysis, but she realized how general was that unspoken conviction. "Not everyone, of course." She added hastily. But if she could doubt someone like Emily, what did that say about her own faith in people?

Mr. Dixon's ruddy face had paled to an expression of sadness. "The more we see of the world, the less I like it. Is this what our lads fought for?"

"Now, Jim..." his wife shot him a look of concern. "There's no call to give up."

He took Alice's arm in his and patted her hand. "It's all right, love, I'm not giving up. There's many a young person like Gwen here, who knows what's right and wrong. I can tell a well-brought-up lass when I meet one."

Gwen didn't know what to say. A confusing war of guilt, loyalty, and an underlying belief in Emily's innocence tore her emotions in a thousand directions. She'd been spying on people, lying, possibly concealing a crime. Were those the actions of a well-brought-up lass?

The Dixons' unvarnished, solid honesty compelled her to be equally direct. "Do you regret coming on this tour?"

Jim shook his head. "Nay, lass. It's been an education. We both left school at thirteen. Me to apprentice in the mills, Alice to go into service. But we both loved to learn, you see. Went to the Working Men's Institute, I did, and the public lectures. And where do you think we met, eh? At the lending library! For years, we talked about travelling, all the places we wanted to see. In the meantime, we worked hard, made our fortune. Had our three lovely lads..." he paused and took a deep, shaky breath. "Aye, and then we lost them." He looked at Alice and squeezed her hand again. "And life lost its purpose. There didn't seem any reason to go anywhere."

"What changed your mind?"

"Our son Edward." He must have seen her look of surprise. "Oh aye, he's been gone since 1917. But he were officially missing in action all this time. Till last September. We got a parcel from the War Office. Gave us both a turn, I can tell you. They keep finding 'em, you see. That's what happened with Edward. They send you a notice of the gravesite and any effects that turn up." He glanced at Alice, who looked ghostly pale but listened to him intently. "There wasn't much in the parcel, except a letter he never had a chance to send. He'd just got back from leave behind the lines. All excited about this talk he went to given by this lady archaeologist."

"Emily," Gwen said faintly.

He nodded. "Aye. Dr. Temple. She impressed him no end. He always was a clever lad. Didn't want to go into the business. Accepted to the university just before he got called up. Couldn't make up his mind what to study, but after going to this talk, he wrote that he'd decided."

"Shouldn't have been a surprise. He was always out in the garden or the woods, digging for treasure." Alice Dixon smiled, but her eyes brimmed with tears.

"Anyway, I wrote to Dr Temple. Stupid, really, to think she'd remember one lad out of the hundreds she must have met. But she was so kind. We exchanged a few letters, then we got to thinking that it was time we got out of ourselves. When she mentioned she was leading this tour, it seemed like a good way to learn about what had so excited our Edward and meet the lady who inspired him."

"You must have been so disappointed..." Gwen murmured.

"Aye." He let out his breath in a long sigh. "The Lord giveth, and the Lord taketh away. Seems like he's been doing more of the taking away." His mouth settled in a grim line.

"Now, Jim," his wife said. "We vowed not to give in to grief."

"Aye, but it's important to see things as they really are. No matter how hard life is." He looked at Gwen and then at his wife, patting her hand again. "In the grand scheme of things, I suppose we've been lucky, Alice and me."

He looked back at Gwen. "Shall we go in?"

* * *

Lying on the bed, she stared up at the yellowed plaster ceiling, wondering for the thousandth time what on earth she was doing here. Emily's calm voice seemed to echo in her head. *Be logical, Gwen. Marshall the facts. What do we know?*

It had all started with the news of Emily's death. The letter, telling her to expect the parcel. Hinting that something was very wrong. Then the arrival of the parcel, and its subsequent theft. Finally, her discovery that the artefacts in the parcel were stolen from Castro de Carballo, stolen not long after Emily visited.

But if Emily had stolen them, which Gwen refused to believe, then why send them to her for safekeeping? Could Emily have thought that Gwen would cover up a crime, out of loyalty to the woman who was giving her the opportunity to pursue her dream? There was a horrible logic to it, but only if Emily was a ruthless and immoral woman who had concealed her true nature. That she simply *couldn't* believe.

And how did Amanda come into it? Because, clearly, she must be involved. Why else steal the photos of the missing artefacts? Whatever the reason, the act was suspicious.

But at least she had one piece of evidence, one item to prove to herself it wasn't all a horrible dream. The golden horseman. Even if the treasure was an incriminating mixed blessing.

She rolled off the bed, landed on her feet, and stepped over to her suitcase, which sat on a low cane table near the door. Unfastening the case, she pulled out the blue velvet bag holding her best pair of shoes. Nestled between the shoes lay the rolled up green silk scarf that had been her Mum's, and wrapped inside it, the precious object.

Except as soon as she put her fingers around the scarf, she felt the absence of the hard, heavy metal shape. She unrolled the empty square of silk. *The horseman was gone.*

Stepping back with an involuntary gasp of despair, she looked down at the items in the case: two neatly folded dresses, three chemises, four pairs of knickers, and an extra cardigan. The shoe bag had been tucked in the corner, otherwise it looked exactly as she had left it before going to Castro de Carballo the day before. Didn't it?

She clutched the scarf to her chest, feeling sick. Who could have taken it?

Amanda? But when? She tried the connecting door leading into Amanda's suite. She'd turned down Amanda's off-handed invitation to use her private bathroom, preferring the convenience down the hall to the prospect of walking in on some sordid scene.

But now she grabbed the handle and tried the door, turning and twisting the knob in vain. It must be bolted on the other side. *What was she going to do?* All the evidence was now gone.

Chapter Twenty-Three

F ather Garrick saw her first. He waved at her from where he sat at one of the zinc-topped tables in the hotel bar. "Miss Armstrong. Do join me, please."

She sank down on the chair opposite, her head still reeling from the disappearance of the gold horseman.

"Can I offer you a sherry, a glass of wine, possibly even a cocktail?"

She stared at him for a moment, trying to focus on what he was saying. "A cocktail? Oh, no, I haven't the head for anything so strong as a cocktail on an empty stomach."

He frowned at her, then stood up, saying, "If you'll permit me, I think I know what you need." He stepped over to the bar, where Amanda stood holding court with Sloan on one side and Colonel Fairlamb and Michael Greville on the other. She still wore her travelling clothes, a divided skirt, and neatly fitted military-style jacket. On her, the practical clothing took on a stylish glamour.

Gwen noticed Mrs. Fairlamb and Mrs. Sloan sitting at another table, silently sipping drinks and balefully watching as Amanda concluded a racy story.

"...and I don't know why the gendarme didn't believe me, you'd think a Frenchman would know cami-knickers when he saw them!"

Sloan and Fairlamb erupted in abrasive laughter while Greville merely smiled. Father Garrick paused in the act of taking a brandy glass from the barman and shot Amanda a disapproving frown. She smiled back at him, serenely contemptuous. "All in good fun, father."

"I'm sure you think so, my child." With that cold dismissal, the priest came back to the table and set the drink down in front of Gwen. "Try this."

She opened her mouth to argue, then took a sip and changed her mind. He was right. The brandy and soda sent a surge of warmth through her chest and somehow helped her focus.

"You seem to have had a shock."

She shrugged, trying to sound nonchalant. "You could say that. The drive from Castro de Carballo was spectacularly beautiful, but the most terrifying journey I've ever experienced."

"Tell me about the dig. Have they found anything interesting?"

She gave him a stumbling account of the items Dr. Hunt had shown them, but her attention focused on the group at the bar.

Amanda worked her coquettish charms with all her might, playing off the three men in turn. Greville seemed least susceptible, leaning back with one elbow on the bar as he drank a martini, and watched her performance with a sardonic smile.

What had happened to Colonel Fairlamb? His glowering disapproval of Amanda had vanished, replaced by a sycophantic adoration that Gwen found repellant. Not least because of the pain and anger in Elsie Fairlamb's eyes.

Still wearing his broad-brimmed Panama, Brett Sloan clearly reveled in playing the grandee. "The French are so easy to fool because they're so arrogant. Especially the officials. They think Americans are all ignorant boobs who know nothing about art and culture. If you understand that, you can put anything over on them! Why I bought this painting last year..." his voice dropped, and he leaned in toward Amanda.

His words were indistinct, but Gwen caught the odd phrase. "Got one of those street artists... told Customs I bought it for ten bucks... sold it in New York for ten thousand." He leaned back again and pulled out a cigar. "Of course, the best opportunities were back in '18. In those days, most of Europe was like one big Goddamn fire sale!" He pulled out a gold lighter, thumbed it into flame and lit his cigar. He regarded the ascending smoke with reflective regret. "Times like that come around once in a lifetime."

"I wouldn't be so sure, if I were him," Father Garrick said. Gwen turned to look at him as he went on, *"The blood-dimmed tide is loosed, and everywhere, the ceremony of innocence is drowned."*

She stared at him.

"The Second Coming, by Yeats. A fine Irish poet and perhaps something of a prophet. Do you know the poem?"

Gwen shook her head.

He went on softly. *"What rough beast, its hour come round at last, slouches toward Bethlehem to be born?"*

She shivered. "What does it mean?"

"The end of an era. The beginning of something even worse." Every vestige of colour had drained from his boyish face. He looked toward the group at the bar, but his gaze seemed focused very far away. And she could guess where.

"There can't be another war. There won't be."

He turned to her with a look of infinite pity. "If there's one thing I know, it's that there is no limit to the human capacity for evil. And the worst evil is convinced that it is doing good."

Silently, she sipped her brandy, as Father Garrick drank his whisky. The priest's gloom seeped into her and made her wonder what point there was in any of this. Emily was dead and gone, the treasures she had entrusted to her were gone too. Completely gone now.

Realistically, there was no danger now to Emily's reputation, unless Gwen herself wanted to make an issue of it, and why would she?

But in her stubborn inner core, she could not let go of the fear that Emily's death had not been an accident. That could not be shrugged off. It cried out for justice.

So, who had taken the Gold Horseman? It seemed most unlikely to be hotel staff. If it was someone in the tour group, it had to be one of those who had not come to Castro de Carballo. The list was short: The Fairlambs, Letitia, Dorcas, and Father Garrick. But was that necessarily true? When was the last time she checked it?

Michael stood at the bar, coolly watching the others, listening to Amanda spin some wild tale about a sheik offering to buy her from the archaeologist in charge of a dig in Amarna. Something secret lay behind his smile. She had the fanciful notion that he knew exactly what everyone was up to. Sloan with his dubious deals. Fairlamb, with his murky past and suspicious present. Amanda using her seductive powers to lead her admirers into intrigue for some hidden purpose.

"Quite the enigma, isn't he?"

Startled, she turned to see Father Garrick smiling at her. "Who?" Her cheeks grew warm.

He leaned back in the cane chair and regarded her with a speculative look. "Greville. He's a dark horse and no mistake."

"Why do you say that?"

His mouth curved in a small smile. "You may have noticed that people talk to priests, inside and outside the confessional. I've heard a great deal about Michael Greville, one way and another."

She wanted to know, without seeming too curious. "Dorcas tells me he's very respectable."

Garrick burst out laughing. "With all due respect to Miss Dorcas, she has a naïve faith in noblesse oblige."

Gwen felt vaguely offended on Dorcas' behalf. "She's an intelligent woman. It's not fair to dismiss her opinions out of some kind of inverted snobbery."

His expression darkened a little. "I can assure you I have more grounds than that. I've had ample experience of women like Miss Bellamy, trained to produce the future administrators of the Empire, just as the Empire starts to dissolve, and the future Colonial administrators get mowed down en masse in France."

He took a large, angry swig of his whisky and soda.

"Sorry. Please forgive me. Perhaps my wartime experience has left me a little raw and apt to be harsh. I met too many gentlewomen who volunteered for the VAD out of patriotic duty, then fled back to the comforts of the family seat when things got too bloody for them. The same women who handed out white feathers and bullied young boys into needless sacrifice."

"That's so unfair! She doesn't strike me as that kind of woman," Gwen replied, then went on quietly. "And were we not talking of Mr. Greville?"

He suddenly gave her a disarming grin. "We were indeed. I'm afraid it's the Irish in me, spoiling for a fight."

She glanced over at Greville, who caught her eye, then turned his gaze back to Amanda. Did he know they were talking about him?

"So, tell me what you have heard."

"He tells everyone that he's a dealer in rare coins, which is true, but he handles much else besides."

"Oh?" She tried not to sound too eager for anything he could tell her. He looked down into his whisky glass. "Miss Bellamy is correct that he's very well-connected. His most useful connections are in the diplomatic corps, at the very highest levels."

Gwen raised a questioning eyebrow.

"Those ambassadorial pouches are big enough for more than dispatches and paperwork. It's rumoured that he managed to get millions of pounds worth of Romanov jewels out of Russia, just before the government fell. No one knows what happened to the fortune. It certainly didn't help the Romanovs." He glanced up and met her gaze. "Apparently, he specializes in small, portable treasures."

Like an ancient gold statuette, for example. But that still didn't explain how he, or anyone else, could have known where to find it.

Gwen watched Greville put down his glass and saunter out of the bar with not even a backward glance. Amanda kept talking to the other men, but surreptitiously watched him leave. She expected men to fall under her spell, but who was the Svengali here?

She tore her gaze away. What did it matter who Amanda dallied with? What mattered was that Amanda held the only remaining link to the stolen antiquities: the sheaf of photographs taken from the dig site. If she could get hold of those...

Abruptly, Gwen got to her feet. "Thank you for the drink, Father. I'm afraid I have some work to do before dinner," she said and hurried back to her room.

One way or another, she had to get those photographs. But even if she did, who in authority would believe her story? And who would she tell?

158

Chapter Twenty-Four

The hotel had been persuaded to provide an early dinner for their party, in order that they could attend the next special event on the itinerary, a private tour of the cathedral crypt.

After the meal, most of the group returned to their rooms to change into warmer clothes. The nights could still be chilly, and the crypt would be colder still.

Gwen put on a woolly jumper over a heavy knit pinafore dress and was just pulling on her warm lisle stockings when she heard sounds from the next room filtering through the connecting door. The peal of laughter was unmistakably Amanda, while the low rumble of another voice indicated a man.

She had been thinking furiously about how to get hold of the photographs. Somehow, she had to get into Amanda's room when it was empty. If only she didn't have to go on this tour.

The voices continued. Her first instinct was to move away. What was she thinking? Of all the times to be stricken by good manners. Annoyed with herself, she stepped over to the door and pressed her ear to the wooden panel.

"You're asking a hell of a price." The deep voice and American accent were unmistakable.

"This is a hell of an item." Amanda sounded equally tough. Very rare. If you don't want it for your own collection, I'm sure you could sell it in New York at a handsome profit."

"With no provenance? That cuts the value considerably."Oh, come now.

The people you know don't quibble about provenance. They throw fabulous dinner parties and show off their collections to a tight little circle of like-minded friends."

"But if I wanted to sell it to the museum…"

"They wouldn't pay anywhere near the price you'd get elsewhere."

"Nevertheless…" His tone hardened. "I might want to have that option. And besides that, in case I get any questions from Customs. They're getting wise to the tricks. They're searching the bags of people like me."

"Then you shouldn't boast about your tricks the way you did today in front of Fairlamb and Greville."

"Fairlamb's a clapped-out old con man. And Greville…"

"Ow…" Amanda gave a yelp of pain. "Don't do that."

Gwen stiffened. What was happening? The double connecting doors didn't quite meet, and there was a scant quarter-inch crack between them. Through the narrow gap she could see Sloan had Amanda's wrist in a tight grip.

"Are you playing us off against each other, me and Greville? Trying to get the best offer? Maybe he's giving you a little bonus?"

"Don't be disgusting." Amanda twisted away from him, and he moved after her. Gwen lost sight of the two figures.

"This kind of rough stuff doesn't impress me." Amanda was back in control, her voice cold and hard. "Keep it businesslike, or the deal is definitely off."

"I want the provenance.""You won't get it from me. I'm not putting my name to anything that can be traced back to Hunt's dig."

Gwen bit back a gasp at hearing this bald confirmation of her suspicions.

"No one's going to be doing any tracing. I just need documentation from a known archaeologist at a respectable institution. Why can't we still use Temple?"

Gwen shivered.

After a frigid pause, Amanda said, "Haven't you noticed? She's dead."

"That's why it's perfect. No one can ask her any questions."

"God, you're a cold-hearted bastard."

"Look who's talking." Sloan strode across Gwen's narrow field of vision.

"This is what you do, get some college letterhead—I bet that Dorcas character has got some, or that cute little redhead secretary. Get a hold of a typewriter and make it sound official. You can fake her signature. And be sure to date it last year. That should be all I need."

"You're making a lot of assumptions." Her voice shook. Gwen had never heard her afraid before.

There was a long silence. Gwen became aware of her pounding heart and the roar of her own breathing. Surely, they must be able to hear it in the other room.

Finally, Sloan spoke. "Look, if you do it, I'll meet your price."

He sounded so close that Gwen jerked back from the door and almost missed Amanda's quiet words. "All right. It's a deal."

After a moment, she heard the hallway door open and close and the sound of someone walking down the corridor. The room next door fell silent.

Gwen sank down on the bed, her legs shaking. What had been nebulous suspicion now crystallized into certainty. Amanda was selling artefacts stolen from Castro de Carballo. Presumably, the items in the photographs, the items in the parcel Emily had sent to her for safekeeping, the items stolen from the cottage, and the Gold Horseman, stolen from her suitcase. Did Amanda have them all now?

It hit her like a revelation. Of course! She remembered the slight, dark-clad figure running from the cottage, the car roaring away into the night. It must have been Amanda who broke in and took the parcel and Emily's papers.

The theft of the photographs suddenly made sense. Without them, no one could prove the origin of the finds. But she still didn't understand the whole story of how Emily was involved and what she was trying to do by sending the parcel to England.

* * *

It had rained while they were having dinner. When they emerged from the hotel into the broad plaza, they found that even though the rain had stopped, the cobbles still gleamed in the lamplight, and a chill crept into the wet night air. Gwen walked alongside Dorcas amid the ill-assorted procession, picking their way through the puddles across the Plaza Obrador towards the looming cathedral.

The entire group was attending this specially privileged opportunity to see the Crypt and all its treasures. The general public was only admitted for strictly limited glimpses.

Instead of entering through the Portico de la Gloria, Colonel Fairlamb led them around to the south side and up a flight of steps.

"This the Puerta de Platerias." The Colonel announced, stumbling over the Spanish words. "Which means the...uh...the..."

"Which means the Door of the Silversmiths," Amanda said briskly. "Courtesy of the medieval silversmiths union."

At that moment, a young priest opened the door and ushered them inside into the main body of the church. Under the lofty barrel-shaped ceiling, he led them towards the glittering altar, then down a flight of stairs and through a narrow stone corridor into the crypt.

Alice Dixon gasped as they turned a corner into the candlelit sanctuary. Gwen recognized the young priest who had been sent to talk to her about Emily's accident. He caught her eye, then quickly looked away. Perhaps he was worried that she would ask more questions he couldn't answer. But right now, all she could think about was the scene she'd overheard in Amanda's room.

Amanda began talking about the history of the building. Gwen glanced around at the listeners. Franz stood beside Amanda, clutching a sheaf of notes and looking up at her anxiously. Letitia and Dorcas, serious and attentive. Jim Dixon, looking around at the gilded splendor with a lost, unhappy gaze while Alice's worried glance kept sliding over to him.

"In this crypt lies the reason for the cathedral's existence," Amanda began, as she indicated an elaborate silver casket decorated with a classical colonnade, each niche occupied by the figure of a saint.

The Fairlambs stood off to one side. The Colonel stood ramrod straight, but Gwen thought she detected him swaying a little. He'd been drinking wine freely through dinner, and just before they left the hotel, she'd seen him down a generous whisky at the bar.

"The reliquary holds the remains of St. James and two of his followers, Atanasio and Teodoro. After James was declared the patron saint of Spain by the king of Asturias, he became a rallying symbol against the Muslim invasion. This crypt is part of the original ninth-century church, which was destroyed by the Moors."

"How did this come to be a pilgrimage site?" Letitia asked. "It seems an unlikely spot."

A slight frown and a tightening of the mouth were the only sign of Amanda's annoyance. If anyone but Letitia had interrupted her lecture, Gwen suspected that Amanda's impatience would have been less restrained.

"It began when the King of Asturias ordered a pilgrimage in gratitude for St. James' supposed help in pushing back the Moors," Amanda said. "The numbers grew very quickly, likely because Jerusalem, the most popular pilgrim destination, had been lost to the Muslims."

Letitia nodded. Beside her, Elsie Fairlamb looked bored, deliberately ignoring her husband, but making an effort at polite attention. Marion Sloan didn't even try. She had her arms crossed, one foot tapping a faint tattoo on the stone floor. She stared fixedly at Amanda, with an occasional darted look at her husband. The very picture of a woman scorned.

Brett Sloan lounged against a wall, but his gaze flickered around the crypt. Cynically, Gwen wondered if he was estimating what he could get for everything he saw.

I wonder who has the money? Gwen thought suddenly. She'd assumed it was Brett, but perhaps not. Perhaps his trading in stolen artefacts was not just the pursuit of a bored dilettante, but an effort to make his own fortune.

Michael Greville stood in the shadow of a stone pillar, so that she couldn't tell where he was looking. Then, the sudden flare of a nearby candle caught his gaze. His eyes stared directly into hers. They met and held for a long moment before she quickly looked away, feeling intensely exposed.

She was sure he was Amanda's lover. Sloan seemed to think he was a rival bidder for the stolen artefacts. Perhaps he was both. But did his involvement go deeper than that? More and more, she felt sure that Emily's death had not been a simple accident. Greville had been here in Santiago at the time. Could he actually be involved?

She shivered.

"Are you all right, my child?" Father Garrick asked softly from behind her right shoulder. She half-turned and nodded. "Fine. Just a little chill."

When Amanda finished her talk, the group broke up and took turns moving into the cramped space that allowed a closer look at the spectacular silver reliquary.

Garrick moved up beside her and said quietly. "Would you care to stay for the Mass? It will begin in only a few minutes." When she hesitated, he said quickly. "Oh, of course, you are a Methodist. No doubt you would be uncomfortable with this Popish ceremony."

Irritated by this rare sign of prejudice, she said swiftly. "Really, Father, I didn't expect you, of all people, to have such a narrow opinion of my character."

To her surprise, he grinned. "Forgive me for teasing. You have shown yourself to be a remarkably open-minded young woman."

The rest of the group went on ahead. Gwen told Dorcas she was staying for the Mass, which got her a small frown and a brisk, "Very well. I'm sure I hope you enjoy it."

When Dorcas moved away, Gwen turned to Father Garrick with a grin. "I think she disapproves." He grinned back. "You seem quite capable of shrugging off disapproval."

As they walked up the steps into the church, Gwen suddenly realized that it was true. A month ago, Dorcas' obvious displeasure would have unnerved her. Now, she just took it in stride. She must have changed.

They sat halfway down the nave. Gwen looked around to see only a scattering of people waiting for the Mass, like themselves.

Father Garrick had his head bent in prayer. What an unusual man he was. His conversation intrigued and stimulated her, his kindness and compassion made her feel safe in this strange new world she found herself moving through. Had he not been a priest, she could not have talked to him so openly.

Right now, she desperately needed someone to confide in, someone to talk to about Amanda and Brett Sloan. About her suspicions of Michael Greville. She glanced over to see Father Garrick still praying, sliding the rosary through his fingers.

Only one thing held her back. Telling him everything would mean talking about Emily, and as she rehearsed the facts in her mind, they implicated Emily far too deeply in undoubtedly criminal activity.

She became aware that silence had fallen. A few coughs and whispers echoed from the vast barrel-vaulted ceiling. And then the Mass began. She noticed the botafumiero hanging high above the altar, evidently not in use for this service. Up at the front, near the altar, the priests were performing a complicated ceremony and intoning the rite in Latin. She wished she could understand. She had the rudiments of the language, thanks to her father, but she must learn it properly, if she hoped to advance in archaeology.

But what kind of realistic hope was that? The tantalizing prospect of Emily's legacy seemed like a fairy tale. The more she learned, the more it felt like a tainted chalice.

She suddenly became aware of clouds of fragrant incense enveloping the altar. One of the priests was swinging a small silver thurible from a chain.

In her mind's eye, she could see how it must have looked when Emily was found. The botafumiero swinging gently at head height, the rope secured but mysteriously slipped lower than usual. The mortal injury and the tell-tale blood trace on the censer.

The apparent solution of a freak accident was clear and understandable. But given Emily's fears and hints of danger, she couldn't believe in that conveniently swinging censer, or the light smear of blood from a blow savage enough to kill her.

What if it was much simpler? What if the botafumiero was a sensational distraction? What if her murderer had hit her with a heavy but portable object, like the small thurible carried by the priest, and simply transferred some of the blood to the supposed weapon?

She looked around the glittering church with its numerous side chapels.

Once she started to look there were all sorts of possible weapons at hand—candlesticks, heavy plates and vessels, small crucifixes. Her mind raced with conjectures. Above all, it seemed ludicrous that someone could aim the swinging *botafumiero* to accurately hit Emily without her seeing it coming.

Whereas sitting in that secluded spot by the pillar, in a virtually empty church, it would be easy to take her by surprise with a swift blow, quickly smear the big thurible with blood and make an escape.

Chapter Twenty-Five

The tour plan used Santiago as the base from which to explore the northwest. The next expedition would take most of them to Corunna, famed as the launching port for the Spanish Armada and for its role in the Peninsular War. But also famous for its Roman heritage.

The next morning, the group gathered in front of the hotel, awaiting the motor bus.

"I do hope the roads aren't too bad." Dorcas fretted. "So dreadful for one's back."

"Do stop fussing, Dorcas." Letitia snapped. "Just be grateful we're not going. And remember that in our day, we had to take the diligence."

"It is rather charming that before the War, they still had stagecoaches here in Spain. Quite like something from the Old West," Marion Sloan said.

"You wouldn't be so charmed after eight hours bouncing around in an old rattletrap, believe me." her husband said. "The bus takes half the time, and those rubber tires make for a better ride."

Gwen set down her suitcase on the hotel steps. Thank goodness no one had suggested driving. Anything had to be better than that nightmare car trip to Finisterre and back.

"Yes. Thank you, Colonel Fairlamb, for hiring the motor bus," Miss Henderson said to him with a gracious nod. "But when precisely do you expect it to arrive?" Clearly, her patrician impulse to see them off had given way to weary impatience.

At that moment, a fusillade of horn toots announced the appearance of a green and white motor coach coming around the corner.

Loading the bags on top of the coach and strapping them down took another twenty minutes of loud arguing between the driver and his assistant—or was he a sort of conductor, Gwen wondered. Then, finally, they were queuing up to get on.

Amanda stood behind her talking to Michael Greville, then she stopped abruptly, "Oh damn," She turned to go back into the hotel. "I'll be back in a moment."

"May I sit with you, Miss Armstrong?" Franz asked at her elbow.

Before she could reply, Michael Greville stepped closer. "If you don't mind, Franz, I'd like to claim that privilege for myself." He looked down at her with a hint of a smile. "Miss Armstrong and I haven't had much chance to get acquainted. That is, if you don't mind?"

She was too surprised to say anything except "Of course not."

She took a window seat halfway down the cramped aisle, and Michael Greville sank down beside her. She felt intensely aware of his physical presence and a faint masculine scent of soap. He said nothing, making her even more self-conscious.

"Have you been to Corunna before?" she said at last.

"Oh yes, several times."

He fell silent again, crossing his long legs with difficulty in the shallow space between his seat and the back of the one in front.

Amanda appeared at the front of the bus, and glanced around until she fixed on Greville, then shifted her gaze to look directly at Gwen. Her eyes narrowed. After a split-second she refocused on two vacant seats near the front, one beside Father Garrick, the other beside Franz. She sat down next to the priest.

With a sputtering cough, the engine started, and the coach headed out of the centre of Santiago, through the narrow, cobbled streets until it emerged onto a wider open road and headed north toward the rocky hills of Galicia.

Now was her chance to find out more about the mysterious Michael Greville, but Gwen felt tongue-tied and strangely shy. She stared out the window at the passing green hillside.

"I understand you have an interest in becoming an archaeologist," he said.

She turned to look at him and said sharply, "Who told you that?"

"Is it a secret?"

"I'm sorry. I didn't mean to sound rude. It's just that... Well, I didn't think anyone would be interested in that."

"Amanda mentioned it."

"Oh." Why on earth would Amanda be talking about her to Michael? "I understand that you are a dealer in antique coins."

"Among other things. But yes, mainly coins. They're very popular with collectors and much easier to transport than statuary."

"I suppose they'd be easy to smuggle," she said without thinking, then almost winced out loud.

The comment didn't seem to bother him. "Yes, very easy. But I can assure you my business is quite above board." He smiled.

"Of course, I never meant to suggest..." She stumbled for words, her cheeks growing warm. Clearly, she had no gift for subtly extracting information. "I'm sorry."

"No need to apologize. It's a field that lends itself to skullduggery."

She turned to him with an embarrassed smile. "I think smuggling is one of those things people have mixed feelings about. We all love those tales of coastal villages conspiring to avoid the excise men."

"It's true." He nodded. "His Majesty's Customs agents must be the most disliked arm of government. Nevertheless, people risk a lot when they try to avoid paying their due. And, of course, there are people trying to smuggle items they are not entitled to have."

"Like antiquities?"

His eyebrows rose a fraction. "Now, there's a thriving black market. Been going on for thousands of years, since the first tomb robbers. Of course, when they started sending young Englishmen off on the Grand Tour, the craze for bringing back a piece of classical marble, or an Italian painting or two really caught fire."

"But it wasn't always illegal."

"It isn't illegal at all," he said, suddenly serious. "But there are rules. Most countries now have strict controls about what is allowed to be exported.

My own family have a few items that I prefer not to take too close a look at." A satirical smile curved his lips.

His family. Hadn't Miss Henderson said something about his connections to an Earl? She imagined him living in some grand country seat, stuffed with objet d'arts and oil paintings.

"Of course," he went on. "Those things were collected a couple of generations ago. These days, the Grevilles are fearfully upright and law-abiding." There was something very attractive about a man with his advantages who didn't take himself too seriously.

She sighed. Probably rode to hounds and sat on the local bench as magistrates as well.

"When it comes to the antiquities market," he went on. "It was the war which threw everything into confusion. Things have settled down now, but a great deal of art disappeared in the chaos and found its way into private collections."

Avoiding his gaze, she said as she looked out the window, "Why would collectors buy stolen goods?"

"You have to understand that collecting can be a kind of mania." His voice dropped, making her turn toward him. "Did you notice Don Alvarez's attitude to his precious objects? It's a drive for possession. Men like him can't stand to look at something through glass in a museum case unless it's their own museum." His voice became warm and resonant as he held her gaze. "They need to touch it. To hold it. To know it belongs to them."

Her cheeks suddenly burned. Imagination supplied a subtle innuendo. What on earth was she thinking? She cleared her throat. "So, they wouldn't care if the things were stolen."

"No, indeed. In fact, items are often stolen to order."

"I heard a very sad story about a shopkeeper in Bilbao who had a coin collection stolen." She watched for his reaction.

"Really?" His tone cooled. "Did this happen recently?"

"Last year, I think. Gold Roman sesterces."

"No shortage of customers for something like that." The atmosphere had changed. His warm interest had become mere politeness.

She'd mishandled the conversation somehow. But she had to make a stab at getting more information.

"You speak the language so well; do you travel in Spain quite often?" Not the most original line, but it would do.

"Often enough."

"I'm curious as to why you came on this tour. After all, you're so knowledgeable about the country already."

"Why, Miss Armstrong, do you think I should be ejected?" A glimmer of humour returned.

"Of course not. I just think it might be boring for someone like you."

"There's always more to learn. And I had looked forward to Professor Temple's lectures. She had a unique ability to put history and culture in context. To tell a story, not just recite facts."

"It sounds as if you knew her." Would he admit to being at her funeral? Should she confront him about it?

"Not exactly, but I had seen her speak on several occasions in different parts of the world." He gave her an intent look. "Amanda told me you were a protégé of Dr Temple. What a terrible loss that must have been for you."

"Yes." She felt an unexpected sense of emptiness.

"What are your plans now? Will you continue with your studies?"

"In case you hadn't noticed, I'm the secretary, not a student." It came out more bitter than she had intended. "Things have changed. I'll have to see what happens."

"Ah, yes." He leaned back as if he had sensed the conversation was at an end.

Gwen could have kicked herself for being so over-sensitive. Just when some kind of connection to Emily was emerging.

She took a deep breath. "Look, I'm sorry to sound so touchy. Dr. Temple's death hit me really hard. She was a very kind friend. And she also tried to help me get somewhere in life."

Before she knew it, Gwen had told him about her early ambitions and the series of blows that had made it all impossible. Until the day Emily found her spending her lunch hour in the empty College library, sitting at a desk tucked out of sight and reading a tome by Woolley on his Mesopotamian excavations.

Like that day at Hildy's, Gwen found that just talking about Emily to someone sympathetic unleashed memories and reminded her of what she had lost. She found herself so caught up, that she almost told him about the will, before catching herself just in time.

How could she have forgotten his intimacy with Amanda? For all she knew, he was just as involved with the missing artefacts. And his reaction when she spoke of the coin theft had made her think that he already knew all about it. Whatever was going on, he could be in it up to his neck. In fact, he could have had something to do with Emily's death. He'd been on the spot. He'd attended her funeral.

Gwen went cold, and turned to look out of the window, in case the shocking thoughts showed on her face. Dark pine woods enclosed the road on either side, but no signs of habitation. "Do you think we're getting close to Corunna?"

"Nowhere near. We have another three hours to go." But they did pull over a few minutes later, at a small roadside inn, for a euphemistic 'comfort' stop. The primitive comfort provided was questionable, but definitely necessary. Happily, Dorcas had sent along a hamper, and they were glad to dig into sandwiches with the staple filling of Iberian ham.

It was not encouraging to see the driver sit down for a beaker of wine, however to her relief, the conductor took over for the next leg.

When Gwen reboarded, she found Greville seated beside Amanda, while two rows back, Franz looked up at her from a window seat in puppyish expectation. She sank down beside him, dreading three hours of complicated Norse anthropology.

To her relief, he was more interested in talking about their visit to the cathedral crypt the previous day and the history of the sanctuary. He chattered on, as the bus jounced and swayed. As noon approached, the air got warmer, and Gwen felt her attention drifting, her eyelids getting heavy, until she gave in to the urge to close them.

Franz continued his monologue, but it became a babbling river of sound, the odd word popping up like flotsam into her consciousness.

"He told me that fifty years ago...accident with the incense burner...but Herr Greville was there. He knew..."

Her eyes snapped open. "What?" she turned to Franz in a daze. "What did you just say?"

He stared back at her like a frightened rabbit. "I...I was talking about the history of the *botafumeiro*. The ceremony of swinging the censer. I am sorry, I forgot that it would upset you to think about Professor Temple."

"You said something about Mr. Greville."

"I did?"

"About him being there."

His gaze darted around, then stared toward the front of the bus. Three rows ahead, blond curls and Greville's dark hair could be seen.

Franz leaned toward her and said in an agonized whisper, "Please don't mention this."

She lowered her voice. "You must tell me what you know. Mr. Greville was at the church when the accident happened?"

He shook his head vigorously. "No, no. Not when it happened. After."

"What do you mean?"

"When we visited the crypt, I stayed to talk to one of the priests, I asked him about Dr Temple's accident. If it had ever happened before. He told me there had been some. Long time ago. But then something strange. He recognized Herr Greville. Told me he had been asking some questions, the day after the... the accident." He grasped her hand in a painful grip. "Please Fraulein Armstrong, I beg of you, do not mention this. I know you want to find out more, but it can make no difference to your friend."

"Why are you so afraid, Franz?"

"This country is not England. The police can put you in jail, say you are a political subversive. It is dangerous to make a fuss."

The homely figure of speech sounded laughable in the context of being thrown in a Spanish jail, but the young German's terror was real. His hands were shaking.

She extricated her hand from his. "It's all right, Franz. I won't tell anyone what you said."

He let out his breath in a gasp and collapsed against the seat. "Thank you."

Gwen sank back in silence. Wide awake now, she stared at the two heads, the blonde and the dark, leaning close together. Whatever Franz feared, she somehow knew it was not the police.

Chapter Twenty-Six

"The Spanish city of La Coruna, known to the British as Corunna, was built on the site of a castro, or Celtic hill fort, which dates back to at least the 3rd-century BC.

"The Romans reached here by the Second century BC and called the city Brigantium. They built a famous lighthouse to guide ships to safe harbor after braving the tempestuous Bay of Biscay and the sinister rocks where many a vessel had been dashed to pieces.

"After the fall of Rome, many of the population fled, and the Normans made increasing incursions. Over time, it became Corunna, the site of a famous battle where the British defeated Napoleon's forces in the Peninsular War. But still, the lighthouse stood guard, now known as the Tower of Hercules."

Amanda paused in her lecture, standing by the balustrade of the observation deck at the top of the lighthouse. She gestured toward the breathtaking view out over the glittering Atlantic. "For seventeen hundred years, this view has endured. Imagine that. Take a moment to savour this. A truly timeless experience."

Despite all the cares which had been preoccupying her, Gwen felt enraptured. The sun poured down like liquid gold from a cloudless sky, tipping the small indigo waves fretting the glassy sea. The sense of being suspended in time engulfed her. If a Roman centurion walked up the stone stairs in full armour, she would not be surprised.

Shaking off the spell, she watched the rest of the group disperse around the tower to look out over the views of sea and town. She had made a decision, during the last stage of the bus ride. The time for tentative investigation was over. Amanda stood by the balustrade, stacking her pages of notes and tucking them back into a folder.

She held them out to Gwen. "Here. I've made some notes in the margins. If they have a machine at the hotel, get them retyped tonight, if you can."

Gwen took the folder and put it in her briefcase. "Do you have a moment?"

Amanda gave her a quizzical look. "Yes. Is there a problem?"

No one stood close enough to hear them. Gwen said quietly, "I've seen the photographs."

Amanda stiffened almost imperceptibly. "My dear Gwen, what on earth are you talking about?"

"The photographs you took from Professor Hunt's dig site. The photographs of the artefacts someone stole from Emily's cottage."

"What an extraordinary imagination you have. But this is hardly the place to discuss your bizarre fantasies." She edged closer, and Gwen moved back, until she felt the stone balustrade pressing into her hip.

Resisting the urge to look down, she kept her gaze focused intently on Amanda's face. "Where should we discuss it?"

"There's a café near the hotel. La Ronda. Meet me there at seven. We'll have a drink and discuss your dreams. Doctor Freud would have a field day, I'm sure." She swept past her, as Gwen steeled herself to resist a push that would send her over the balustrade to smash her body on the courtyard almost two hundred feet below.

The moment passed and she watched Amanda disappearing down the circular stone stairs. The fear was irrational. Amanda would never do anything so stupid in front of witnesses.

* * *

Gwen waited until five past seven, making sure that Amanda sat alone at the café table. She looked around the plaza but saw no signs of Franz, Greville, or any other member of the tour.

Steeling herself, she walked over and sat down, facing Amanda across the small table. A glass of red wine sat in front of each of them.

"I ordered you some Rioja," Amanda said. "That's what I'm having."

"No, thank you."

She sighed impatiently. "For God's sake, don't be such a prig. It might not be Beaujolais premier cru, but it's not poisoned!"

"I'll take your word for it." After a moment, Gwen picked up the glass and took a sip. The wine tasted astringent but no different to any of the others she had tasted. That gibe about poison made her feel foolish, which was clearly Amanda's intention.

Well?" she said at last. "Tell me more of this extraordinary story."

"The night we spent at the dig site—I saw you take those photos from the filing cabinet. The ones which show the artefacts that were stolen from there last year."

"Leaving aside the question of what you were doing prowling around at night, one must ask how you know what the subjects were in the photos."

"I opened your briefcase and looked." She admitted it boldly, but nevertheless felt embarrassed to admit to snooping.

Amanda put down her glass, sat back, and crossed her arms. "Now, how on earth could you know what they were?"

"From Dr Hunt's description, and...because I saw them."

"You saw the stolen items? Where?" Amanda looked at her intently.

"They were in a package delivered to Emily's cottage, then stolen again the same night." She remembered the frightening sound of shattering glass and the dark figure fleeing across the garden. "But I think you know that."

"Clever of you to work that out." Amanda still leaned back, apparently unconcerned. The corners of her mouth curved in a small smile. "But aren't you rather ignoring how the parcel got to England?" She gave Gwen a pitying stare. "You're a clever girl, Gwen. Surely, you can see what this adds up to. Your sainted benefactor was the one who actually had possession of stolen goods and sent them out of Spain. What does that suggest to you?"

"I'm not sure what her intentions were, but I know Emily sent them for safekeeping. She would never steal."

Amanda sighed and rolled her eyes. "You're very sure of that, aren't you?

But how well did you really know her? A year of being her adoring protégé hardly permits an understanding of her morals."

"Emily loathed antiquities thieves. She said they robbed the world of knowledge and stole people's cultures."

"But the facts contradict you." She waved at the passing waiter and ordered another glass of wine. He looked inquiringly at Gwen, who shook her head.

"Frankly, I'm not sure why you are telling me all this," Amanda said. "Am I supposed to confess something? Are you going to the authorities? If so, you're asking for a world of trouble. Emily is dead, but you're very much alive and liable to be arrested for receiving stolen property. Except of course, you can't produce any evidence aside from some photographs which I borrowed from Professor Hunt." She sighed. "So you see, darling. It's quite hopeless. You might as well have another drink."

The waiter placed a full glass in front of her, and she ordered another for Gwen. From her bag lying on the table, she extracted a compact and powdered her nose. "Must protect the complexion in these foreign climes."

"What about the Gold Horseman?"

"The what?"

Embarrassed, Gwen realized she didn't know the proper name to call the object. "The thing someone stole from my room, from my suitcase. Was it you who took it?"

"Perhaps you mean the fibula stolen from Professor Hunt's safe? The one in the picture you showed to Franz? A photo that was definitely not taken in Spain, so you must have photographed it in England, when you had possession of those stolen artefacts."

Amanda picked up her glass and took a deep draught of the ruby liquid. "Really, my dear, I wouldn't mention it if I were you. After all, Emily was there when the items were found, and they disappeared not long after she left. That could be considered suspicious, especially if you tell anyone that she sent them back to you in England, in a parcel. And now you're saying that you brought the most valuable item back here with you in your luggage. Then, it subsequently disappeared. How *extraordinary*." Her words burned with cynicism.

A tide of despair washed over Gwen. How naïve and foolish had she been to think she could surprise Amanda into some kind of confession.

She stood up abruptly. "Emily didn't do anything wrong. I'm sure of that."

"Unfortunately, we'll never know, will we?"

Retreating back to the hotel, Gwen went straight to her room and sat looking out of the window, or rather, she stared out toward the distant sea without seeing anything except failure. Without tangible evidence, she couldn't prove Amanda's involvement in the theft, but the woman had virtually admitted it.

She felt a sudden keen awareness of being very much alone. Hundreds of miles away from friends and family. *Vulnerable.* A very convincing case could be made against her as Emily's accomplice.

What she needed was an ally, but who could she trust? No one in Corunna, that was certain. Franz might have some sympathy for her, but he was Amanda's creature through and through. The Sloans were unapproachable; the Dixons might be nice people, but she couldn't imagine telling them her story. It would sound like a tall tale. As for the Fairlambs, she couldn't trust them after hearing what Hildy had to say.

Hildy! She felt a surge of hope. But Hildy was back in Bilbao. Gwen sighed. They'd return there eventually, but she needed someone to talk to now. There was Father Garrick, of course, but she needed help from someone with influence. Letitia Henderson would be her best bet, but Letitia had stayed behind in Santiago. When they returned tomorrow, she'd go straight to her and tell her everything she'd found out. The thought gave her a small measure of comfort.

In the meantime, she had better try to go on as usual. She did have work to do. The hotel reading room had a typewriter, so like a good secretary, she spent the next two hours typing up Amanda's amended notes from Corunna and the lecture at Finisterre. Then, she requested dinner on a tray in her room. She had no desire to see anyone. Feeling exhausted, she changed and settled down for an early night.

The hotel was old, the room cavernous and only dimly illuminated. Needing fresh air, she opened the casement window a little, felt a cool breeze, and heard the mingled evening sounds of the town: rolling carriage wheels on cobbles and the sounds of laughter and talk in the staccato, mysterious Spanish rhythm. Looking for something to read, she dug into her suitcase and pulled out *The Ancient Monuments of Northern England*, a slim volume she had found on the bookshelf in Emily's cottage. There was Emily's name inscribed on the title page in her familiar hand. The sight gave her a stab of pain.

Remembering Hildy's stories, she turned to the section about Corstopitum. Emily had once mentioned working with Leonard Woolley on the first professional excavation of the Roman fort site, but somehow, she had never gone into detail about her time there. As was often the case, their conversations digressed into other years, other digs, far away from that English summer of 1906.

The photographs showed stones and relics, but no people, nothing of what she really longed to see.

A knock on the door startled her. It sounded again. She got up and stood by the door. "Who is it?"

"We need another chat."

Gwen opened the door to see Amanda leaning against the frame. She had changed into a flowing black slip, topped by a dramatic scarlet kimono with matching beaded slippers.

She hoisted a bottle of gin in one hand. "You wouldn't believe how much it cost to get this from the barman."

"What do you want?"

Amanda shouldered her way into the room. "We didn't finish our conversation."

"Oh, but I think we did."

Amanda set the bottle down on the table by the window. "Tooth glasses? There should be two on the sink."

Gwen shut the door and got the glasses. What did Amanda want? It might be worthwhile to find out.

Amanda poured the gin. Gwen took hers and sat on the only chair, an ancient and uncomfortable bentwood armchair by the window.

"Now let me tell you a story," Amanda began. "About how a woman can use her wits to get ahead in this big, bad world." She sat down on the bed and plumped up a pillow, took out her cigarette case, extracted one and lit it, before leaning back, inhaling deeply, and blowing out a plume of blue smoke. "Believe it or not, I used to be an idealistic young girl. I grew up in a family that worshipped intellect and learning but had the benefit of hardheaded ancestors who accrued more than their fair share of earthly goods. Of course, I took it for granted. I went to university, dreaming of financing my own explorations, discovering another Troy.

"And then my father died." She took a deep drag of the cigarette. "And I discovered it to be all an empty shell, built on a crumbling foundation of debt and unpaid mortgages. My elder brother Stephen had been killed on the Somme, and so young Gerald got everything. He sold off the townhouse and some of the land. Managed to save the estate, to which he retreated to live the life of a country squire." She toyed with the cigarette. "Did I mention that father was famous for his support of women's suffrage, for equal education, for every radical cause you could name? But when it came to his own daughter..." She ground the cigarette into the ashtray on the bedside table. "You see, he knew how bad things were. He changed his will after the war, made sure that Gerald got whatever could be salvaged from the wreckage. For me—he left the advice that with my beauty and brains, I could be sure of a good marriage to secure my future."

Gwen felt an involuntary surge of sympathy. "I don't suppose you were impressed." She knew what it felt like to be bitterly let down.

"To put it mildly. Papa was content to see me sell myself to some brainless sprig of the aristocracy, or a social-climbing captain of industry."

There had to be a reason for Amanda sharing her tale of dispossession. "So, what did you do? I assume this is leading up to something."

She smiled. "By that time, I was a graduate student, working with Flinders Petrie. I saw other women in the field prostrating themselves before the male professors like servile handmaidens, desperate for opportunity and attention. I met Gertrude Bell before she went off to sort out the Near East and envied her fortune as much as I admired her fearlessness. But I couldn't

181

see a model for what I wanted to be, except it wouldn't be some dowdy frump grateful to be washing the potsherds."

Gwen gave an involuntary smile. The sainted Gertrude would not have cared for *that* description.

Curious despite herself, she asked, "What answer did you come up with?"

"It was in Paris, I was visiting my Uncle Jack, the family black sheep. He took me to a party at the home of this obscenely rich man, who showed me what he called his cabinet of curiosities. It was a secret room filled with the most amazing examples of Scythian gold objects. Absolutely dazzling. It rivalled any museum I had ever seen. And I was quite sure he hadn't come by it in an above-board fashion. Then I met his 'finder' as he called him, a young man who seemed quite taken with me. I asked Jack not to mention my profession. I was already thinking that there had to be a way to render myself independent, while pursuing my scholarly interests."

"So you became a thief."

She shook her head with a tolerant smile. "Why is it more virtuous to put beautiful things on a museum shelf to gather dust, than to put them in the hands of people who will treasure and care for them, who will really appreciate them?"

Gwen shook her head. "That's just a cheap justification for stealing."

"Oh, nonsense! Do you know what I hate about most archaeologists? They are utterly blind to beauty. They care more about their cracked old pots and primitive arrowheads than the intricate lacework of a Celtic gold bracelet. They look for fossilized corn and wonder what the peasants ate. How unutterably boring!"

There was no denying her passion. Gwen felt a twinge of guilt, knowing she had sometimes felt that way herself. "Why are you telling me all this?"

"For some strange reason, I've taken a liking to you. Even with your deplorable accent and your uninspiring clothes, you're one of nature's aristocrats. You're intelligent and ambitious, and you want to better yourself." She topped up her gin. "I can understand Emily taking you under her wing. She knew quality when she saw it." She sighed. "Such a shame about Emily."

"That's the first time you've shown any real compassion towards her." A touch of acid crept into Gwen's voice.

Amanda gave a sardonic laugh. "Don't go by appearances, dear. I learned long ago to put up the façade I wanted others to see. I don't bare my soul to anyone. What happened to Emily was a dreadful accident. It also put a serious spanner in the works of our operation."

Gwen caught her breath. "What do you mean, exactly?"

"Look, I think it's time to put our cards on the table. You deserve to know what Emily was up to."

"Up to?" Had she been hopelessly naïve? Perhaps Emily had really been the idol with feet of clay.

"It all started a few years ago, not long after I met...after that day in Paris with Uncle Jack. It turned out that he knew a fair few collectors and on my travels that year in Greece and Egypt I was able to send some choice little pieces his way."

"You stole them."

"Certainly not." She shrugged. "Let's just say I gave some of the workmen an incentive to pass on small, valuable finds to me. I outbid the archaeologists."

"You haven't said how Emily comes into it."

"Patience, darling. I'm getting to that. I met her at a conference in Oxford where she was giving a talk. I made rather a point of meeting her because I knew she'd be useful to me." She caught Gwen's expression and laughed. "Oh, come on. We all do it, if we're honest. Anyway, it was clear at Oxford that Emily knew every eminent archaeologist and that all the most important dig sites and museums would welcome her, no questions asked. It was absurdly easy to get information from her about the most rare, valuable, and lightly guarded ancient treasures she'd run across in her travels. After a while, I asked her to bring back parcels from the continent for me, fragile things, presents from friends who didn't want to trust the post."

Gwen felt ashamed of doubting Emily, even for a moment. "You used her. You got information out of her and gulled her into smuggling for you. It's despicable."

Amanda shrugged. "It worked well, at first. A harmless, elderly female academic goes through customs with never a second look. Her innocence was also her shield."

"You said, *at first*. What happened?"

"I'm not sure. Somehow, she got wind of what was going on."

For the first time in their conversation, Gwen knew Amanda wasn't telling the complete truth. "You mean, she threatened to tell the authorities."

She sidestepped the question. "It was a little awkward, but once everything was explained to her, she started to see reason."

"I don't believe you!"

"After all, she was nearing retirement. I persuaded her to see it as a way to earn a little nest egg."

"But…" Gwen stopped. Emily had no need of a nest egg.

Amanda looked her up and down. "You could earn a little nest egg yourself. Of course, you don't have Emily's connections, but you could prove very useful."

Gwen shook her head. How predictable. The inducement, combined with the veiled threat. "And what if I'm not interested? Will I end up like Emily?"

"For heaven's sake! You make it sound as if something sinister happened to her, when it was just a dreadful accident."

But what about the parcel, and that strange letter? *A series of untoward episodes that have left me uneasy…*

Amanda had drunk a lot of gin. She lolled back against the pillow and sipped from her glass, but there was nothing relaxed about her expression. "I'm not sure you realize what a very precarious position you're in. I told you already that there's no evidence connecting anyone to the Castro de Carballo items except Emily and you."

"But I don't have them any longer. So that's an empty threat." Her defiant attitude didn't fool either of them.

Amanda ignored her protest. "If you have any notion of pursuing a career in the field, I'm in the position to help you in the same way Emily helped you."

"You're not exactly at her level, though, are you?"

Amanda narrowed her eyes. "Is there any particular reason you're being deliberately offensive? Because it's rather foolish of you."

"Perhaps I'm just tired of kowtowing."

Amanda sighed. "Well, I will give you points for courage. That's one of the reasons I'd rather recruit you than get you into trouble. You can think on your feet, and you won't be slapped down." She lurched to her feet and picked up the half-empty bottle. "You've got until midnight to let me know if you're interested. Think very seriously about my offer. It won't be repeated."

Chapter Twenty-Seven

"What do you mean the bus will be late!" Fairlamb loomed over the terrified desk clerk, red-faced and furious.

"Beg pardon, *Senor*, he sent a boy to say he was delayed." The small man cowered behind his counter, waving a crumpled note. "It will be here at ten."

The group sat collected in the hotel foyer beside their suitcases. At least, most of them. A quick glance told Gwen that Amanda and the Sloans hadn't come down yet.

"Ah, Miss Armstrong," Mrs. Fairlamb hurried toward her. "Professor Spenser wants you to collect some books left in her room."

It was on the tip of her tongue to say Professor Spenser could bring her own books down. "Is she still at breakfast?"

"Oh, no. She left an hour ago with the Sloans." She bit off the words. In her well-bred way, Elsie Fairlamb was clearly incensed. "They hired a car, as did Mr. Greville. I'm afraid the bus didn't quite suit them." Evidently, she took their decision as an affront to her husband's arrangements.

"I see," Gwen said. "That's an early start." Especially given the amount of gin Amanda had put away last night.

After their talk, she had lain awake until the early hours, wondering how to use Amanda's offer to her advantage. Was it possible to convince her that she might accept? Or should she go ahead and tell all to Letitia? She was just as happy not to face either of them yet.

The bus didn't come until eleven, so they didn't reach Santiago until after five. Weary from the hours of rough travel and agonizing over what to do,

Gwen desperately wanted a bath and a rest before dinner. However, she had finally decided to confide in Letitia after all and knew she couldn't put it off any longer.

After a quick wash and brush up, she hurried to Letitia's suite and knocked on the door. Dorcas opened it. "Gwen! You're back." Her face looked drawn and anxious.

"I'd like to speak to Miss Henderson."

"Well, I'm not sure…" She looked over her shoulder into the room, then turned back to Gwen. "Come in."

Letitia sat on a couch near the window with a book on her lap. She set it on a low table in front of her and indicated a chair facing her. "Please sit down." She turned to Dorcas. "You can leave us."

Her impassive expression and icy manner struck a chill in Gwen. Something was *very* wrong. "I wanted to talk to you about something important," Gwen began. "But I'm not sure how to start."

"Really." Letitia's voice had a freezing edge. "Best just to begin then."

"It's about Emily. I've found out some things…" Gwen hesitated.

"For Heaven's sake," she said impatiently. "Spit it out, girl!"

Gwen took a deep breath. "You know what Emily said in her letter… Now I'm more and more certain that her death was no accident. She'd been tricked into something… something criminal."

Letitia raised an eyebrow. "Criminal? In what way?"

Now, she had no alternative but to plunge in. "Stealing antiquities from digs and dealers. Smuggling them into England."

The anger in Letitia's eyes was unmistakable. "You're talking about one of my oldest friends. A woman of unimpeachable integrity. This is a disgraceful slur against a woman who went out of her way to help you, and moreover, is not here to defend herself. Not that she should have to. What you're saying is not just insulting, but absurd."

Gwen leaned forward urgently, willing her to understand. "She didn't do it deliberately! She would have died rather than…" She gulped, her mouth dry. "I told you, she was tricked, she had no idea, until…until somehow she found out."

Letitia's face appeared carved in stone. "And how did *you* find out about this... story."

"From the woman who got her involved in this crime. From Amanda Spenser."

"Dr. Spenser?" Letitia stood up and turned toward the window, her shoulders sagging, abandoning her usual ramrod posture. "I am so disappointed, Gwen. Emily deserved better from you."

The disillusionment in her voice gave Gwen a deep pang of sadness. "Believe me, I hate to be the one telling you this. But you must know the truth."

Letitia turned back to face her. "But which truth, Miss Armstrong? I must warn you that Dr. Spenser has told a very different tale."

"Dr Spenser?" Her thoughts reeled. "What did she say?"

Not a shred of sympathy could be seen in the other woman's grim face. "She revealed a sadly plausible story. Some arrangement with one of the young men at Dr. Hunt's dig. Facilitating illegal trade in valuable finds, not to mention an illicit liaison. All apparently confirmed by Mr. Heider."

"What?" Gwen said faintly. It felt as if the ground suddenly disappeared from beneath her feet, as if she'd fallen into deep water and begun to sink. "But I don't know any of the young men at Dr. Hunt's dig, not for smuggling or...or anything," She protested. "Miss Henderson, how could you believe it of me?"

Letitia clasped her hands together in an agonized gesture, betraying raw emotion for the first time. "Frankly, I don't know what to believe."

"Whatever Dr. Spenser might have said, I had nothing to do with this scheme," Gwen insisted. "But I've been trying to find out what really happened. Emily was tricked into helping them through her tendency, to believe the best of people. I think that she found out that something untoward was going on, and it led to her death."

"Surely, you're not implying that Dr. Spenser had anything to do with Emily's accident?" She rapped out the words with remorseless certainty.

"Please just listen to me," Gwen pleaded.

"Miss Armstrong, your motives may not be malicious, but I cannot believe these accusations. Dr. Spenser's family are old friends of mine, and I know she could not be mixed up in anything questionable. However, I realize that Emily's death has been a terrible shock and a deep disappointment to your hopes. I could see that you resented Dr. Spenser stepping in." Sorrow shadowed her face.

Gwen felt a wave of heat rise into her cheeks. "That's not what this is about at all," she insisted.

"This situation is quite untenable," Letitia cut in. "I cannot allow it to go on, But I don't wish to be unfair." Her expression softened a fraction. "I can see that you believe what you are telling me, however mistaken you may be. However, for me, one consideration is paramount—the reputation of the school must not be compromised."

She turned to where the communicating door stood ajar. "Dorcas! Come here, please."

Dorcas rushed into the room in her outdoor clothes, her face flushed, with a sheaf of papers in her hand.

"I am afraid I must send you home." Miss Henderson nodded at her companion. "Dorcas has your train ticket to Vigo and funds that will cover the cost of a steamship back to Plymouth. You will be leaving immediately. Your salary is paid up to the end of this month. When we return, I will give you a letter of reference. With your abilities, I'm sure you will be able to secure another good position."

"You're sacking me?" Gwen felt her throat thicken and tears spring to her eyes. "This is so unfair."

"I'm afraid there's no alternative. I must do what's right for Seathorne." Letitia's crisp tone softened a fraction. "Dorcas will accompany you in a taxi to the station. She has already had your luggage taken to the foyer."

Letitia Henderson stood immobile, as tall and rigid as a marble column. "I'm very sorry to have ended our association." She did not offer her hand but gave a regal nod. "Goodbye, Miss Armstrong."

Back in her room, Dorcas watched silently as Gwen packed up her overnight bag again and put on her coat and hat.

They walked down the staircase and Gwen prayed they wouldn't see any other member of the tour group. She felt utterly humiliated. All the fire had gone out of her, leaving a cold, empty feeling inside.

In the taxi, she looked out the window at the passing wagons, the laden donkeys, the peasants with their bundles, and the smartly dressed couples perhaps going to some dark restaurant. This foreign world she had briefly been a part of.

At last, she mustered up the energy to turn to Dorcas and ask the miserable question. "What could I have done to convince her?"

Dorcas looked away. "Nothing, I'm afraid. It's very delicate. The most important thing to Miss Henderson is protecting the college."

"But how does ignoring the truth protect Seathorne? What lies has Amanda been telling her?"

Dorcas shook her head. "I really can't say anything. Miss Henderson would be most upset to know I was gossiping."

Gwen realized that the older woman's livelihood rested on the good graces of her employer and had a sudden vision of how precarious life could be for someone elderly, poor, and alone. After all, she had youth and energy on her side. Even if, right at this moment, it all felt dark and hopeless.

She patted the other woman's hand. "You've been very kind to me, Dorcas. This must be very difficult for you."

"Oh, Gwen, I will miss you!" The blue eyes swam with tears. "It's all so unfair! That wretched hussy!" She suddenly stopped, as if realizing she had said too much.

"It's all right. I can guess who you mean." What a fool she had been to be taken in by Amanda's charade. That farcical pretence of inviting Gwen to participate in her crimes had merely been an attempt to find out what she knew. Amanda must have guessed what her next move would be. No doubt, the car had already been hired in order to get back ahead of her and get to Letitia first.

The taxi arrived at the station.

"Just a moment, driver." Dorcas handed Gwen a large envelope. "There's a train ticket and the steamship fare and enough money to get you back home." She grasped her hand tightly. "I'll write to you when we get back. I want to know that you'll be all right."

"Of course, I will. But Dorcas…"

"Yes."

"Do *you* believe me?"

Dorcas nodded her head rapidly. "Of course, I do. Emily was a brilliant woman, well-travelled and more knowledgeable about the past than anyone I've ever known. But she could be terribly naïve in some ways." She sighed. "You're so young; you might not have seen that in her. She could be quite dazzling, but it's not hard to imagine her being taken in by someone who seemed to share her enthusiasms."

"Amanda."

"Yes, well…" Dorcas' gaze shifted away.

"I suppose I shouldn't be surprised that Letitia would believe her stories."

Dorcas winced. "Amanda can be very plausible. And Letitia's known her family since she was a child."

"And they belong to the same class," Gwen added cynically.

"As do I," Dorcas said quietly, "But I believe you." She looked at her wristwatch. "You'd better go, the train leaves in ten minutes."

Feeling wretched, she turned and entered the dark cavern of the station. A hooting whistle echoed in the stygian depths as the train for Vigo pulled up to the platform where Gwen stood waiting with her suitcase. A porter whisked away her trunk to the baggage car. She climbed up the steps into the carriage and began walking down the corridor, looking for an empty compartment. At least Letitia had the grace to get her a first-class ticket. Or perhaps she had Dorcas to thank for that.

Unexpectedly, a lump rose in her throat, and sudden tears sprang to her eyes. The unfairness of it all! A wave of hopelessness washed over her, and she sagged against the wood panel of the compartment. How could she have imagined that Letitia would take her word against Amanda? Why would anyone pay attention to her?

She slid open the compartment door and stepped in, taking one last look out the window through blurred eyes, at the colourful placards lining the platform, advertising the charms of travel to the tourist haunts of Spain.

Sailing in San Sebastian, flamenco and orange trees in Seville, bullfights in Bilbao.

Bilbao. She swiped at her eyes and took a deep, shaky breath. Bilbao! A shrill whistle sounded, accompanied by a loud, incomprehensible shout. A shudder ran through the carriage as the engine gathered steam.

Suddenly, Gwen made a dash for the carriage door. A porter exclaimed as she jumped back down onto the platform. Only one person in Spain might possibly be on her side, and she needed to see her as soon as possible.

Chapter Twenty-Eight

I sabella shook her head again and repeated, *"La Señora Scott no está aquí. Ella esta en San Sebastian."*

Gwen's whole body sagged in dismay. It hadn't occurred to her that Hildy might be away. San Sebastian was many miles down on the coast. She hadn't enough money to travel there in the hope of tracking Hildy down.

"When will the Senora be back?" At the maid's uncomprehending look, she resorted to the phrasebook again, quickly leafing through the pages. *"Cuando se volvera?"*

Isabella had one floury hand on the door, obviously anxious to shut it and get back to her baking. *"La proxima semana."*

Another week! She heaved a weary sigh. *"Gracias."*

Hefting up her suitcase, she made her way back down the stairs to the cobbled street. The first-class ticket to Vigo had only got her a second class to Bilbao, on a train that stopped at every halt and crossing along the way. After a night of sitting up in a crowded carriage, every joint and muscle ached. A long and jouncing ride to Portugalete in a crowded tram had not helped. But she had no money to waste on carriages now.

They remembered her at the hotel, where she took the cheapest room available. That evening, she carefully counted out her money. Setting aside enough to get home, she could just barely afford to stay here another week.

Unless…. She pulled out everything from her suitcase that had any value. Her good leather handbag, the thin gold-plated wristwatch that Gran had left her. She opened a small velvet bag, pulled out a single string of pearls, and fingered the smooth, lustrous beads.

Oh, Mum. Why did you have to die? Over seven years now, but the memory of that awful night never faded. She would give anything to feel her mother's comforting arm around her shoulders and hear her gentle, encouraging voice.

Warm tears spilled down her cheeks, and she held the pearls to her lips. *No.* Whatever else she pawned, it wouldn't be these.

* * *

"Mr. Stevens will see you now." The sleek young man at the Consulate front desk waved toward the stone staircase. "Turn right at the top. First door."

Gwen hurried up the steps. The consulate had the power to get things done that were impossible for her. They could insist the police reinvestigate Emily's death and the theft from the Castro de Carballo dig site. Couldn't they? She really didn't know exactly what a consul could do in a foreign country, but they were certainly supposed to help British travellers in trouble.

She knocked at the first door as instructed.

"Come." A middle-aged man sat behind an enormous mahogany desk. Presided might be a better word. "How can I help you, Miss...?"

"Armstrong. Gwen Armstrong." She took a seat across from him. "It's about a very serious matter...." She stopped as he held up a hand. He was filling in some kind of form.

His pen nib scratched slowly across the paper. Finally, he placed the densely written page in his 'Out' box, took another form from a drawer, and wrote something at the top of the page.

Finally, he looked up. "Address in Bilbao?"

It took an age to go through every detail demanded by His Majesty's representative before he would deign to hear the reason she had come to see him.

"It's about the death of Emily Temple," The words rushed out in a spate. "She was killed in Santiago de—"

"Yes, yes," he said impatiently. "We know all about that. It was dealt with by our people over there very expeditiously. Thankfully, fatal accidents of that sort rarely happen to British travelers. Rather complicated case that, but it was all taken care of."

"But you don't understand. It's possible that it wasn't an accident. And there's more to it. Theft and smuggling of antiquities and..."

"Good heavens, young woman, what are you talking about?" He glared at her. "You'd better explain yourself. In detail. First of all, what is your connection with the deceased?"

Gwen took a deep breath. "I'm a secretary at Seathorne College where Emily, I mean Professor Temple, worked." She paused with a sigh. "At least, I was until yesterday."

She told him an edited version of the story Amanda had told her, emphasizing Emily's innocence and the hint in her last letter that she felt threatened.

He laboriously wrote down every word, making her pause every sentence or so in order to get caught up. "And this Professor Spenser, what is her full name?"

"Amanda Spenser."

"Spenser with an S?"

Gwen nodded.

"One of the Suffolk Spensers?"

"I...I'm not sure. I think that's where she's from."

He frowned. "Good Lord! I think I went to school with her brother, Gerald." He shook his head.

Holding up a hand to stop her speaking, he continued writing for another minute or so. The scratching of the fountain pen was the only sound in the stuffy room, with its clutter of dark Victorian furniture. The Consul's frown got deeper.

He looked up at her at last. "Well, Miss Armstrong. This will have to be looked into most carefully. *Most* carefully. These are very serious accusations." He stared at her in silence until she realized that she was being dismissed.

Gwen got to her feet. "So, you *are* going to do something?"

He gave her a cold stare, took off his spectacles, and polished them with his handkerchief. "We will send a message to you at your hotel after we have investigated these…claims."

"When? How soon?"

His gaze even chillier, he replaced the spectacles on the bridge of his nose. "Matters like this are unpredictable. But I should imagine that, in a day or so, we can determine the proper course of action."

"Thank you," she said uncertainly.

He nodded. "Please close the door on your way out," then bent his head and began reading over the notes he had just taken.

Her footsteps echoed loudly on the marble as she went down the stairs, her spirits so much lower than on her arrival. As she told the consul her story, it had struck her own ears as utterly far-fetched.

Somehow, she had to stay long enough to see Hildy. Something about her sympathetic commonsense made Gwen feel that she, of all people, would be on her side.

After her accounting exercise of the night before, she knew that finding a pawn shop had to be her priority. But how to find one? Then she realized there was one place she could try.

* * *

The proprietor of the *Casa de Antiquedades* was just locking his door when Gwen turned the corner and saw him.

"Senor!" she called out as she hurried down the narrow street.

He turned to look, peering intently. His look of confusion changed to recognition as she got closer.

"Senorita! How nice to see you again." His little monkey face wrinkled in a broad smile.

"Oh dear, are you closing for the day?"

"Si, si, but…did you wish to buy something?"

Her cheeks burned with embarrassment. "No. Quite the opposite, I'm afraid."

He looked at her intently, then patted her hand in a paternal gesture. "I think you are in need of some help."

She nodded.

He put the key back in the lock and turned it. "Come in then and share a glass of sherry with me and tell me all about it."

As they sat at the little table again and sipped from the tiny, elegant glasses, she told him an edited version of the truth. That there had been trouble with her employer who had discharged her. That she needed to stay for at least another week until Dr. Temple's great friend Mrs. Scott returned, who might be able to employ her, but that her funds were running low.

She opened her bag and took out the gold wristwatch. "I thought you might know where I could find a pawn shop."

He took the watch and examined the delicate case, then turned it over. "*To Doris, with love,*" he read, then lifted his gaze to her.

"It belonged to my grandmother," she said. "A wedding gift from my grandfather."

"This is a very fine piece. He had good taste."

She nodded. "He was a bit of a rogue, actually. Too fond of the cards. By the end, Gran didn't have much left...except this. She gave it to me before she died."

"And now you are going to pawn it?"

Shame welled up in her. "I don't know what else to do. If I can't raise some money, I'll have to go home, but I can't until—"

"Until you see this, Mrs. Scott, yes." He took another sip of the sherry. "I do know a pawnbroker, but I would not send him any friend of mine. He is not exactly, shall we say, scrupulous? He would give you a fraction of what this is worth and I'm afraid it would not be there when you went back to redeem it." He shook his head. "No, I cannot allow you to do that."

He poured them each another glass of sherry, then got to his feet. "*Uno momento, por favor.*"

He disappeared behind the velvet curtain at the back of the shop and returned a few moments later. He handed her a small envelope. Mystified, she peered inside to see a sheaf of banknotes.

"I think you have not told me the complete truth about why you need to stay here." He stilled her protest with an admonishing finger. "But I can tell that it must be important. I also know that any friend of Professor Temple is my friend. It was a pleasure to talk of her with you, and I could tell that you were very fond of her. She was a great lady. So I am happy to lend her friend some money that will take away her worry."

She didn't know what to say. "That is so...so incredibly generous of you. Of course, I'll pay it back as quickly as I can." She picked up the watch and tried to hand it to him. "Please take this as a surety."

He waved it away with an offended expression. "One does not ask friends for sureties. It is clear that you share Miss Temple's honourable nature."

The mention of honour stabbed at her conscience. In all her innocence, Emily had been unwittingly responsible for the loss of this man's greatest treasure. The thought made Gwen more determined than ever that the real criminals should be made to pay. She shouldn't neglect the opportunity to discover more information about the coin theft. Perhaps she could help restore his property.

She told him that she had discovered his shop through Emily's diary. "I wonder if she told other people about your wonderful establishment."

He gave a little smile of indulgence. "Perhaps. But no one has spoken of her as you did. Many Americans come here, not so much the English. They think Bilbao means steel and coal and shipbuilding. Like your Glasgow or Newcastle." A thought sparked in his eyes. "But wait. There was one English visitor last year who was unusual. He could have been a friend of Senorita Temple. Very educated. His Spanish was excellent. He was interested in some of my Roman glassware and also the coins. Sadly, I had nothing. It was not too long after the robbery."

"What was he like?"

"He said he was a dealer, but...." He shook his head. "He did not seem like a dealer to me, more like an academic, perhaps.... A man who had been to the best schools. He had the aristocratic bearing, tall, dark, distinguished."

"An older man?"

He shook his head. "Oh, no. Not a boy, but perhaps in his thirties. We talked for a long time about history, art, politics… Yes, a most interesting man."

It sounded so much like…. But the thought was ridiculous. The description could fit thousands of Englishmen. "I don't suppose you remember his name?"

He shrugged. "Alas, I do not think it arose in conversation." He frowned. "Which is strange, come to think of it. The English are usually so punctilious about introductions. But perhaps to him, I was a mere shopkeeper."

Gwen bid Senor Ochoa farewell, repeating her profuse thanks for his generosity and vowing to pay him back as soon as she possibly could. He had given her enough to stretch her existing funds to cover at least two weeks' expenses. Now, all she needed was to find out what the consulate intended to do about her information.

* * *

The answer came sooner than expected. Taking the tram back to Portugalete, she arrived at the hotel to find a message waiting for her.

With an expression that bordered on distaste, the desk clerk handed her a folded note. She opened it to read: *Miss Gwendolyn Armstrong is required to present herself at the British Consulate at 9 a.m. on the 18th of June, 1928.*

It read like an order, rather than an invitation.

Chapter Twenty-Nine

"I don't think you understand the seriousness of your situation, Miss Armstrong. Slanderous accusations will land you in jail if you're not careful."

Stunned, she could barely speak. "But—"

The Consul glared at her, his voice rising. "Perhaps you are not aware that in the current political situation, disruptive foreign elements are highly unwelcome. It is the job of the Consulate to protect the reputation of the Crown and of British subjects in general. We don't need troublemakers, and we are more than happy to expedite their return home."

She struggled to repress her anger. "But surely the Spanish authorities would want to know about the theft of historical treasures?"

"These matters are handled by the proper authorities and involve cooperation between our governments at the highest levels. They don't rely on the tittle-tattle of female clerks, or malicious stories told by jealous women."

Jealous? She felt a wave of heat rise up into her face.

"I have spoken with Miss Letitia Henderson." He shuffled a pile of handwritten pages that lay in front of him, tapped them smartly into alignment, and then tucked them into a folder, which gave a loud smack as he threw it into a tray at his left.

His voice rose an octave higher. "And may I say that it is only due to her intercession that I will refrain from sending you home to be prosecuted? That distinguished lady asked that you be treated kindly, which was most generous of her. Also, I understood that publicity of that sort would be damaging to her respected college."

An icy shiver washed away the burn of embarrassment and anger. "Did you speak to Amanda Spenser?"

He looked affronted. "I did speak to Miss Spenser, who was most gracious about the whole thing. A young lady of her esteemed social and professional position is particularly sensitive to these tawdry personal insults, no matter how baseless. For this reason, you are forbidden from repeating any of these stories to anyone else, on pain of immediate deportation. Do you understand?"

She could only trust herself to nod. So, Amanda had got to him too. Her brother Gerald's public school chum.

Gwen swallowed hard. What right did she have, a jumped-up secretary with the wrong kind of accent, to expect an equal hearing from those in power?

"Are you sending me home?"

"No, not immediately." He sighed impatiently. "In consideration that you have been in distress after the death of Miss Temple and that you are waiting to meet with her friend, Mrs. Scott, we have decided to be compassionate in this case. You say she is expected back next week. Very well, you are permitted to stay until then, but you must be on the steamship which leaves for Plymouth next Saturday. I shall expect you to show us proof of purchasing a ticket."

So, did that mean Hildy had influence with the powers-that-be? The thought gave her a faint spurt of hope.

"But what if Mrs. Scott isn't back before Saturday?" she protested.

"That is no concern of ours, Miss Armstrong." He took another folder from the tray on his right and opened it.

"Now." He lowered his gaze to another stack of official papers, his tone dismissive. "In light of all that has occurred, for the remainder of your stay, you should comport yourself quietly."

* * *

"This is a respectable establishment, Senorita." The hotel manager's voice was low-pitched but insistent. "A young unmarried woman such as yourself must be above suspicion. When you were here as part of an established group that provided a kind of umbrella of respectability, but now..."

She stared at the little man behind the counter in disbelief.

Returning to the hotel, depressed and despairing, all she had wanted was to curl up and sleep, hoping that the morning would bring her some kind of inspiration. Instead, when she asked for her key, the manager emerged from his office and indicated her suitcase, tucked beside the desk.

"A man has been calling here, asking for you, refusing to leave his name. Now we have a report that you are considered persona non grata by your own consulate. It is best if you leave."

"Leave? But where can I go? I don't know this city."

The manager sighed in exasperation and reached under the counter. "You have five pesetas?" He pulled out a small book bound in red, with a gold engraved title. *Baedeker's Spain and Portugal.*

She could ill afford the price, and the worn corners told her it was a few years old, but the famously thorough guidebook might be invaluable if she had to fend for herself over the next week. At the very least, the maps would be a great help. She fumbled in her bag until she found her purse and counted out five silver coins.

Ten minutes later, she sat at a café in the nearby plaza with her suitcase at her feet, sipping a small coffee and wondering what to do next. It occurred to her that her trunk was on a ship to England at this very moment, leaving her with nothing but a few clothes in her small suitcase, but she couldn't summon up the energy to care.

According to the Baedeker, there were no other hotels in Portugalete, although it did say that there was the equivalent of boarding houses, *Casas de Huespedes.* However, the dry comment that such accommodation 'might afford a good insight into the domestic life of Spain', and that a good knowledge of Spanish was indispensable told her such places were not for her and 'few are fit for foreign ladies.'

Gwen sighed. She'd have to take the tram into the centre of Bilbao, where there were many hotels, but they were bound to be more expensive.

CHAPTER TWENTY-NINE

"May I join you?"

She jumped at the sound of the voice behind her and turned to meet the deep blue eyes of Michael Greville. Her heart began to pound. He was supposed to still be in Santiago with the rest of the tour group.

He sat down in the wrought-iron chair across from her. "I didn't expect to see you here."

"I could say the same." A million questions hammered in her brain. Why was he here? How much did he know? And how deeply was he involved in Amanda's exploits?

He waved over a waiter and ordered a coffee. After it was swiftly set in front of him, he took a sip from the small cup, then set it down in the saucer and looked up at her in a way that made her feel exposed and vulnerable. "By now, I thought you would be boarding a steamer at Vigo on your way home."

"Where did you hear that?" She met his gaze directly, hoping she looked confident and unconcerned. The table between them seemed very small.

"I believe it was Miss Bellamy who told me." He raised his eyebrows. "Something about a family emergency?"

Of course, they would have to concoct an excuse. Heaven forbid any implication of conflict, or criminal allegations. She looked down and sipped at her coffee, furiously debating what to tell him. An emergency telegram from her father, perhaps...

"I didn't believe it," he said firmly.

Her gaze flew up to see a slight frown creasing his brow. "What!"

"A family emergency wouldn't find you sitting here drinking coffee after being thrown out of your hotel."

She drew herself up in alarm. "How on earth did you know..."

He held up his hand. "It's actually my fault." In reply to her bewildered stare, he sighed.

"I phoned the hotel several times, looking for you. I'm afraid that I didn't give my name. I'd forgotten how sticky they are here about unmarried women. If I'd given it a moment's thought, I would have claimed to be your brother." A fleeting smile curled his lips. "Then I went in to inquire, and of course, the man on the desk recognized me. The story emerged about the phone messages and your precipitate departure. Since I am, of course, eminently respectable, it soon became apparent to the manager that he had overreacted—perhaps he'd been having trouble with a wayward daughter himself." He smiled again. "At that point, his honour wouldn't allow him to back down, so he made up some other patently false stories of your wanton behavior."

Had the man also mentioned her trouble with the consulate? If not, no reason to tell. "Might I ask what you are doing here?"

He paused a moment. "Here in Bilbao, you mean?"

"Yes. And at the hotel looking for me, and here in this café?" She gave him a challenging glare.

"I had some business which required me to pop back here."

"Business?"

"In my sort of work, one is never really on holiday. Apart from being an invaluable learning opportunity, this sort of tour enables one to see the dig sites firsthand, to meet the archaeologists in situ. If one's really lucky, one sees actual discoveries being made."

"Cutting out the middleman," she murmured, remembering Mr. Sloan's avaricious comment.

"What?"

"Common business practice, or so I've been told." She took another sip of the coffee and grimaced. It had gone cold.

"As a matter of fact, I'm seeing Dr. Hunt this evening. He's giving a talk for the local Antiquarian Society before he goes back to England on his lecture tour." He smiled. "Amusing to think they have such a quintessentially English body in a place like this. Thanks to the steel works and the shipyards, they have enough British residents to populate a small town. Apparently, even engineers and boilermakers like to fancy themselves the next Howard Carter."

"How very presumptuous of them."

He raised an eyebrow at her cutting tone, then started to laugh. "You're right. That was a rather snobbish remark."

She had to be careful. He couldn't be trusted an inch, but his seductive charm threatened to lower her guard. "Are you hoping to buy some of the finds from Dr Hunt?"

"It's a rather more delicate process than bargaining at a street stall. But essentially, yes." He gave her a long, considering look. "Would you care to accompany me to the lecture?"

She didn't know what to say. "There is the small problem that I have nowhere to stay."

He waved away her objection. "No problem at all. I'm at the Grand Hotel de Vizcaya; we'll get you a room there."

"Sounds expensive."

"If one knows the management, they can usually find a reasonably priced cupboard somewhere on the premises." He grinned.

"But there's my objectionable status as a single woman."

He chuckled. "I think you'll find attitudes a bit more enlightened down in the city. For all its charms, and despite the recent influx of advanced industry, Portugalete is essentially still a fishing village. Bilbao itself is rather more cosmopolitan. They are quite used to eccentric Englishwomen gadding about the continent alone."

He waved over the waiter and asked for the bill.

"Let's finish our coffee and get things squared away at the hotel. The lecture is at seven. We can dine afterwards at the *Café Iruna,* it's rather good. Excellent Iberian ham and other specialties of the region."

Gwen felt trapped in a web of conflicted feelings. Despite her suspicion of Michael, her instincts told her that he couldn't hurt anyone, least of all Emily. But she couldn't risk trusting him on the basis of mere intuition. She needed to keep her guard up.

In the meantime, she had to take the opportunity to eat a decent meal that didn't cut into her meagre resources. And use the occasion to extract as much information from him as possible.

He took another sip of his coffee. "You never did tell me the real story of why you parted ways with the tour."

"And you never did say why you called the hotel," she said firmly.

He looked a little embarrassed. "Seems we both owe each other an explanation." He leaned back in his chair and gave her a quizzical look. "So why did you come back to Bilbao?"

"I wanted to see Hildy Scott." That much was true.

"Dr Temple's friend?"

She nodded. "There was a… a misunderstanding with Miss Henderson and Dr. Spenser." She didn't quite meet his eyes. "I had to give notice."

He raised an eyebrow. "Rather a brave move to make so far from home."

"More like foolhardy," she admitted. "But it was a matter of principle. I'd rather not go into detail." More like she couldn't think of a convincing falsehood. "I'm hoping that Mrs. Scott can help me find a job. I'd like to spend a bit more time in Spain if I can."

"I must say, you're a very enterprising young lady," he said with a faint grin. "And coincidentally, that's why I came looking for you." He smiled again. "When I discovered you were at liberty, I thought you might be in need of a job. If so, I have a proposition to make."

Her cheeks warmed. "I'd better tell you that the Consulate has told me to leave on the ship for Plymouth a week from now."

In a welcome diversion, the waiter came by with the bill. As Michael dug in his pocket for a handful of coins, he said, "My admiration is unbounded. You've managed to put *their* backs up, too."

His amusement irritated her, but she didn't respond by revealing any details.

"As to the Consulate, I think I might be able to help you there." He reached into his inside pocket and pulled out a small leather-bound notebook. "I have a few useful contacts who can pull some strings."

"I don't need your help." The last thing she wanted was him talking to the consul and hearing about her 'wild accusations.'

"You misunderstand me. I think *you* can help *me*."

She hesitated, then said, "Tell me about this job you want me to do." It could be a golden opportunity to discover what kind of role he was playing in this shadowy trade.

He stood up, came around the table, and picked up her case. "Let's get you settled at the hotel. I'll tell you about it on the way."

Chapter Thirty

In the carriage heading south into the city, Michael Greville leaned back on the battered leather upholstery and looked at her with the hint of a smile curling his lips.

Gwen turned to look out at the river, sporadically visible between the massive shipyard cranes and the hulls of naval vessels being fitted out with guns. How much of the truth should she tell him? If she lied, it would need to be very plausible.

"For an innocent abroad, I'd say you've stepped on quite a few toes in a short space of time," he said.

She turned back to him with a start. "You make me sound like some naïve fool."

He laughed. "Hardly. You are no fool, Miss Armstrong. But I do have the feeling you may have got in far too deep, out of a misplaced sense of loyalty."

"What do you mean?"

He shook his head. "Never mind." He went on briskly, "You asked about this job I would like you to do. Here's the thing. There are a number of items I am interested in purchasing. The problem is that I'm too well-known amongst the dealers. I'm quite sure the price goes up when they see my face. What I'd like you to do is visit a few antiquaries as a simple English tourist and find out what sort of price they are looking for."

"I'm not sure that makes sense. After all, wouldn't they try to take advantage of an ignorant tourist by charging more?"

"They know I have money. Without wishing to offend you, Miss Armstrong, you don't give the impression of affluence."

Nevertheless, she was offended, even though it was perfectly true. At that moment, she longed for a wardrobe of elegantly cut dresses, exquisite beaded gowns, heeled silver sandals—Amanda's wardrobe. Then, he wouldn't regard her with that superior hint of amusement.

"I still don't think it makes sense," she said stiffly. "The kind of things you'd be buying require affluence to afford."

"I'm sure we can get you a wardrobe to play the part. A cotton heiress with intellectual aspirations, perhaps?"

His quizzical look made her laugh despite herself. "Now you really are making fun of me."

"I would merely suggest that, in your present situation, can you afford to ignore an offer of employment?" he said.

"You mean, beggars can't be choosers," she said tartly.

He sighed. "My dear Miss Armstrong, you do make things difficult for yourself."

Gwen reviewed the situation. If she turned down the offer, she had barely enough money to keep her for another two weeks, even with Senor Ochoa's help, assuming there was an affordable room at Greville's hotel. She had to pray that Hildy would return before the Consul's deadline. And what if she didn't? What would the consular officials actually do, if she didn't board that steamship? Would the police search for her? She didn't trust Greville's assurances about his consulate 'contacts', but if she took the job, then he had an incentive to help her.

All she had were questions. And no weapons except common sense and an instinct for self-preservation. And the good old Boys Brigade pocket-knife. She slid a hand into her pocket and felt the weight of metal. Bless Reg for insisting she take it with her. It wasn't much of a weapon, but it gave her a reassuring sense of comfort.

She took a deep breath. In for a penny, in for a pound. "All right. I'll do it."

"Excellent." Unexpectedly, he reached over to shake her hand.

The warm clasp made her skin tingle. She let go and sat back in her seat, feeling a little breathless. Whatever chemistry might be bubbling under the surface, she had to keep it forcefully suppressed. This unexpected opportunity could be the key to finding the truth about Amanda's schemes. And, more importantly, the real story of Emily's death.

* * *

"I think I'm getting too accustomed to champagne!" Gwen said.

Tucked into a corner table on the lower floor of the Café Iruna, Michael refilled her coupe glass with the straw-coloured bubbles of Veuve Clicquot. "One can never tire of proper champagne."

Gwen smiled and sipped the wine, aware that she was practically simpering. It had seemed like an excellent plan: pretend to fall under his spell and ask ingenuous questions that would reveal his real motives.

However, it was all very well to set out on purpose to be entranced, but not if she found herself *actually* falling under his spell. It wasn't at all difficult to be charmed by Michael Greville. She had to keep reminding herself not to stare too long into those sea-blue eyes that crinkled at the corners so attractively.

The surroundings didn't help. Candlelight flickered on a Moorish fantasy of glazed tiles and delicate murals, with shadowy nooks and low archways.

"This is lovely," she looked around. "Straight from the *Tales of the Alhambra*."

Michael leaned forward and said softly, "One almost expects to see Scheherazade, or the Forty Thieves."

The mention of thieves was too apt for comfort. During Dr. Hunt's lecture, she had been listening for any mention of the stolen artefacts, however unlikely. He had covered much the same ground as their own recent tour of the dig and its finds. To her relief, Michael decided it was too crowded to talk to Hunt. They had slipped out halfway through the question and answer period, and Michael had led her to the restaurant—an ancient building tucked away down a narrow sidestreet.

Somewhere between the aperitif and the sweet, he had managed to extract her life story, up to the moment of getting the job at Seathorne. Her own attempts to find out more about him seemed to inevitably wend their way back to the subject of herself. Some sleuth she was turning out to be.

"Now, Mr. Greville…"

"Michael, please," he interjected.

"All right, Michael, I've talked far too much about myself. What about you? How did you come to be a dealer in rare coins? Is it a family business?"

He laughed. "Hardly. My family are deeply disappointed that I'm not running an estate deep in the Cornish countryside, but I could never work up much enthusiasm for the care and feeding of hops or barley."

Running an estate. Surely, as lord of the manor, not a hired hand. "So, your family are farmers?"

He had that amused look again. "You might say that. According to my Great-Aunt Prunella we go back to the year dot, or even farther, when some Roman general declined to go home with the troops and stayed on to run a tin mine and plow his acres. Fifty years ago, they turned up evidence of a small villa. You know, scraps of mosaic and random tiles. Since then, it's been a bit of a family hobby, walking the fields and investigating suspicious mounds."

"Is that how you got interested?"

He nodded. "The fever caught me at the vulnerable age of ten, when I found a small pot filled with coins. Nothing spectacular, all small denomination bronze pieces. The savings of some poor labourer, no doubt. Hidden away and never retrieved. But I was as excited as if I'd found Blackbeard's treasure chest." He grinned. "After that, I read everything I could get my hands on about the Romans, ancient coinage…. Suddenly, I started astonishing my History Master and the Latin tutor with my newfound enthusiasm." He chuckled.

"Is that what you studied at university?"

"I read Classics. Loved it. Never did finish, unfortunately." A shadow fell across his face.

She knew, without him saying it. "The War."

"The calamity that marks us all." His mouth tightened, and a look of pain crept into his eyes. He caught her gaze and seemed to see the leap of sorrow and sympathy that sprang in her breast.

"My family were lucky, if one can use such a grotesque word. Three sons, who all survived. Me without a scratch, Rupert without a leg, and Giles with only a fragile hold on sanity." His mouth tightened with bitterness. "Oh yes, we did survive, though." He stared down into his wine glass.

Silence fell between them, but for some reason, it didn't feel awkward. Gwen sipped the last drops of her brandy. At last, she said. "Are you the eldest?"

He nodded. "Fortunately, my father is hale and hearty, still very much in charge. He insists I must inherit the estate to keep it intact, but Rupert knows I'll be turning it over to him. In many ways, he's running the place already and very capably, too. He loves every acre of that land like his life's blood. He never wants to stir from there again. And Giles... in the peace and quiet and the gentle rhythms of country life, I like to think he's healing."

But she recognized the wishful tone in his voice as an emotion she knew well. "Do you think they can? All these broken men like your brother and my father."

He met her gaze, an expression in his eyes compounded of pain and hope. "They must. Or else what was it all for?"

It came to her that perhaps he carried a burden of guilt to have survived with his mind and body whole.

She stared down into her brandy glass as the silence lengthened. There had been a moment of real connection between them, and it left her feeling vulnerable and confused. She needed to get this conversation back to a more detached plane.

"I really want to know more about how your sort of business works," she blurted out, awkwardly aware of the non-sequitur. "I mean, it's not like an antique shop, is it?"

She glanced up to see him giving her a thoughtful look. "Hardly. But the principle isn't much different from any other business. A dealer is the intermediary, bringing together those who want to buy, with those who want to sell..."

"Like a sort of introduction service."

"If you like." He smiled, and once again, she felt the tug of a physical

212

attraction she couldn't afford to acknowledge.

"Do you buy things first and then find a customer?" she asked, genuinely curious. "How would you make the most money?"

"I can see you have an instinct for business. Perhaps you might take up the trade."

"Oh no, I want to be an archaeologist." It spilled out unintentionally and sounded as naïve as a child declaiming her intention to be a princess.

"Like your late, lamented Miss Temple." There was something ironic in his voice that gave her a chill. Together with the fact that he had been at the Cathedral the day after Emily died, asking questions. Had he been there the night before? Suddenly, the chill penetrated right down to the bone.

He could at least give her the honour of her proper title. "*Doctor Temple* was a brilliant archaeologist. She taught me so much. She was going to help me get a job on a dig this summer and recommend me for a special scholarship." Her throat tightened. "Of course, that's all over now." She dismissed the fleeting thought of the legacy. At this point, it remained a distracting chimera.

"Do tell me more about Dr Temple. I only met her once," he said, with a curiously sardonic tone that raised her hackles. "A brief exchange in passing."

"Really? Where was that?"

"At Dr. Hunt's dig."

Icy fingers ran down her spine. It kept coming back to the excavation at Castro de Carballo. How much did he know, and how involved was he in this whole sinister affair?

Chapter Thirty-One

As they left the restaurant, Michael took her shawl and courteously draped it around her shoulders. His fingers grazed her bare flesh, and she shivered.

"I hope it's not too cold for you to accompany me to the *Casa de Antigüedades*."

Alarmed, she pulled the wrap more tightly around her. Should she have told him that she knew about Senor Ochoa's being robbed and his friendship with Emily? But it was too late now to regret her openness.

"Is it normal in your business to call at a shop at this time of night?"

He steered her toward a wide, moderately busy, cobbled street. Couples strolled arm-in-arm, while the jingle of bridles and ring of horseshoes announced the occasional carriage, "You must have learned by now that Spaniards keep late hours."

"I take it that you know the shop."

He nodded. "When you told me about your benefactor, it didn't surprise me. Senor Ochoa has a weakness for damsels in distress."

The phrase smarted, but she couldn't really take offense. "I will, of course, be paying him back. But he did strike me as a very kindly man. I hope he doesn't get taken advantage of."

He laughed out loud. "He's a good man, but in business, one of the wiliest old birds you can imagine. No one ever gets the better of him."

"Except thieves."

He instantly sobered. "Rotten luck. But it's a hazard of doing business." That sounded rather cavalier.

"Why are we going there?"

"I heard he had acquired a rather lovely marble piece. If it's good, I have a client who would be interested."

"So, I'm not playing the cotton heiress just yet."

He chuckled. "No, we'll have your debut another day." They turned into a familiar narrow side street, where a lamp glowed in the window of the old-fashioned shopfront.

Senor Ochoa greeted them with joyful recognition. "Miss Armstrong, how delightful! And you, Senor, we have met but..."

Michael formally introduced himself, and the shop owner swiftly brought out the sherry decanter. "I am so delighted that you are a friend of Senor Greville." He seated Gwen at the little table, while Michael strolled around the room, perusing the items in the tall display cases. "When he introduced himself the other day, I was delighted to recognize him from last year."

He poured a sherry into a tiny, delicate crystal glass and handed it to her. "I have been quite worried about you, *querida*. All alone in a strange place. But now I know you have a protector like Senor Greville, I am relieved."

She didn't care for that word, *protector*. Uncomfortably redolent of some heavily mustached cad visiting Theda Bara in her boudoir.

Michael was looking intently at an object on an upper shelf, but she noticed a brief smile flit across his face. For some reason she felt sure the image of a Victorian lothario had also passed through his mind. Her cheeks suddenly felt warm.

"Yes, well...Mr. Greville is a friend," she emphasized. "A fellow Englishman who has kindly helped me. As have you, Senor Ochoa."

The whole discussion made her deeply uncomfortable.

"Well, Emilio," Michael said, "Where is this head of Venus you promised me?"

The shop owner chuckled and got to his feet. "A Spaniard would observe the courtesies a little longer. You Englishmen can be so blunt." He vanished behind the velvet curtain, and silence fell.

"Is he right?" Gwen asked. "Do we do business so differently?"

"The Spanish do place great emphasis on formality and ceremony,"

Michael responded. "But there are many variations between the different areas. Catalunya and Vizcaya might be different countries. You may have noticed that the working classes here don't speak the same language as their superiors."

"They speak Basque?"

He nodded. "The steel and shipbuilding here form the industrial heart of Spain. It has developed thanks to far-sighted businessmen who sought to bring in British workers and industrial methods, not to mention British investment."

"That's why there's such a large English colony here."

"Indeed."

She wondered how the Spanish workers felt. "Are we welcome, do you think?

He frowned. "Good question. There's a lot of political turmoil right now, and something always seems to be brewing, but so far, the English haven't been targeted as they have elsewhere."

Senor Ochoa emerged from behind the curtain with a flourish. "Forgive the delay, Senor and Senorita. I wanted to ensure the shutters were barred and the back door secured."

"Wise of you," Michael murmured, watching the older man unwrapping a bundle shrouded in burlap and kapok.

Cushioned by the wrapping, Senor Ochoa placed a carved marble bust on the counter. "Exquisite," he breathed.

Michael ran his fingers delicately over the white features of a serenely beautiful face, the hair carefully curled and coiled in an elaborate style. "There's a chip or two."

"She's been in the ground for two thousand years, then dug up in some peasant's orchard a month ago," Ochoa said indignantly. "You'd have lost a chip or two in her situation and counted it lucky!"

Michael laughed out loud. "Very true." He addressed the sculpture cradled in his hands. "I beg your pardon, senorita."

"Is it really a bust of Venus?" Gwen asked, getting to her feet for a closer look.

216

Ochoa shrugged. "One can never be absolutely sure even with a full-length statue, but the dressing of the hair is similar to the Venus of Milo. Our first question might be, is it Greek or a Roman copy? The Romans plundered thousands of statues from the Greeks, but they also manufactured copies of such masters, as Phidias and Praxiteles. However, this…" he delicately stroked the head.

"The most striking thing is that she does not have the idealized classical features," Michael went on, gazing into the translucent marble face, clearly captivated. "She may actually be a portrait of a real person."

Gwen stood beside him and stared at the woman's image. She could feel the allure of this timeless beauty. At the same time, a feeling of melancholy rose within her. So long ago, this woman had lived and died.

"Someone loved her very much." The quiet words slipped out without thinking.

She felt embarrassed by her impulsive response, unable to look at Michael, but very much aware that he was looking at her. To her relief, he changed the subject.

"I'm assuming you have good provenance," he turned to Senor Ochoa. "This peasant can testify to digging it up?"

"Of course. I have his signature on the relevant document."

"Signature?" Michael shot him a wry smile.

Ochoa shrugged. "All right, so he made an X. The man's illiterate. But I had the priest witness it."

"I suppose that will do. Where is his farm?"

Ochoa shook his head. "You're too late. An official from Madrid has got an archaeologist digging away there. The peasant is furious; it's going to ruin his crops."

"Do you know the archaeologist's name?" Michael asked, rather offhandedly.

Ochoa peered at him a little more closely. "Cabrera, I think. Miguel Cabrera. University of Salamanca. Do you know him?"

Something unspoken seemed to pass between them. A look of curiosity on the part of Ochoa, or was it suspicion?

Michael responded with an impassive shrug. "Not a man that I know. It will be interesting to see what else he turns up." He set the bust back down. "Well, Senor Ochoa, we will have to discuss the price, but I believe my client would be interested."

"Indeed. I am glad to hear it. Let us leave the dickering over money to a time when we will not impose it on Senorita Armstrong."

"I shall call tomorrow and finalize the arrangements," Michael told him.

They left the shop, ushered out with many courteous bows.

After they had walked a little way along the narrow, cobbled street, lit intermittently by flickering gaslight, Gwen turned to Michael. "What was all that about?"

He only lifted an eyebrow in reply.

"I thought you only dealt in coins?"

"One must be flexible in our business." He didn't seem inclined to elaborate.

They walked on for a few more minutes in silence; then she voiced what was on her mind.

"When Senor Ochoa said you were too late and that it wasn't an archaeologist that you know. What did he mean?"

"Sounds like you suspect me of something nefarious."

Too true. Had she overplayed her hand? "I only meant...I can imagine it would be an advantage in your business to know a lot of archaeologists. Like Mr. Sloan said. Going to the source."

He smiled. "I like to deal with people I can trust."

After that enigmatic declaration, he remained silent, and so did Gwen, as they walked through the quiet streets back to the hotel, pondering the irony that he was the last person she herself could risk trusting.

Chapter Thirty-Two

M ichael escorted her to her door and bade her a distant goodnight. True to his word, he had got her a small, but very comfortable room at an affordable rate.

After slipping into her nightdress, she sat up in bed, wondering what on earth to do next. Her instincts were at war trying to decide what role Michael Greville was playing in this complicated game. Nothing directly connected him with any of the thefts, but he was undoubtedly involved with Amanda, and the conversation at Senor Ochoa's had rung numerous warning bells. And above all, why had he been at the cathedral asking questions about Emily?

It was tempting to accept the job with Michael as an opportunity to find out more. But the Consul's threat still hung over her, and she couldn't be sure Michael's influence was enough to nullify it. Alternatively, now she had a bit more money, she could perhaps go in search of Hildy Scott. And tell her what, exactly?

She slipped out of bed and got her bag to look for the Baedeker. That would tell her how to get to San Sebastian. Digging through the contents, her fingers encountered something cool and weighty. She pulled out a key with an enamel tag reading 208. In her hurried departure from Santiago, she had forgotten to return it to the hotel desk.

Staring at the heavy iron key filling her palm, she blessed her own absent-mindedness. The only real evidence that remained to back up her story lay in the photographs from the Castro de Carballo dig. If Amanda hadn't destroyed them, and if the golden horseman was hidden in her luggage....

It might be a slim chance, but she had to take it, and the sooner, the better. The room might be occupied already, and who knows what Amanda might do with the photos and the horseman.

At five the next morning, she left a rapidly scribbled note at the desk for Michael, saying there had been a telegram from her family and she must return to England. He hadn't believed it from Dorcas and probably wouldn't believe her either, but any story that would confuse and mislead would do if it gave her a head start.

* * *

Her meagre funds bought a third-class ticket on the slow train. Wedged into the corner of a hard bench for the lengthy journey, she stared out the window, not really seeing the wooded landscape. If she was ever to get justice for Emily, she had to work out what was really going on and how everyone fit in. And then prove it.

If she could believe what Amanda told her, her uncle Jack Spenser presided over a network of thieves and smugglers, like some sort of obscene spider in his Parisian nest. But his role was static. A mere marketplace for treasures. Amanda had mentioned his *finder*, then shied away quickly from the subject, as if she'd said too much.

Gwen knew instinctively that this was the true presiding intelligence. The man who directed operations, darting around Europe and the Mediterranean, snatching irreplaceable fragments of human history and selling them like so much scrap iron in a wrecker's yard.

Amanda was probably not his only agent, and certainly Franz was her willing helper. She had used Emily as an unwitting tool, then tried to recruit her with blackmail. *And then killed her?*

Gwen shook her head. For all that she hated what Amanda had done, she didn't believe her capable of violence. In some ways, she felt sorry for her and even understood the bitterness that led her to flout society's rules. Besides, she had no reason to think Amanda had been anywhere near Santiago when Emily died.

220

No, it was the man in charge who threatened and finally killed Emily. She felt sure of that. And he was one of the tour group, she was convinced. But who?

Jim Dixon, Father Garrick, and Franz, she dismissed out of hand. Colonel Fairlamb, perhaps? His record told against him, but somehow, he seemed too weak under all his bluster.

Brett Sloan seemed a likely candidate. He was a tough man, clearly prone to violence, as she'd seen in his treatment of Amanda. Could he be playing the role of a buyer, maintaining anonymity within his own organization? Possible, but far-fetched.

And then there was Michael Greville.

She drew in a deep breath, focusing on the scene outside the train window. A deep plunging ravine split the mountainside, clothed in emerald trees and broken by misty silver streams, like something out of a fairy tale.

Michael. He couldn't be more perfectly fitted to the role. An educated product of the aristocracy. An attractive man who could move in any society. A man who had impeccable contacts in the world of antiquities and archaeology.

Could he also be a cold, calculating monster who could murder a defenceless woman with impunity?

A blaring hoot from the engine startled her. Suddenly, she saw the tumbledown farmhouses lining the track on the outskirts of the city. The cathedral spires split the distant skyline. Santiago de Compostela at last.

She extracted her stiff, aching body from the cramped corner seat. Stepping over chicken cages and trying not to hit any children or livestock with her case, she stumbled out of the train. The station clock read quarter past one. She was exhausted after more than twenty-five hours on the train with two changes. Quite a difference from the first-class sleeper.

After checking her case at the left luggage office, with much pantomime and recourse to the phrasebook, she went in search of the omnibus. So as not to pollute the holy city with soot and noise, the railway station for Santiago de Compostela was in the hamlet of Cornes, almost a mile out of town.

Gwen doled out twenty-five centavos and climbed into the rackety bus. There was little chance of encountering any of the tour party in this humble vehicle. Nevertheless, she darted a nervous glance around, then sank down into the back corner.

She got out at the post office, placed a telephone call to the hotel and asked for Amanda.

"Scnorita Spenser is not available." The desk clerk informed her. "I believe she is out for the day."

She couldn't hope for a better opportunity. Pulling down her grey cloche hat to hide her face, she belted her raincoat tighter, hoping she looked unremarkable among the bustling crowd. Slipping along the back streets, she reached the rear staff door and poked her head in. She had counted on everyone being busy serving lunch, and to her relief, no one was in the corridor leading to the kitchens. She hurried up the backstairs to the second floor, hoping that the maids had finished cleaning the rooms.

Still, if her old room was already occupied, this could be tricky.

Stopping in front of Room 208, she lifted her hand to knock. The lock rattled in the door of the next room. Amanda's room.

Frantic for cover, she looked around and saw a green-draped alcove halfway down the hall. She dived into it, retreating into the darkest corner, surrounded by mops and buckets. A mop wavered, threatening to topple, but she grabbed it just in time.

Not daring to breathe, she risked peeking through the narrow gap between the curtain and the wall. She could hear the door being closed and locked, then saw a man's back as he paused on the landing. Dark hair, broad shoulders on a lean torso. He quickly moved past the cage lift and ran up the stairs. But she saw enough of his face to know. It was Michael Greville. Her hands began to shake.

She could hardly believe it. What was he doing back here? What did he think when he found she had gone? He'd made no mention of returning to Santiago. Was it for an assignation with Amanda? But why else would he have been in her room?

That meant she might still be in there.

Get a hold of yourself, Gwen. She couldn't stay hiding in the cleaning cupboard forever. She had to take a risk.

She knocked on the door of room 208. No sound came from within, but she waited a few seconds before pushing the key into the lock. She turned it with agonizing care, then slipped inside. Her breath escaped with a gasp of relief as she shut the door softly behind her. The room was empty.

Her heart pounded against her ribs as she moved across to the connecting door, praying Amanda hadn't shot the bolt. She pressed her ear against the door and listened for a long time. Nothing but silence on the other side. She had to take the risk. With agonizing care, she slowly turned the knob and opened the door a crack, gradually widening the gap until she was almost sure that it was empty.

The wardrobe stood open, and a frothy evening dress lay across a chair. Gwen frowned. It wasn't like Amanda to be so organized about her clothing plans. She usually pulled out a dress at the last minute. Gwen picked up the frock and stroked the filmy violet silk. It seemed too slinky for an afternoon tea dress. She glanced at her watch. Almost two-o-clock! Amanda could be back any moment to change.

Hurriedly, she searched through the suitcases and went through every drawer, trying to carefully put things back as nearly as possible the way they had been. She could only hope that Amanda would assume anything out of place could be blamed on the maid.

Nothing. She heaved an exasperated sigh. It looked as if the photographs were not there or had been destroyed. And there was no sign of any golden horseman. What had Michael been doing in here? Had he also been searching for something?

She took one last despairing look around the room and saw a tweed jacket hanging on a peg by the door. Something distended one of the deep pockets. She reached in and pulled out a thick envelope filled with a sheaf of photographs. A quick look told her these were what she sought.

Elated, she tucked the envelope inside her jacket. As she turned to go, her foot slid from under her, and she only saved herself from falling by grabbing onto the bedpost. She looked down and saw the reason for her slip. From under the bathroom door, a puddle of water spread out on the terra cotta tile floor. Surely, even Amanda would not leave that sort of mess. And it seemed an odd time to take a bath.

She didn't know what made her reach for the bathroom doorknob. A white clawfoot tub stood in the centre of the room, full to the brim. Near the taps, a thread of water overflowed the curved rim, and a steady drip echoed in the stillness.

A pale arm hung over the edge. A slender hand with long, elegant fingers.

Like an automaton, Gwen stepped closer. A halo of golden hair floated on the surface. For a moment, she couldn't make sense of what she was seeing. Her heart seemed to have stopped.

Under a foot of water, Amanda's eyes were wide open, her lips slightly parted, as if taken by surprise. A beautiful Naiad. And very clearly dead.

Something bumped against her foot. She looked down to see an empty champagne bottle rolling across the wet tile floor.

A sudden fusillade of heavy knocking shocked her out of her frozen state.

"Amanda! What's going on? Everyone's waiting for you." Franz's loud, anxious voice came from the corridor. "Are you ill? I'm so worried I got the manager to come." He sounded on the verge of tears.

Another voice intervened "This is the manager, senorita. Your friends are worried about you. I am afraid I will have to open the door if you don't answer."

Gwen backed toward the connecting doors, trying not to make a sound on the wet floor. She had to get out. Slipping back into the other room, she closed and locked her side. She pressed her ear against the wood panel, listening to the manager's repeated pleas, then heard the rattle of a key and the opening door.

A confused series of bangs and splashes ensued, followed by a tortured wail that made gooseflesh rise on her arms. Poor Franz.

Somehow, she had to get out of here. Peeking out into the corridor, she heard the commotion through the open doorway. At this moment, the hall was empty, but for how long?

Gwen slipped out and ran for the backstairs, taking two at a time. A noise below made her freeze and shrink back into the corner of the stairwell. In an instant, the shock of that dead face hit her, followed swiftly by the full realization of just how much danger she was in.

It may have looked like an accident, as if Amanda had had too much to drink, then fallen asleep in the bath, but somehow Gwen didn't think so.

Amanda had accused her of spreading lies and got her kicked off the tour. Now Amanda was dead. If the authorities knew she was here, they could easily see her as a prime suspect.

And what about Michael? Why didn't he raise the alarm instead of hurrying away? Unless...

Unless he had killed her.

From the floor above, Franz's high-pitched voice rang out in a desperate cry of anguish. Right now, she had no time to think about anything but escape.

A few flights below, a commotion sounded from around the back door. A cacophony of harsh voices rang out in Spanish. Had they already called the police?

Only one possible refuge remained. She flew down another flight and into the first-floor corridor. She knocked quietly at the door, pressing her body against the panel and whispering urgently, "Let me in. Please let me in!"

Father Garrick opened the door. "Gwen!" He stared at her in surprise, then poked his head out into the corridor. "What on earth is going on?"

She edged into the doorway. "Please let me in."

He stepped back and let her enter, closing the door behind her. "I thought you were en route to Vigo. Something about a family emergency?"

She shook her head, suddenly close to tears. "It's awful. It's all so hard to explain, but... I need your help."

"Is it something to do with all that shouting and commotion? It sounds like something very serious is going on."

She nodded. "Oh, yes. It's serious. Amanda is dead."

He stared at her, aghast. "Dead? But that's... I can't believe it. I just saw her last night at dinner. She seemed perfectly alright. I was asking her why you had left, that's where I heard about the family trouble."

Gwen shook her head. "There was no family trouble. Miss Henderson sent me home. She'd been told lies about me, stories about disgraceful conduct. She believed them."

"But who on earth would malign you in that way?" He stared at her in confusion. "And what happened to Amanda? I don't understand."

"She drowned in the bath. And I don't think it was an accident."

"Drowned?" For a long moment, he just stared at her, then crossed himself and waved distractedly at the armchair near the window. "Look, you'd better sit down."

He poured them each a tot of brandy before sinking into the opposite chair. "Tell me the whole story."

He listened intently as she poured out the full sequence of events in which she'd been caught up, from Emily's death onward. What a relief to confide all her fears and suspicions to someone who believed her. Her only omission was that, for some reason, she didn't tell him about seeing Michael leaving Amanda's room. Was that because she couldn't face the implication?

She still hesitated for a moment before pulling out the envelope from inside her jacket. Then she took out the photos and handed them to him.

"This is what I'm talking about."

He leafed through them, the expression on his face changing from anxious to dismayed.

"I'm no expert," he said finally. "But I know one can get in a lot of trouble over antiquities. Dr. Hunt would have reported the theft to the authorities, I should think."

She nodded miserably, but reflected that at this point, being accused of theft was the least of her worries.

Father Garrick handed the photos back and rose to his feet. "Look. I'll find out what's going on." He stopped at the door, his hand on the knob. "Don't worry. I'll do what I can to help you."

"Thanks." Her shaky smile disappeared with the priest as he shut the door. Gwen stood up and inched the door open again. A muffled noise sounded in the distance. She could distinguish the voices coming up the stairwell from the floor below.

Above the babble rose the sharp, commanding tones of Letitia Henderson. "A British subject has been killed. I insist that the Consul be summoned immediately."

A rising torrent of Spanish submerged Miss Henderson's next words like a tidal wave. Gwen shut the door again and locked it.

She watched the minute hand on the bedside clock tick over with agonizing slowness. When Father Garrick returned fifteen minutes later, it felt like hours had passed.

He slid into the room with a wary, backward glance at the hallway. "It's bad news, I'm afraid. Apparently, Colonel Fairlamb saw you on the street near here, behaving... suspiciously." He looked embarrassed. "I'm sorry, but that's the word he used."

Gwen shook her head. "So, they're not treating Amanda's death as an accident."

"It seems not. The Guardia Civil are in her room and down in the lobby. I think they're going to search the hotel."

Gwen jumped to her feet. "I have to get out. I'll go to the Consulate. Tell them everything. They'll have to help me!"

Father Garrick shook his head. "I wouldn't put much faith in His Majesty's representatives." His lip curled in disdain. "They're more interested in maintaining good relations with the government and greasing the wheels of commerce. They'll visit you in jail and get you a lawyer, but that's about all you can expect of them."

Thinking of the reception she'd got before, Gwen had to admit he was probably right. A rising tide of panic threatened to engulf her. "I've got to get out."

"Look here, your best plan is to get back to England. Much better to get legal help there, and it's harder for the Spanish authorities to throw their weight about in another country."

"But how can I get out of the hotel if it's full of police?'

"Do you have enough money?"

She nodded, feeling in her pocket for the pile of banknotes. Would she be able to retrieve her case at the station? If not, she'd have nothing but the clothes she stood up in.

"I've got an idea!" Garrick took a suit from the wardrobe and looked her up and down. "Fortunately, I do go out in mufti occasionally. Put this on. They're looking for a woman. We just might be able to fool them."

Gwen rolled up her skirt and slipped on the trousers. With a pair of braces to hold them up, they would do. Fortunately, Father Garrick was a slim man, not much taller than herself. "What about my hair?" She had never been shingled, and her neat rolled bun concealed a mass of auburn curls.

"Here." He handed her a soft felt hat with a stylish turn of brim. "Put your hair up under it, then pull it down low."

When she had done as instructed, he looked her over. "Good thing that jacket's loose on you." A curious expression fluttered across his face. "There's a night train to the coast; it leaves at ten. It'll get you to the steamer dock at Vigo in time to get the Plymouth boat."

She clasped his hand with both of hers. "You've been so good to me. How can I thank you? This is such a risk for you."

Brushing aside her thanks, he cautiously opened the door, then ushered her into the corridor. "Follow me."

He led her down the backstairs, but instead of going out the main staff door, he took a narrow side corridor filled with empty crates and boxes and the pungent odors of food. It led out into a cobbled courtyard stacked with the detritus of the hotel kitchens.

He pointed to a ramshackle door in the high brick wall. "Through there, you'll find a narrow passage that brings you out near the Plaza Mayor. You'd better walk to Cornes Station. Stick to the busiest streets, and you won't be noticed."

"I'll never forget this. I can't tell you how grateful I am." She slipped out into a stinking alley.

Father Garrick gave her an encouraging smile. "Go with God, my dear." He closed the battered wooden door.

Gwen hurried down the alley, trying to avoid the slippery rubbish underfoot. She had never needed divine help more than she did right now.

Chapter Thirty-Three

Gwen shoved her hands into the unfamiliar jacket pockets and attempted a relaxed masculine amble. Above all, she must not draw any attention.

She paused to glance in a shop window, not looking at the merchandise, but at the reflection of her surroundings. No policemen could be seen, and no sign of any disturbance, just the usual confusion of horses and donkeys pulling carts and carriages in every direction, and pedestrians taking their lives in their hands without turning a hair.

Motorcars were still rare, and so she noticed the elegant touring model moving slowly in her direction. The hairs rose on the back of her neck as she recognized the dark-haired man at the wheel. Michael Greville.

She kept her face toward the window until the car had passed her by.

It took only fifteen minutes to reach the station, but it felt like hours. She was able to slip into the empty women's lavatory and take off the suit in the privacy of a cubicle. It was tempting to stay disguised, but a few odd looks from people she passed in the street made her realize that the imposture didn't stand up to close scrutiny. She kept the hat, however, as it covered her distinctive hair and shaded her face.

After retrieving her case from the left luggage, she bought a ticket back to Bilbao. Despite Father Garrick's good advice, she knew what she must do—find an out-of-the-way hotel and sit tight until Hildy returned.

The next train went to Gijon, roughly in the right direction. She leaned against a pillar and looked up at the massive clock. It was nearly four. The train was due any minute. Her anxious gaze darted around the platform and toward the station entrance. The platform was getting crowded now, the babble of voices around her rising in pitch. As people pressed urgently forward, their bags and packages jabbed and banged painfully against her legs. She looked for the distinctive cocked hats of the Guardia Civil. Would the police have already put a watch on passengers?

A distant roar swiftly grew louder until the clank and scream of pistons filled the air. Clouds of steam and the pungent smell of coal announced the train's arrival. As it slowed down, Gwen lifted her case and moved forward. The steam whirled around her, giving a treacherous sense of protection.

With a massive hiss and final burst of steam, the train came to a halt. The crowd surged forward, even as conductors opened the doors and shouted at them to move back and let the arriving passengers off.

Gwen scanned the crowd around her and saw no recognizable figures. If Greville were here, his height would make him stand out.

"Ticket, Senorita."

The conductor's demand startled her. "Oh, of course." She had it ready in her hand. He gave it a quick glance, then waved her on.

The packed crowd pushed and shoved, and it seemed to take ages to get anywhere near boarding. She had just reached the carriage steps when a hand closed over her arm in a painful grip and pulled her aside.

"Fraulein Gwen!" Franz's anxious face stared into hers. His round face had become drawn and haggard. He looked distraught.

"What are you doing here?" She tried to yank her arm from his grip.

"You must come with me! You must!" He started to drag her away from the train toward the exit.

She tried to hang back, her gaze darting around, looking for the police. "Where are we going?"

Over the roar of the train engine, she heard the shudder of the pistons starting to turn and the shrill whistle that heralded departure. She wrenched her arm again, but his grasp was like iron. Her hope of safety picked up speed, and went roaring out of the station.

As if in answer to her thought, Franz said, "I take you away from Santiago. To somewhere safe."

Her tense muscles fractionally relaxed, and she let him pull her toward the barrier and out into the street. A strange passivity crept over her. None of this made any sense, but somehow, it was all mixed up with Emily's death, and this might be a way to get to the truth.

"You know Amanda is dead," he said flatly, his wan face streaked with tears.

Franz was involved in whatever was going on, but he seemed genuinely grief-stricken over Amanda.

"You are in danger, too. You must come." She felt so terrified of falling into the clutches of the authorities. Whatever he had in store, it couldn't be worse.

A small, closed motorcar stood at the kerb. Franz pushed her into the passenger seat and got behind the wheel.

"You're being followed," he said, as he started the motor. "Sit lower. He'll see you."

"Who?" As they pulled away, she saw the touring car she had noticed earlier parked in front of the station. She recognized the tall figure running up the steps that led inside.

"He almost caught you." They picked up speed as the buildings grew less dense, until, in only a few minutes, they were out in open country.

"Why would Michael Greville want to catch me?"

Franz glared. "Can't you guess? He'll pin Amanda's murder on you. You make the perfect scapegoat."

The fear that had dogged her ever since she fled the hotel welled up and choked her. "Why me?" she whispered. "Why would he do that?"

He glanced at her briefly in disgust, then back at the narrow road. "Isn't it obvious?"

He shook his head. "You are like them all. A naïve schoolgirl. The high and mighty Mr. Greville. So cultured. So handsome." He spit out the words. "Even Amanda was taken in. Until he killed her."

Gwen's head was spinning. "But why?"

"He was looking for this." Franz dug into his jacket pocket, pulled out the Gold Horseman, and lay it on the seat between them. It gleamed a buttery soft yellow in the sunlight.

"You stole that from my luggage."

He snatched it back and tucked it into his pocket again. "*I* stole it?" he said with a bitter laugh. "Greville stole it. Before that, your precious Emily stole it. I'm taking it to its rightful home."

"Emily was duped." But it was useless to protest. Her head was spinning as she tried to understand. "Who are you working for, Franz? Who's in charge?"

He ignored her questions. She became aware that they had gone from open country to hilly forest and now raced along an unmetalled road that twisted between high stone banks.

The sun hung low in the sky ahead of them. So, they were heading west. "Where are we going?" But suddenly, she knew.

* * *

"It is the mark of a great warrior, you see," Franz said softly, breaking the long silence that had fallen between them.

His words penetrated her drifting consciousness. Exhausted from lack of sleep and days of fatiguing travel, she had leaned back into the leather seat and closed her eyes. She woke to see that the sun had nearly hit the horizon, as they emerged from the trees. The wooded landscape had broken into steep hills and rocky outcrops patterned with long shadows.

"Such a large and mighty cloak broach." He seemed to be speaking almost to himself. "The fibula represents a horse and rider with a severed human head hanging from the bridle, the trophy of a defeated enemy." He spoke with such relish it made her shiver. "The Celt-Iberians were precursors of the Nordic Race." He glanced triumphantly in her direction. "We...*they*, are destined to rule Europe. This should have happened by now if not for..."

"The War?" she guessed.

"That villainous treaty!" he spat out. "They ground us into the dirt and made us pay for the privilege."

"I'd say we all paid," she said sadly. "All the families on every side of that dreadful war."

He lifted his chin. "Next time, there will be no need for conflict. Once we establish the scientific proof of superiority, everything will become clear."

She stared at him, chilled, as it dawned on her the degree to which this belief fired his life and gave him purpose.

As to a child, he explained patiently that forces were already at work in Germany and Italy, laying the foundation for new political systems, but it was vital to educate the people so they could understand their glorious past and reclaim it.

"The Gold Horseman will be the centrepiece of an important collection. This will establish my academic credentials with authority."

"You can't establish academic credentials with stolen artifacts," she said, shaking her head. "They can be identified. You can be prosecuted."

He laughed. And suddenly, she realized the hopelessness of her situation. At least an hour had passed since the last sign of human habitation. Despite the speed of the car, she looked for an opportunity to jump out. As they slowed to take a corner, she grasped the handle and jerked hard. It didn't move. The door was locked.

At any moment, he could stop and do away with her.

"Where will you establish this collection?" Her only faint hope was of somehow persuading him to show mercy. The longer she could keep him talking, the better. "Do you have a particular university in mind?"

He glanced at her and gave a smug smile. "We in the party know. We have important connections. Once our leaders are in control, the University will be revealed. They have promised me an excellent post. In the meantime, I will guard the horseman. It will be kept safe and secure."

The party?"

"The DNVP."

"What is that? Something like Herr Hitler's party?"

"We are nothing like those hoodlums!" He banged the wheel for emphasis. "The *Völkisch* movement is an expression of the true Germans. Our people have always been here, from the most ancient times. This decadent era is coming to an end, and we will reassert our legitimate claims."

233

"Claims to what?" she asked, though she knew the answer.

"To Europe, of course. Kossinna has proved that Germanic peoples occupied central and Northern Europe from the Bronze Age to the present day. Gunther established that this Nordic race was superior in every way. The pure-bred Germans of today carry forward their achievements. Only by restoring this dominance can we cure the sins of our modern condition."

He spoke as if explaining the obvious to a backward child. Gwen shivered, chilled to the bone. "I can understand why it appeals to you." She tried and failed to sound intrigued. "By the way, you haven't told me where we're going." All at once, she felt detached and hopeless. Her flat voice sounded like it came from someone else.

"Can't you tell by now?" As they turned a corner, the ground fell away into a deep valley. Beyond the distant hills, the last light gleamed on the sea. Dusk had slowly fallen until now the sky darkened to indigo overhead, and stars began to appear. Behind them, in the east, the moon had just risen and threw long, eerie shadows.

As they rattled up the track to Castro de Carballo, the headlamps swept the road ahead. Why on earth did he bring her here? She had to shake off this sense of hopelessness. Once he stopped, she must seize the chance to escape into the darkness.

Against the faint light of the Western horizon rose the outline of the stone hut. A light glowed in the window. Dr. Hunt had told her that the dig was closed down while he did his lecture tour. Perhaps it was a watchman?

She looked around and saw the gleaming bonnet of another car peeping out on the other side of the hut. "I think your boss is here." Her voice rasped in her ears. She felt deeply afraid and bitterly conscious that, after all, this was what she had wanted: to finally confront the man behind this vicious criminal scheme. The man responsible for Emily's death.

Franz did not reply. He got out and came round to open her door. The key turned in the lock. She braced herself to push him over and run; then she caught sight of the gun in his hand.

He stepped back and waved her out of the car and toward the house. She moved as in a dream. The dark headland, the stone house, the moonlit sea.

So unreal, she almost expected to wake in her bed back home. But as she walked towards the door, the cold night air stung her face, and the rocky ground beneath her feet felt all too real. She was going to die here.

With a flood of anguish, she thought of her father and the boys and the pain this would cause them. She thought of all the chances she had had to avoid this moment. How rash and stupid she had been.

At the closed wooden door, she stopped. Something hard jabbed painfully into her spine. "Open it."

She obeyed and stepped inside. A man stood with his back to her, warming his hands at the log fire blazing in the hearth. "A chilly night out there," he said as he turned to face her.

She could only stare in shock. *"You?"*

Chapter Thirty-Four

Father Garrick smiled at her benevolently. His priestly garb had been replaced with a tweed suit and an open trench coat.

"Come in and get warm. Sit down." He waved her to a chair by the hearth, then turned his gaze to Franz. "There's soup in the pot. Heat it up on the fire; there's a good chap."

"I'm not your servant," Franz muttered, but he did as he was told.

Garrick held out his hand. After a moment, Franz gave him the gun. Garrick slipped it into his own coat pocket. He leaned an elbow on the rough stone mantel and looked down at her in appraisal.

"I must say you led us on a merry chase."

"What do I call you?" she asked faintly, her senses still reeling.

"Pardon?"

"I can't call you Father. You're not a priest."

"Oh, but I am, my dear. At least...I used to be. But you can call me Matthew." Seeing her look of disbelief, he smiled. "That is really my name, I assure you."

At this moment, she couldn't be sure of anything. "Why have you brought me here?"

He sighed. "You had your chance to go home. You didn't take it. Isn't it obvious why you're here? We can't have you running around Spain telling wild stories."

"Why not? No one believes me."

"We prefer not to take chances in our business."

"The business of theft?"

236

He shrugged. "Theft from whom? The real owners of these things have been dead for millennia."

"From the archaeologists. From the museums and the citizens to whom they belong."

He looked amused. "My, my...such passionate rectitude." Abruptly, he turned to Franz. "You're sure you weren't followed?"

Franz snorted. "Of course."

"Alright, go outside and get started. We need to be out of here well before dawn." As the other man turned for the door, he added, "And give me that fibula."

Franz glared at him. "You promised me. For my museum." But the look on Garrick's face made him dig in his pocket and pull out the statuette.

Matthew snatched it from his grasp with a sudden swipe. "You heard what I told you. Go and get started."

"Not until I've had something to eat." Franz served himself a bowl of stew and sat down at the table.

Matthew contemplated the gold object in his hand with avid pleasure. "You do realise that the vast majority of museum holdings never see the light of day? At least private collectors venerate and care for these treasures."

She shook her head. "You're just rationalizing your crimes. You said you used to be a priest, a man of God—"

"God!" His face contorted with pain. "He disappeared in the trenches. Buried alive in shell-holes and rotting on the wires of no man's land. I walked away from all that. There's no heaven after you've seen Hell on earth."

Another casualty of war. For a moment, Gwen almost felt sympathy. "I'm sorry."

"Don't be. It stopped me wasting my time."

The deadness in his eyes banished her moment of compassion. She had caught a glimpse of the dark hole inside him.

"What about Amanda?" she asked.

"What about her?" He looked down into the fire, the flickering orange light reflected on his face and on the gold horseman he still held in his hand.

"Did you kill her?"

He straightened and stepped away from the hearth, shoving the fibula into his pocket. He held her gaze for a long moment before speaking. "You know, we were a good team for quite a few years. We met in Paris, at her uncle's gallery. He dealt in objets d'art and curiosities. Some very curious indeed." He gave a reminiscent laugh, but there was no humour in it. "I'm still not sure how I ever got to Paris. It was just before the Armistice. The country was in chaos. Roads choked with refugees. Whole towns and villages reduced to rubble. Sometimes, it was impossible to know what side of the front line you were on."

The pieces were falling into place. Amanda's story and his were like a jigsaw puzzle that fitted together. But there were pieces missing, and either of them could be lying to her.

She hazarded a guess. "You deserted."

He looked at her with loathing. "It's so easy for you to sit in judgment without a clue of what we endured, we who were used as cannon fodder by those murderous lunatics."

"You're wrong. I do know something about it. My father—"

"Your father was in the war. Yes, you told me. But you still have no idea what it was like, do you?" he demanded passionately.

"No," she admitted softly. "No, I don't."

Silence fell, broken only by the crackle of the fire and Garrick's fast breathing as it slowly quietened. He shoved his hands in his pockets, and she could tell he was fingering the gun. Her only hope was to keep him talking.

"You were telling me about Paris. About the gallery."

"Yes. I took Jack some...finds that I'd made during the war. You'd be amazed what people will tell a priest when they're dying." A cold smile curled his lips.

She stared at him in horror.

"In those days, his delightful niece Amanda was just a student, but we took to each other immediately. If you know what I mean."

Gwen could tell that he wanted her to be shocked and repelled. She remained unmoved. "You became lovers."

He sank into the rustic chair on the other side of the fireplace, a bemused smile on his lips. Gwen perched forward on her own chair, surreptitiously looking around for any means of escape.

Garrick had a smug look of satisfaction. "She learned quickly, in every sense of the word. At first, we used her uncle's contacts. We travelled around Europe. A couple of times, we even slipped into Russia. Rich pickings there, let me tell you."

"That story about St. Petersburg was true?"

"In essence…" He smiled in reminiscence. "After that, Amanda pursued her career and began to make contacts of her own in the archaeological community. We developed a system of identifying targets. I did the removals, and her uncle found the clients. For several years, it worked exceedingly well. And then Jack died, and suddenly Amanda seemed to think she was in charge."

He took a silver cigarette case from the small table beside him, extracted, and lit a cigarette, taking a long drag before exhaling.

"Was that why you killed her?"

Sitting at the table, hunched over a bowl of stew, Franz stopped eating and sat up a little straighter. She could tell he was listening.

"It was her own taste for intrigue that got her killed," Garrick said harshly. "And the delusion that she was in charge." The cold contempt in his eyes chilled her to the bone.

"So, you put an end to that delusion. You killed her." She wanted to hear him admit it. and for Franz to hear it, too.

"The stupid bitch thought it a good idea to recruit Franz, and then she made the most stupid mistake of all—using your precious Emily Temple."

"She tricked Emily. She took advantage of her."

"I admit it was a clever idea at first. It was so simple. Amanda cultivated Emily like any senior, influential colleague, but, with a vengeance. She used her to meet as many important people as possible. Travelled with her to many a dig site. It's astonishing how naïve academics can be. They tell their colleagues every detail of their marvellous finds. They gossip like fishwives."

"So, Amanda stole from the sites."

He shook his head, the throb of anger in his voice. "Our superior, Amanda, would never stoop to that. No, Amanda identified the targets. I did the dirty work. And always long enough afterwards that it couldn't be connected with her."

"And Emily didn't know how she was being used."

"It all worked so well at first," he conceded. "Sometimes it was tricky to get things across borders. Especially into England. That's when Amanda asked Emily to take things back with her. Presents and souvenirs, she was told. That sort of thing. The damn Customs and Excise men usually love a good snoop through one's luggage. But, an elderly, respected lady academic? Carrying gift-wrapped presents? They just chalked up her baggage and waved it through."

"But then Emily found out, and she was willing to risk everything in order to put a stop to all this." Gwen found that her hands were shaking.

"Those damned coins."

"Senor Ochoa's coins?"

"After that little episode and Hunt's finds vanishing from the dig, Emily began to ask awkward questions. At that point, Amanda had enough on the woman to destroy her reputation and put her in jail." He gave her a speculative stare as he put the cigarette to his lips and sucked in the smoke.

Gwen asked the question that had nagged at her. "Why did she mail the dig finds to her cottage?"

He shook his head. "She had some absurd idea of telling everything to some trusted colleagues and using the antiquities as evidence. She wanted to do all that in England, out of some naïve faith in British justice. At the end, Dr. Temple was willing to risk everything, for the sake of her principles. A brave woman."

"Don't be a hypocrite!"

He spread his hands in a gesture of resignation. "I saw her send off the parcel in Santiago. I was too late to stop her. But I thought I could persuade her to be sensible."

"I don't believe you for one minute! You killed her." Disgusted and furious, she clenched her fists, wishing they were around his throat.

He gave a careless shrug. "It was an accident. The incense burner should have swung harmlessly over her head. Unfortunately, she stood up from her chair at the wrong moment and…"

Gwen shook her head, angry tears stinging her eyes. "You're lying. The botafumeiro didn't kill her. That was all a setup. You hit her with something, what was it? A crucifix, a candlestick?"

"You should write detective fiction, my dear. What an imagination!" He sighed and leaned back into the chair. "You've got that revengeful look, but I wouldn't bother. There's absolutely no way you could prove it."

Not that she'd have the opportunity. From the moment she found the car door locked, Gwen had known she wouldn't be leaving there.

"I still don't understand why Amanda died." As long as she kept him talking, there might be some faint hope.

"Another unfortunate accident." He glanced toward Franz, whose gaze was fixed on him. "But really, her arrogance killed her. She liked men dancing to her tune. She was a whore."

Gwen flinched. It was personal, then.

He paused for a long, considering moment, gazing into her face. "You're an unusual girl. Intelligent, resourceful…certainly brave. You have great potential. Perhaps I can offer you an alternative. You could study archaeology, travel the world, make very good money."

She stared at him in disbelief. "Stealing for you, you mean."

He was like a cat toying with some small, helpless creature, and she didn't care to be the prey.

He shrugged. "Depends how you look at it. We both know what it's like to live on the edge of poverty. The world is awash with money if you know where to look."

What if she pretended to play along? It might be the only way to get out alive.

Gwen clasped her hands together and leaned forward. "How does it work?"

He regarded her for a moment without replying, then scooped some soup out of the pot on the fire, ladled it into a cup, and handed it to her. "Here."

He sank down again and watched her gulp down a mouthful of hot liquid and fatty gristle. Her stomach revolted, but the stew would give her energy.

"Why are you here at Finisterre?" she said between mouthfuls. "I thought you'd got the choicest pickings last year."

"Not quite. Franz has his faults, but when Amanda got him taken on to help Dr. Hunt for a short time, he worked away assiduously and found some items that were a little too bulky to carry off immediately. He cleverly concealed them in an area that had already been excavated, and now we're getting them out."

She clasped her hands tightly around the warm mug, trying to sound confident, instead of frightened. "And how do you see my role in all this?"

"I'm still thinking about it." He got to his feet. "Have you finished your soup? Then come on."

As they moved toward the door, she saw the gun appear in his hand again. Could she convince him that she wanted to work with him? It might be her only way out of this nightmare.

Chapter Thirty-Five

The cold night air cut through her thin jacket like a knife blade. The moon had risen higher, spreading a shining path on the water and picking out the rocky landscape on the headland in dramatic black-and-white, like a theatre spotlight.

What could she do? Distract him, run off, and hide? But run where? Only one direction offered any hope. On the landward side of the castro, a steep slope led across a few hundred yards of bare rock to the beginnings of a dense pinewood. There, she could find cover. She just had to reach it unseen.

The light dimmed for a moment. A shred of cloud obscured the moon. To the west, a bank of clouds was approaching, and she felt a spark of hope. *Stay alert.* This could be her chance.

Franz came up to the house pushing a squeaking wheelbarrow with a lantern hanging on one handle and bearing a shovel.

"Lead us to it," Garrick said. He took Gwen's arm and pushed her ahead of him.

With Franz leading the way, they crossed the headland. She stumbled on the rough stones and tripped on one of the circular foundations emerging from the earth. Garrick kept a firm hold on her arm as they reached the outer wall of the settlement.

"This interest you have in working with us indicates a rapid change of heart." He sounded amused but not dismissive.

She had to strike a realistic note. Most of all, she mustn't sound frightened. "I'm still angry about Emily, but you're right about my ambitions. Why should I give all that up?"

A light wind began blowing in from the sea as Franz rammed the shovel into the soil and started digging.

In the stark light, she could see Garrick watching her intently. "You certainly burned your bridges at Seathorne," he said.

Gwen shrugged, watching the clouds coming closer. The first thin drifts of mist barcly dimmed the moon for more than a few seconds. She tensed every muscle and scanned the route to the woods.

A small, satisfied sound from Franz drew Garrick's attention. He had unearthed a bundle wrapped in sacking and heaved it out of the hole. Throwing the cloth aside, he raised the lamp, and Gwen drew in her breath.

A gleaming hoard lay heaped before them. Two massive torcs of twisted gold wire lay there, the ends worked to resemble boar's heads and wolves, beneath them a pile of gold broaches and women's necklets. An incredible treasure trove. Beside them lay the carved stone head of some ancient idol.

Franz rewrapped the hoard and loaded it into the wheelbarrow. "Very good," Garrick breathed. "Very good indeed."

He let go of her arm, but now she saw the service revolver pointed at her.

"We're not finished digging." He nodded at Franz, then looked at Gwen and laughed quietly. "Did you really think I believed you? I'd be delighted if it were true, but I'm afraid you are far too good for me. Not a larcenous bone in your body. Such a delightful body, too. What a shame."

What a fool she had been to think, even for a moment, that she could trick him. She looked at Franz. "How can you trust him not to do the same to you?"

He stood with the lamp held high enough that she could see uncertainty in his eyes. In the sky behind him, the clouds scudded closer. In the blink of an eye, the moon disappeared, and darkness fell like a black shroud.

At the same moment, she punched with all her might and knocked the lantern from Franz's grip, then ran off into the darkness as the light snuffed out.

A shot rang behind her. A chunk of stone spurted from the wall at her shoulder, and searing pain ripped across her arm. She stumbled and gasped but kept running as she heard the desperate grunts of men in deadly combat.

Another shot rang out.

She followed the outer wall, barely visible in the darkness. It would take her past the dig house, where the faint glimmer of a candle outlined the cottage window.

With a jolt, she cannoned into a hard body in the darkness.

"Be quiet!" A low male voice said softly.

"Michael?"

Stunned, she felt him grip her shoulders and push her down into the shelter of the wall. What was he doing here?

In the distance, the lantern flared to life, then started moving closer. Who was it? Garrick? Franz? Or both of them?

Greville pulled her toward the cottage. Whose side was *he* on?

As she pulled away, struggling to get free, she felt a weight in her pocket and a moment of exhilaration. She found the penknife and eased out the blade. In one swift move, she stabbed at one of the restraining hands.

Greville let go with a startled cry. She darted away as another shot echoed behind her, and the lamp dropped and shattered.

She ran blindly across the headland as more shots echoed around her. Something caught her foot, sending her flying. Instinctively putting out her hands, she winced in pain as her palms grazed the rocks. Somehow, she managed to keep hold of the knife and clutched it more tightly in her hand. She stopped and looked wildly around, all sense of direction gone. Her heart pounding like a hammer in her chest, she tried to still her breathing and listen.

With the clouds thickly covering the moon, faint starlight barely revealed the outline of the cliff edge against the sky. She thought she saw dark figures moving and heard the thud of footsteps.

She crept in the opposite direction, suddenly tripped over a wall, and fell on top of someone who gave a grunt of pain.

"Aaach, Fraulien..." he whispered.

Franz. She huddled down beside him; her hand touched his chest and felt something sticky. He winced.

"Have you been shot?" she whispered. "Please believe me, I never wanted him to hurt you."

His frantic, laboured breathing sounded terrible. "I know."

She dug in her pocket for a handkerchief and squeezed it against the wound. "Press hard; it'll stop the bleeding. I'll get help." What a hopeless promise to make.

He clutched at her feverishly. *"Bitte...* Please... take this."

She felt something hard being pushed into her hand and knew immediately what it was. The Gold Horseman.

He clung to her. "I could not let him have it. He is not fit to guard this relic. You must keep it safe."

She'd be happy never to see the cursed thing again but would agree to anything to keep Franz quiet. She shoved the heavy fibula into her pocket. "Yes, all right. But I must get help."

"Follow the line of this wall to the left and back to the cottage." He coughed convulsively. "The key is in the car."

"What's Greville doing here?" she whispered, but Franz did not respond. She shook him gently and found he had gone limp.

She listened intently. The sounds of struggle and pursuit had stopped, so she couldn't tell from which direction danger would come. Should she run to the woods and hide, or risk going for the car? There were two men out there and she feared they lay between her and either goal. Garrick wanted to kill her, and Greville...? Was he a disgruntled partner? A rival thief? Whatever he was, she had to treat him as a threat. At least the unbroken cloud cover gave the protection of darkness.

Bending low, she crept along the wall as quickly as possible in a crouched scramble, trying not to make a sound. Up ahead, she could see a faint glimmer of light that must be from the cottage window. To her left, on the other side of the wall, she heard the roar of waves and picked her way carefully between the tumbled stones.

Without warning, a shaft of moonlight broke through the clouds, and suddenly, Garrick stood right in front of her, the cold blue light carving his face into a livid mask.

"Full marks for effort, my dear." He raised the gun.

In one swift movement, she rammed a hand into her pocket, pulled out the golden horseman, and slammed the heavy weight against the side of his head.

A bright flash exploded and rushed past her ear, leaving her momentarily blinded and deaf. A dark shape blocking the stars crumpled and staggered, then suddenly the stars shone again.

The night split with an appalling scream that stopped abruptly. He had gone over the cliff. Garrick had gone over the cliff.

She had killed him.

Chapter Thirty-Six

For a long moment, she couldn't seem to breathe. The gold fibula in her hand gleamed silver in the moonlight, marred by a streak of dark liquid, that ran down her arm.

Somehow, she shook off the shock that immobilized her, slipped the horseman into her pocket, and began to move. Clouds hurried across the moon, giving fitful light.

Stumbling forward, sometimes scrabbling on all fours, she moved towards the lighted window of the stone cottage.

After edging around to the front of the building, she could make out the shape of the car. She made a dive for the driver's side door.

"Stop." Strong hands clasped her upper arms from behind and immobilized her against the car.

She struggled against his grasp. "We've got to get Franz some help."

Michael relaxed his grip. "I'm surprised you care. Wasn't it your partner's idea to shoot him?"

She turned to face him and found herself shaking. "Garrick's not... I mean, he *wasn't* my partner. But who are *you*? I thought you were mixed up in all this, working with Amanda."

There was enough light to make out his face, puzzled and dismayed. "I've been trying to stop them. Look, there's no time for explanations right now; we must get Franz some help. You'll just have to trust me."

"How can I?"

"I think we have no choice but to trust each other." He switched on a torch, but it fell from his fingers.

She picked it up and ran the beam over him. "You're shot too!" His muddied coat was torn, and a vivid patch of blood covered his white shirt, where it protruded at the right shoulder.

He shrugged irritably. "Never mind about that. It's just a surface wound. I think Heider caught it in the ribs. He's breathing, but we'd better get him to a doctor."

Between them, they carried Franz to the car, laid him in the back seat, and covered him with a rug. She could tell Greville was in pain and trying to hide it.

"Can you drive?" he asked. She nodded, and got in. "There's a small town twenty minutes away. I'll tell you where to turn."

At first, nothing but the hiss of tires on the stony road broke the silence as they drove the winding route downhill.

"Are you all right?" she asked at last and glanced over at him.

He lifted the stained handkerchief from his shoulder. "It's stopped bleeding, I'm glad to say."

Gwen glanced anxiously in the rearview mirror. "How is Franz, do you think?"

Michael twisted around and glanced into the rear seat. "His breathing sounds well enough." He looked back at her. "I think it's time we told each other the truth."

She kept her eyes on the road, the headlamps illuminating a corridor of rough track between onrushing trees.

"For me, it all started when Emily died." Haltingly, she told him the whole story.

"It seems we have been unwittingly on the same side," Michael said at last. "And I have been very mistaken. I told you I was a coin dealer, and that is true, but primarily, I work for the British Museum. We have arrangements in the archaeological world to buy antiquities which help to fund digs.

"My job is to identify stolen and faked antiquities, and we do a decent job of vetting our own acquisitions. A larger problem is all the finds that never reach us. Theft and smuggling exploded during the war."

"I can imagine." Gwen thought of Garrick's story and wondered how many others had taken the opportunity offered by chaos. "So, does that mean you're a sort of detective?"

He smiled. "You could say that. For a number of years, we've known about exceptionally large thefts from many of the digs we subsidise. On most digs, it's common for small items to vanish, usually into workers' pockets. That's efficiently dealt with by offering them rewards. What's unusual about these crimes is that the items have been documented and carefully stored before they disappear. Investigation led us to link Dr. Temple and Amanda Spenser to many of these places, although usually some time before the actual thefts. Clearly, someone else carried them out."

"How did you know it was Garrick?" She glanced over to see Michael wince as he eased himself deeper into the seat. Hopefully, the town wasn't too far away, and hopefully, there was a doctor.

"I tracked him all across Europe," he went on." But always one step behind. For a while, I thought he was several different men."

"So, the priest wasn't his only disguise."

"Businessman, doctor, professor… He was a remarkable chameleon. But he did like the priestly role, perhaps because it was genuine, in its way." He waved to the left. "The turn is coming up."

She slowed down, suddenly overcome by a wave of anxiety and horror. "I killed him," she whispered, seeing again the terror on his face as he fell backwards into the darkness. "I killed a man. I hit him with the gold fibula. What will they do with me?"

"Listen to me. You must tell them the fall was an accident. The man was chasing you and missed his footing in the dark. Don't say anything about the fibula. Where is it?"

"In my pocket."

"When we get to the village, give it to me. I'll take care of it."

"Gladly." She shuddered. "I never want to see that thing again."

* * *

The next three days were a blur of activity. After a doctor tended to Franz and Michael's wounds, the Guardia Civil arrived, and there followed hours of tense, aggressive questions and answers in torrents of Spanish, which Michael handled with aplomb.

They were taken to Corunna, where Franz was hospitalized under guard. The British consul came to their hotel and explained where things stood.

"I think we've squared things away with the police and the government," he said with an air of satisfaction.

He was a plump little man in faultless tailoring who sat back in a leather chair addressing Gwen and Michael, who sat at either end of a long sofa in the empty hotel lounge.

"Fortunately, Greville, your credentials persuaded them to believe you, despite the preposterous tale of rogue academics and murderous priests." He sighed. "However, I must say, Miss Armstrong, I do wish Garrick hadn't gone over that cliff."

"He was going to kill me!"

Michael shot her a warning look.

"That may be true, my dear young lady," the consul went on. "But I had the devil of a time persuading them not to charge you with murder."

She sat up swiftly and opened her mouth to protest, but Michael cut in. "You know very well it was an accident..."

The diplomat put up a hand to stop him. "Do not distress yourselves. The Guardia like things tidy. I merely meant that only Heider survives to answer questions, however his story confirms everything you said. He seems to have been only a minion, with little knowledge of their wider activities. However, he has been arrested. When sufficiently recovered he will be tried, and no doubt jailed for quite some time."

Gwen felt terribly sorry for him. "Poor Franz..."

After the Consul left, they stood facing each other. She felt suddenly shy. "I'm not sure how I'm going to explain this to Miss Henderson, or if I can persuade her to give me my job back."

"Do you really want that?" Michael asked.

It surprised her to realize that she hadn't thought of any other option.

Greville looked down at her with an expression in his blue eyes that kindled warmth inside her. "Thank you for everything you've done. You'll be happy to know that we've recovered most of the artifacts from Hunt's dig. You saved the most valuable of all. Any time you're in London, you must come to the British Museum and see it on display." He hesitated. "Unless the memory is too painful."

She shivered. "I'm afraid I'll always find that object very sinister. How ironic that Garrick was killed by the very thing he sought so urgently."

"The pagan gods have got their sacrifice." Greville's expression looked infinitely sad.

"You thought that too," she whispered. "I thought that was just me being fanciful."

He shook his head. "The evil is certainly real; we both know that." He took a step closer, reached out, and took her hand. "I'm sorry to say I'll be leaving soon. I have to meet the Museum trustees in a few days and report on all this. I sail from Vigo tomorrow."

His hand felt warm and reassuring on hers. She suddenly realized how very much she would miss him. The regret must have shown on her face.

"Don't worry. Everything is straightened out here, and the Consul is going to see that you get back to Bilbao. His counterpart there will ensure your passage back to England, and I believe he has already spoken with Miss Henderson, whose group has returned there."

"Thank you." All of that was reassuring, but she knew it was Michael's departure that made her feel hollow. The powerful attraction she felt might be pointless, but over the past week, she had realized it was more than physical. His intelligence, strength, and kindness had touched something deep within her.

Nevertheless, it was ridiculous to dwell on the impossible.

"I'm afraid it's time to say goodbye." He clasped her hand in both of his. His warm, firm grip enclosed her fingers. For far too long, she stared into his blue eyes, then caught herself, shook his hand, and swiftly let go.

Later that day, in the rocking railway carriage on the way to Bilbao, she stared out the window at the passing countryside. She would never see him again.

Chapter Thirty-Seven

Hildy came rushing out of the door just as Gwen alighted from the carriage.

"Oh, my goodness," she cried, as she enfolded her in a warm hug. "When I heard what had happened, I felt just dreadful! You poor girl."

Hildy whirled her into the house and sat her down to an enormous tea, then had her tell her story in detail.

After the maid cleared things away, she handed Gwen a crystal tumbler filled with a double tot of whisky. "My goodness, you must need this."

She went to the tall, carved escritoire and reached into one of the pigeon-holes overflowing with papers. "I have something for you."

Hildy turned back to her, holding an envelope clutched close to her chest. "This was delivered while I was away. It seems that, when Emily was in Corunna, she entrusted this to the assistant manager of the hotel to post for her. I suspect he forgot about it."

She held it out to her, and Gwen opened it. The outer envelope was addressed to Hildy and contained another envelope and a note.

The note read:

Dearest Hildy,

This will sound terribly melodramatic, but I must ask you a great favour. In the event of my death, can you please send the enclosed to Miss Gwen Armstrong?

I hasten to assure you this is a remote possibility, and I expect to tell you all about it when we meet next week. I have been embroiled in rather a mess and may, in fact, be in terrible trouble. But never fear, I have a way out.

I close in haste, as I must catch the train to Santiago. Emily

Gwen looked at the envelope addressed to her home in Seathorne. With trembling fingers, she tore it open.

Dear Gwen,

This is a difficult letter to write, because if you're reading it, that means I'm dead and can't explain anything that I forgot to tell you.

It will also mean that you've heard from my lawyer and are wondering why on earth I have left you my estate. It's a long and complicated story, but you deserve to know the truth.

Twenty-seven years ago, Leonard Woolley invited my friend Hildy Scott and I to work on a new dig of Corstopitum. We had hoped for Egypt, or at least Italy, but we women archaeologists were still fighting to be taken seriously. So there we were, up on Hadrian's Wall, enjoying an English summer as we scraped away the clammy mud.

Fortunately, we were blessed with an army of volunteers. Local antiquarians came out in droves. Educated, hard-working amateurs, retirees, teachers on their summer holidays. We got chummy and ended many a day in the local pub where we were billeted. Perhaps you can guess where that led. I was nearly forty, but one of the men took a fancy to me, and I to him. He was intelligent, kind and treated me like a desirable woman—a feeling I had not experienced for years. Predictably, this led to an affair which lasted through the summer. That is, until I discovered I was pregnant.

When I told my lover this bombshell news, I discovered, to my horror, that he was married. Not only that, he had a young child at home. Naturally, I broke things off; not only did I feel furious and betrayed, but I was left in despair. Not least because I realized how deeply I loved him.

I had to give up an offer from the British School in Athens and go away to have the baby. For a while, I thought my career was over. I made plans to find a teaching post and pretend to be a widow. And then it all came to naught. I had a horribly difficult confinement, and in the end, the baby died.

I barely survived myself. My dear elderly mother nursed me back to health and told me bluntly to accept it as a fortuitous ending to a disastrous episode. In the end I did resume my career. I went to Athens, feeling like the shell of a human being. Over time, I came back to myself, and after many years, I eventually came to Seathorne.

Just when I thought that whole episode was in the distant past, you were engaged as the department secretary. Armstrong is not an uncommon name in the North, but there was something about you. Remember that first day you came for tea, and told me all about your family?

Then, of course, I knew immediately. Edward Armstrong, teacher from Corbridge. When you told me that, I felt myself go hot and cold, shocked at the depth of my reaction. You may not have noticed, but I rather rushed you out. I had realized that you were the daughter of my lover.

It brought everything back. That wonderful summer, our bitter parting, and then the utter heartbreak of losing the child, a girl. I confess that I wept unreservedly. Not just for myself, but for everything Edward had suffered too. I think that night, I finally forgave him.

In a strange way, I started to think of you as the daughter who might have been mine, if things were different. So bright, so ambitious. It was a crime to deny you the education you dreamt of. That same night, I vowed to help you in any way possible.

You may know that I came to Seathorne at Letitia Henderson's request. We have known each other from girlhood, since I spent summers there with my Aunt Sarah. She lived to a great age, then left me her estate, which included the cottage. Rather ironic to inherit a fortune in one's fifties. But it decided me to accept Letitia's invitation to teach a few classes at Seathorne and spend most of my time writing up my years of research.

This is a roundabout way of explaining why I made you my heir. It will enable you to get the education you deserve and to do everything you might want to do in life. It will also enable you to help your family, which I know means so much to you.

If you are reading this letter, it means I am dead, which is a shame, as I had hoped to tell you all this in person. I would like to have given you help and advice on your education. But I trust your good sense in that respect.

The final thing I wish to say is, be kind to your father. He was an unhappy man when we met. I hasten to say that this had nothing to do with your mother, but with his situation. Like you, he had intended to take up an academic career, but poverty led him to school teaching. He told me he'd never been happier than that summer, feeling like a real archaeologist. It doesn't excuse his shameful neglect of his family, but I think he deluded himself that he could move between two separate worlds without pain. When you told me of his present situation, my heart ached. I hope you may be able to bring him comfort in his declining years.

In the year since we met, you have brought me great joy, and I hope my legacy enables you to have the life you deserve.

God Bless You, Emily

Gwen sat staring at the letter for a long time, tears running down her cheeks. At last, Hildy said quietly, "Are you all right?"

She shook her head, her heart almost too full to speak. "I don't know. I have a lot to think about." She took her leave, with a promise to keep in touch.

About to close the door, Hildy said suddenly, "Wait a moment!" and disappeared inside. She came back and handed her a slip of paper. "I found that quote Emily was fond of."

Gwen put it in her pocket as she walked back to the hotel. When she reached the riverside, she sank onto a bench and reread the letter, then stared sightlessly toward the other bank.

The revelations about her father had left her reeling. Anger and pity fought for dominance as she thought about his betrayal of her mother and then what a sad and miserable life he had ended up with. It explained so much about his reaction to Emily's cultivation of her friendship,

What would she say when she saw her father again? It would take a lot of thinking about. Well, she had three days on the boat ahead of her, then another day on the train. She sighed, folded up the letter, and put it in her bag. So much to consider. So much to plan.

Letitia had offered her job back, and she would take it. For the time being.

Every time she thought about the inheritance, she felt a thrill of excitement before telling herself not to count on anything. But if she had learned one thing over the past few weeks, it was the nature of her own capability. One way or another, she would make her dreams a reality.

Something crinkled in her pocket, and she pulled it out. The quotation from Marcus Aurelius that Emily thought of so highly. Gwen read it and smiled. How utterly apt.

It's the truth I'm after, and the truth never harmed anyone. What harms us is to persist in self-deceit and ignorance.

About the Author

Carol Bruce spent her childhood in north-east England where she developed a lifelong fascination with history and archaeology. A winding career path began in forensic chemistry, followed by documentary production and writing romance novels. As a lover of classic mysteries, and an avid reader of literature from the inter-war period in England, all these strands came together in the creation of *The Pilgrim Road to Death*, the first novel featuring Gwen Armstrong.

AUTHOR WEBSITE:
  carolbruce.com

Also by Carol Bruce

Co-wrote 2 novels with Debra McCarthy-Anderson for Meteor Publishing
as RACHEL VINCER
  Hot Copy
  Prim And Improper

Co-wrote 5 novels with Debra McCarthy-Anderson for Harlequin Romance
as DEBRA CARROLL
  Obsession
  To Catch a Thief
  Man Under the Mistletoe
  One Enchanted Night
  An Inconvenient Passion

www.ingramcontent.com/pod-product-compliance
Lightning Source LLC
Chambersburg PA
CBHW020611110726
47899CB00002B/467